The Sex Surrogate

–

Jessica Gadziala

THE SEX SURROGATE

Copyright © 2015 by Jessica GadzialaAll rights reserved. This book or any portion thereofmay not be reproduced or used in any manner whatsoeverwithout the express written permission of the author
except for brief quotations used in a book review.

"This book is a work of fiction. the names, characters, places and incidents are products of the writer's imagination or have been used fictitiously and are not to be construed as real. Any resemblance to persons, living or dead, actual events, locales or organizations is entirely coincidental."

Cover image credit: Shutterstock.com/ AS Inc.

Dedication:

To those who know all about the
safest place in the world.
And to those who so lovingly provide it.
xx

THE SEX SURROGATE

Author's Note:

Sexual Surrogacy is a legitimate profession in the United States and has been a way of dealing with various forms of sexual dysfunction for many years. In real life, all sessions are overseen by a third party licensed sexual therapist. In this story, in the interest of creating more intimacy between the leads, Dr. Chase Hudson is both the surrogate AND the sexual therapist.

It is also important to understand the root of Ava's dysfunction is not based on a trauma. Her anxiety and panic attacks have stemmed from irrational, uncontrollable fears based on previous experience. Such is how anxiety and panic disorders often work.

THE SEX SURROGATE

Before The Sessions

"I am going to see a sex surrogate." There. I said it. Out loud. Granted, only to myself and in the privacy of my car with the windows up. But, hey, it counts. It's not like it is something I could share with my family, or my coworkers, my roommate or... well, that's about all the people I have in my life. And they wouldn't get it. They hear "sex surrogate" and they think "prostitute". Besides, admitting it would mean admitting to them that I am dealing with some form of sexual dysfunction. Which, I am. Totally. But they didn't need to know that. That would be so humiliating. It was bad enough that the guys I had (tried) to date are all too aware.

This was for me. No one else needed to know.

I pulled into the parking garage, three floors up, and parked my car. I was early. They said to come early because, apparently, there was a detailed questionnaire to fill out. But I was pretty sure they didn't mean... an hour and a half early. Honestly, I had to leave my apartment or there was no way in hell I was going to go through with it. So, I just got to sit for forty-five minutes and freak the heck out wedged between a van and a SUV, in perfect seclusion.

Six months before, I had no idea there was even such a thing as help for me. I thought I was doomed to uncomfortable discussions with men I was interested in for the rest of my life. Or, more likely, a lifetime of being a spinster. Because, let's face it, how many times can you be expected to sit down and tell someone that you don't like sex? To see that look cross their face: confusion, disappointment, arrogant male pride. Because every guy thinks they'll be different. They will change it. They can make you writhe and moan and get over the fears and insecurities that make you lie there like a dead freaking fish, internalizing a panic attack because you're terrified of what they would do if you pushed them off like you wanted to.

No one changed it.

Four men down. And I was so over it.

I was supposed to be out enjoying sex. Hooking up. Dating. Having one night stands. All those things that normal twenty-seven year olds do before they finally get serious and give thought to settling down in their thirties. I had already lost so much time.

And it wasn't like I didn't want to want sex. I totally did. I could get as turned on as the next girl just thinking about it. But when it came down to it and he's there and you're there... and clothes need to come off, and touching needs t happen... I just flip out inside. And then that makes me lose the drive and then... yeah, dead fish, someone plowing into me, pissed off because I was not enjoying it.

Something needed to change.

Especially because... I had no trauma. I hade no legitimate

reason to be afraid of sex. I was never abused as a child. I never witnessed anything twisted or gross. I had never been raped or coerced into doing things I was uncomfortable with.

There was no good reason why I couldn't enjoy a healthy sex life.

Except my own stupid head.

And I had tried the traditional therapy route. Actually, I had been in and out of treatment for my anxiety issues since I was a teenager. The current therapist was a middle aged woman with startling green eyes and a soothing voice. To her, I spilled it all. All of the sordid, awful tales of my quest to have physical contact with men. She did her best, bless her, to help. She gave me workbooks meant to help me bolster my confidence, talked to me about sex in as frank a manner as possible to get me comfortable with the idea, hoping the action would be easier for me afterward. But nope.

Finally, frustrated with her inability to help, and sorry for me in her detached, professional kind of way... she had produced a card. It was small and white with raised black writing.

Dr. Chase Hudson
Psychologist/ Sexologist/ Sexual Surrogate

"Call his office," she urged, nodding for emphasis. "I know it seems far-fetched, Ava, but it's worth a shot. You've tried everything else."

Afterward commenced a long, drawn out internet search on the topic of sexual surrogacy. It was a profession, I found, dominated mostly by women. Which, I guess, made sense. Men were a lot more likely to suffer from sexual dysfunction. But there was a growing subset of male practitioners. It was a legitimate, legal business. They could talk with me, touch me, have sex with me. It was all perfectly safe and, from the law's standpoint, acceptable.

I researched Dr. Chase Hudson, finding an amazing, upscale-looking website with information on his degrees and certifications, a brief outline of all his services, and a place to set up an appointment online. Which sent a tiny surge of gratitude through my body, because, well... there was no way I could have set up that kind of appointment over the phone.

I got a call from a secretary the next day, confirming my appointment and telling me to arrive at least a half an hour before my scheduled time on the first visit so I could fill out paperwork.

My alarm went off at eight in the morning and I crawled out of bed, showered, and stood in front of my mirror for the better part of twenty minutes.

There was nothing wrong with me physically. My face was soft, slight cheekbones, a straight and well-proportioned nose, a slightly pointed chin, brown eyes with light brown lashes, a somewhat plump lower lip, and long blonde hair. If I caught myself on a good day, I would say I am pretty. It was not a good day.

My body was perfectly average. I was not super thin, but not heavy either. I had a slight flare of hip, a decent rack, and an ass that didn't live up to current beauty standards (meaning big enough to be seen from the front), but it wasn't flat either. I liked my legs most of all, I guess. They were long, lean, and slightly muscled from from all the squats I had done to try to get my butt to be seen from the front.

I dried my hair, applied a little eye liner and lip balm, and made my way to my closet. I hemmed and hawed over an outfit for forever. What, exactly, does one wear to meet a man who you were going to be paying (three thousand dollars for ten sessions!) to, essentially, sleep with you? I was assured, however, that the introductory meeting (not included in the ten sessions, thankfully) was just about getting acquainted. There would be no touching. There would be no nothing but a little talk therapy. But still, I would be sleeping with him eventually.

In the end, I decided on skinny leg blue jeans and a long sleeve v-neck white shirt. It was tight, but chaste. And comfortable. Lord knew I was going to be uncomfortable enough, I didn't need to be worried about flashing my panties when I crossed my legs in a skirt or pulling up my bodice because it kept showing too much cleavage.

I ate dry rye toast, had a cup of tea, and started losing my cool.

Which put me in my car, frantically tapping my fingers on the steering wheel, trying to listen to the music on the radio instead of the voice inside my head.

Because, seriously, what a strange situation. I was paying a psychologist, not some two-bit hack calling themselves a therapist, but an actual psychologist, to touch me and... yeah, didn't need my mind to go there. He was going to *do things* to me. Because I gave him a huge chunk of my savings to do it. Who else could say that?

I didn't even know what the hell he looked like for goodness sakes. He could be as old as my father with a belly spilling over his waistband and clammy meat hands. Literally. He could look like that. I had no clue. But I had spent the last few days trying to convince myself that that didn't matter. What mattered was learning how to feel comfortable in a man's presence, comfortable with them looking at me naked, touching me. That was what was important. Not whether or not he had huge ears or man boobs.

And I wasn't expecting miracles. Maybe just some small breakthroughs. Maybe just not... cringing when someone reached out to touch me. Maybe not feeling completely horrified at being naked in front of someone else. I wasn't expecting to walk out of the office being some kind of sex goddess. Just... normal. I just wanted to be normal.

So, if that meant I had to sleep with some sixty year old with fake teeth... so be it.

I took a deep breath, checking the time, then grabbed my purse and got out of my car. I was still too early, but I could take my time with the paperwork. Check out the office.

I shivered against the late Fall air, grabbing the office door and pulling it open. And I stepped into straight up elegance. There was no other way to describe the waiting area of this office. The wall straight ahead, behind the white reception desk, was painted black with the doctor's name emblazoned across it. The rest of the walls were covered in some sort of white, shiny, textured panels. The hard wood floors were pristine and dark stained. There were two captain's chairs upholstered in a aqua color in front of a low white coffee table with two books on top.

Neat, clean, expensive.

Those were the three words that came to mind immediately.

The woman behind the desk was in her mid or late forties with a kind round face with large brown eyes and had her brown hair pulled back at the nape of her neck. She looked up when I walked in, a kind, non-judgmental smile on her face.

"Miss. Davis?" she asked, standing behind the massive desk that kept her body under her chest hidden from view.

"Y... yes," I said, shaking my head slightly.

"Great timing," she smiled, reaching around for, I assumed, my paperwork. "You'd be surprised how many people take 'come at least a half an hour early' to mean 'show up five minutes after your scheduled appointment time'," she laughed.

I walked up to the desk, swallowing past the sudden fist in my throat.

"Nervous?" she asked, leaning closer, like she wanted to keep it between the two of us, despite the office being empty except for her.

I knew she was just being professionally kind, but I felt a bit of the flurries in my stomach subside. "Only in the way that I am ready to turn and bolt out the door at any moment," I admitted.

She smiled, producing a pile of papers on a white clipboard. "Then you picked the wrong shoes," she said, her eyes bright. I felt a giggle rise up, shaking my head and looking at my feet, wrapped in beige boots with a three inch stiletto heel. "Don't worry," she said, putting a hand on the paperwork, "everyone is always nervous. It's completely normal."

I nodded. "So, I just... fill all these out?"

"Yep," she said, pulling back, away from me. Back into professional mode. "Some are just basic medical questions. Mental health questions. And then the last few pages are an in-depth sexual questionnaire. You seal all of it into that manila folder in the back," she said, flipping the pages. "No one but Dr. Hudson will be privy to that information."

Thank God.

"Great," I said, forcing a wobbly smile. "Thank you."

I walked over to a chair, sitting down and trying to power through the pages before I got myself too wrapped up in the awkwardness of the situation. It was good to have something to focus on.

That was, until I got to the sex questionnaire.

It started off tame enough, asking about my upbringing. What (if anything) I was taught about sex. If I had ever caught adults engaged in sexual activities. If so, what? Then how many sexual partners I have had. What acts I had engaged in. What my comfort level was with each act on a scale of one to ten.

I figured I would put myself at a four for each, though I was pretty sure it was more like a one or two. A little fibbing never hurt anyone.

I took my time filling out the open ended question, asking me what I *thought* caused the onset of my dysfunction. I sat there

THE SEX SURROGATE

for a long moment, completely blank. Because I honestly didn't know. I had been young and inexperienced and completely terrified during my first time. And it hurt. And I reacted. And he reacted. Badly. And from that day on, even the thought of getting kissed sent me into a full blown panic attack. Because a kiss led to touching. Touching led to sex. Sex led to pain. Pain led to men freaking out on me.

So that was what I wrote down, more or less, praying it didn't make me sound silly or pathetic or weak. I knew there were women with more issues than me. With more legitimate reasons to freak out. But I wasn't one of them. I had a bad experience. It set a bar (in my mind) for how all sexual encounters occurred. It was irrational. But, then again, nothing about an anxiety disorder is rational.

I took a deep breath, signing the end of the last page, putting all the pages into the folder, sealing it, then handing it to the receptionist.

I went back to my chair with my heart slamming in my chest, my hands getting clammy.

I was saved from my misery a short five minutes later.

"Miss. Davis," the receptionist called, making me jump, then spring to my feet. She smiled sweetly, moving toward me with an extended arm, but kept her distance. "Dr. Hudson would like you to wait in his office, get comfortable for a moment, while he looks over your paperwork," she explained, leading me toward a door down at the far end of the large waiting room, "then he will be in to see you."

She opened the door, standing outside of it, making it obvious she was not going to go in. "Thank you," I said, stepping past the threshold a few steps.

The door clicked quietly behind me, the sound slamming somewhere in my mind, screaming out:

This is it. There's no going back now.

Introductory Session

His office was in complete contrast to the waiting room. Whereas the waiting room was crisp and clean, almost feminine, his office was all man. The wall straight across from the door had windows covered in heavy drapery, a brown leather couch situated in front of it. To the right was a floor to ceiling bookshelf with a dark wood executive desk in front of it. Books spilled from the shelves, heavy tombs of, I imagined, psychological origins. Or sexual origins, I thought with a strange hysterical little laugh. To the left was a small, intimate seating area. There was another brown couch, this time in a soft suede material, with two end tables with lamps, and an arm chair across from it, on an angle. Dr. Hudson's four degrees and certificates were displayed above the couch.

The walls were a deep green color, the floors the same dark wood as the waiting room. There were a few framed pictures, one on either side of the door. One, a black and white of a man and woman, half in shadow, with the edges of their heads turning into birds. The other, another black and white, the same man and woman, still half in shadow, embracing.

I turned away from them, walking into the room which was nothing like I had been expecting. I guess, maybe, a part of me had been expecting, well, a bed. Which was ridiculous because Dr. Hudson wasn't just a sexual surrogate. He was also a psychologist. He took on normal patients like every other shrink.

I shook my head, making my way over to the suede couch, situated slightly into a small alcove. I sat, placing my hands out on the cushions beside me. To ground myself, to stop my hands from being clammy.

There was a clock above the door and I sat there watching it, time tick tick ticking away. Still no sign of the good doctor. Music started to come through some hidden speakers, the song slow and bluesy. Calming. The heat clicked on, warm and comforting.

I was almost, just barely at the point where I didn't think I was about to vomit all over his perfect office, when the door slowly opened.

And in he came.

And...

Oh,

my

God.

So, yeah, he wasn't middle aged. He had no hangover of a waistline. He had no moobs. He didn't have meat hands or elephant ears. No. This was, in a way, almost worse.

He was a freaking monument to male perfection.

His hair was black, longish but pushed back from his face. He had strong dark brows over startling blue eyes. He also had a sharp jaw with the slightest trace of a dark beard. His body was large. He was tall, wide of shoulder, and solid in the center. Looking impossibly fit underneath his open black suit jacket and white button up, the first two buttons undone, casual yet professional.

He was gorgeous.

And I was going to be having sex with him.

Jesus Christ.

"Miss. Davis," he said, looking up from the paperwork in his hands, almost like an afterthought.

His eyes on me felt like an invasion. Like he saw it all. Because, I reminded myself, he knew it all. He had it all scribbled carefully on those pages in his hands.

His brows were drawn together in confusion, like he was trying to figure something out.

"Dr. Hudson," I said, swallowing hard, moving to stand.

"Chase," he corrected, shaking his head once. "Don't get up," he said, holding up a hand and moving toward me.

His massiveness seemed to completely overtake the intimate little seating area, making me push into the back cushions to give myself the breathing space I felt like he was taking from me. His head quirked to the side slightly, watching me as he put the paperwork down on the closest end table, and took the chair across from me. "Can I call you Ava?" he asked, sitting back in the chair, looking completely at ease. Like he had done it a thousand times before. Which, well, maybe he had. Oh, God. Had he slept with that many clients? Maybe this wasn't such a good idea after all... maybe...

"Ava," he said, a little firmly, making my eyes snap up to his face.

"Sorry," I rushed, shaking my head. "I just..."

"You're nervous," he said, shrugging a shoulder.

"Yeah." You have no flipping idea.

"We're just talking," he said, his voice too deep to sound comforting, but it somehow did anyway. "Think of this as any normal therapy session, okay?"

"Okay," I said, taking a breath and letting it out slowly. I could do that. I had plenty of practice with that.

"Your chart says you started therapy when you were fifteen for anxiety issues."

"Yes."

"And now you are..."

"Twenty-seven," I supplied automatically.

"Any success with the treatment?"

A small half-laugh, half-snort, escaped me, as I reached up to run a hand through my hair. "Yes and no. Every time I get over one thing that makes me anxious..."

"A new anxiety develops," he answered.

"Yup."

"That must be incredibly frustrating."

"You have no idea."

He hadn't stopped looking at me. Literally. His eyes were just... on me. Since the second he walked through the door. Why couldn't he just... look away?

"What are your current anxieties?"

I was going to sleep with this man, what did it matter if he knew all the weird little things that gave me massive panic attacks?

I tried to keep his gaze and failed, looking down at his hands instead. Strong, wide. Capable. Of what, I wasn't sure. "I have issues feeling trapped. So, work can be a problem. Someone else driving me, especially public transportation. Public speaking. And..."

I couldn't even say it. How the hell was this going to even work if I couldn't...

"And sex," he finished, making my head snap up, eyes a little wide.

I felt a blush creep up into my cheeks. "Yeah."

"Okay," he said, casual. Like it was the most normal thing in the world. "I read in your chart that you don't ever remember not having a phobia about sex."

"Right."

"But you have tried to get more comfortable with it."

I laughed nervously, shrugging. "Exposure therapy," I suggested and he surprised me by laughing, a low, rumbling sound that reverberated somewhere deep in my chest and belly.

"With no success though."

"No."

"Yet you kept trying."

I looked down at my hands, pale and thin fingered. "Yeah." Four times. More than enough to start hating myself a little bit. And not be able to even kiss anyone anymore.

"So, why are you here?"

My head shot up, my brows drawing together. Was he serious? Wasn't it obvious why I was there? I mean, seriously. "I'm... frigid."

"Are you?" he asked, leaning forward and resting elbows on his knees, way too close. He was taking up all my space. "Being frigid implies an absence of interest in sex and a lack of sexual fantasies."

"Oh," I breathed the word out.

"Seeing as you are here," he went on, his lips twitching slightly, but not breaking into a smile. Seemingly always set in a firm line. Which I thought I preferred. I wasn't sure I could take him smiling, "I wouldn't call you frigid."

"Okay."

"Do you have sexual fantasies, Ava?"

Holy hell.

That question, with my name like a secret on his lips, sent an unexpected ping of desire between my thighs. My eyes focused on the watch on his wrist. "Yes."

"Do you get turned on?"

You mean like how I was right that second? Nooo. Not at allll.

"Yes."

"Good," he said. "Ava, can you look at me?"

Um. No. Don't think so. But my eyes moved slowly up anyway.

"There you are," he said, a smile slightly lifting his lips. "It's good that you get turned on. This process will be much easier. Now, I'm sure you did some looking around on my website, but would you like a bit more in-depth information on how this works?"

"Sure."

"Today, we talk," he started automatically. "If all goes well and you are comfortable enough with the situation, we will set up the dates for the next session. Each session will gradually lead up in intimacy. Provided things go par for the course, sex will likely happen around the sixth session."

Six. I had six sessions of non-sex. Well, that was good. I swallowed hard. "Okay. What... what will the first five sessions be then?"

He gave me a small, encouraging (I think) smile. "The first session is just getting comfortable with contact. At most, it would be kissing. From there, the next session would include undressing. Learning to get comfortable with your own nudity as well as... someone else's..."

His. His nudity. Oh, geez. Him naked... looking at me... naked.

"Ava," he broke in, his voice firm. "Don't go there," he said, reading my mind. His hand moved out, landing on top of my knee, solid, strong. Completely disconcerting, but somehow reassuring at the same time. "Anxiety doesn't exist in the moment. It is only in the past and the future. So, let's not think about those things, alright? Just be in this moment."

The moment. With his hand on my knee. It still hadn't moved. He was just sitting there, arm all stretched out, no doubt less than comfortable, with his hand on my knee.

"This moment makes you uncomfortable, doesn't it?" he asked, his hand squeezing my knee.

"Yes," I admitted, looking away from his hand and back up toward his face.

"But not enough to push me away," he observed.

"Not yet," I said, and he chuckled, taking his hand away, my knee feeling almost strange without the contact.

"The purpose of this is to push you out of your comfort zone. It's important that you don't push me away with the first twinge of anxiety. As I'm sure you learned in your previous therapy sessions, anxiety can really only be treated with exposure to that which makes you anxious."

"Right."

"So, if kissing makes you anxious..."

"I have to let you kiss me."

His eyes darkened for a second, just a quick flash that was just as quickly gone. "Exactly," he agreed, sitting back in the chair. "Only pull away or push me away if you can't talk yourself down. If you can't take it any more. That being said, I am going to be communicating with you the entire time, trying to work to dispel the fears before they become overwhelming. The point is for you to get to the point where you can enjoy being touched."

By him.

I was going to be touched by his six foot three, dark-haired, blue-eyed, ridiculously sexy self. All the while he talked to me in that low, deep, confident way he spoke that was making my skin feel tingly. Which... was good. That was good. But the initial arousal had always been easy for me. As long as he was... arousing me outside of my personal space.

"You're a very beautiful woman," he said, shocking through my internal stream of thought.

"I'm sorry?" I asked, sure I misheard him.

"I said you are a very beautiful woman."

Oh, for Christ's sake.

I felt the flutter in my belly, followed immediately by a strange rolling, my eyes dropping to my lap as my cheeks started to blush. I was awful at taking compliments. For as long as I could remember.

"Compliments make you uncomfortable?" he asked and I knew he was watching me. Always freaking watching me.

"Yes."

"Why?" Now, that was a loaded question. "Because you don't believe them?" he asked, hitting the nail on the head.

"Yes."

"Ava," he said, that same firm, yet pleading sound that I was learning to take for *look at me*. I sighed, looking up. "I don't feed women compliments for fun. If I tell you something, I mean it. It is an observation. You are a beautiful woman. Case closed."

"Right," I said, hoping it sounded like agreement.

His lips quirked up, turning into what I could only call a smirk. "Ava, what do you think the main reason men compliment women is?" He paused, like he was going to let me answer, but I didn't. "To get women into bed," he finished for me. He leaned forward, that smirk etching wider, almost devilish. "You are here to go to bed with me. Eventually. Do you really think I need to give you compliments?"

He had a point. "I guess not."

"Exactly. So, you're beautiful. It's a biological fact." Right. So it didn't really mean anything. Everyone finds different people attractive. For all I knew, he hated blondes, and brown eyes and lack of seen-from-the-front-buttage. "And," he cut into my little insecure tirade, "I find you incredibly attractive."

Oh, lord.

Feeling like I needed to find something to say, I mumbled, "Thanks."

To which, he chuckled.

"Do you find me attractive?"

"I think the entire continental US would find you attractive," I said, hedging the question. It was a skill I had learned early on, to answer, but not to include myself in the answer.

"That's wonderful," he said, leaning toward me, "but I wasn't asking the entire continental US, I was asking you."

Mother fucker.

I averted my eyes slightly, looking at the edge of his ear, "Yes."

"Good," he said, getting up from his chair suddenly, moving away from the alcove and making the air feel a lot thinner, easier to breathe. "So, I will see you... Tuesday for your first session."

It was a question, but also a statement. Like there was no doubt in his mind I would agree.

And, hell, I was in this deep. I might as well keep going.

"Okay."

"Okay," he said, opening the door to the waiting room and standing there, waiting for me to pass through. "Seven at night work for you?"

Odd hours. But I guessed it wasn't easy to get in the mood to pay a stranger to touch you at eight-forty in the morning.

"Yes," I agreed, moving into the doorway.

His hand pressed hard into my lower back, guiding me through, then dropping as he walked to stand next to the reception desk.

"See you then, Ava."

He needed to stop saying my name.

I couldn't freaking think straight.

"Okay," I said, walking numbly toward the door.

After the Session

Okay. So, maybe I ran to my car. Literally. Ran. In heels. Then threw myself into the seat and turned it over and started my way home. Because, well, I needed something to focus on.

That wasn't what I had expected.

Well, I mean it was. It was sufficiently embarrassing and awkward. But there was also that weird *'I find you attractive, do you find me attractive?'* thing. What was that about? If he didn't find me attractive, would that make a difference? I couldn't imagine all of his clients were good looking. Which must have made for a lot of time rolling around the highlight reel in his head to get the, ah, juices flowing.

And was he attractive? Seriously? Would any woman answer that with an *'eh, seen better'* ? Because I was pretty sure I hadn't. He was like a walking model for a suit catalog. And those eyes...

Alright. Enough of that.

If I concentrated on how good looking he was, it would only make me more nervous. Because, apparently, I only had one more session before I had to get naked with him.

I sighed, unlocking my apartment door and stepping inside.

"Still frigid?"

"What?" I asked, my heart flying up into my throat.

"You left your computer up," Jake, my pain in the ass roommate said, walking into the living room with an enormous bowl of cereal, wearing nothing but a pair of thick gray sweatpants slung low on his hips. Jake was extremely good looking. He was also completely aware of it.

He was slightly over six feet with sandy blond hair, longer on top and pushed back from his forehead, bright green eyes, and tan skin over the body he spent endless hours in the gym working on.

He was also a jerk.

"So, you thought that meant you could just... go through my browser history?" I asked, slamming the door and dropping my keys on the table.

"That wasn't the plan," he said, dropping down onto the couch and staring at the TV.

"What was the plan then?" I asked, kicking his gym shoes out of the middle of the floor.

"You have that huge screen," he said, turning to me with a smirk I didn't trust. "I'm tired of watching porn on my phone."

"Oh, gross."

"Well, some of us have sexual urges."

"You're such an asshole," I growled, grabbing the box of cereal off the kitchen counter and putting it back in the cabinet.

I didn't know why I put up with him. He was a slob. He

was insensitive. He had wild parties in the middle of the week. He brought an endless barrage of women home. Then he would leave early in the morning to hit the gym and make me to deal with them. God, I couldn't count how many of those awkward morning talks I had had. The *'he's an asshole, you can do so much better'* talks.

Fact of the matter was, it was an expensive freaking city. And my job didn't pay that great. On my salary alone, I'd have to live in one of the crummy areas, worrying myself to ulcers about all the unseemly characters I shared a building with. So, unfortunately, my only other option was to find a roommate to live in a better neighborhood.

So, I tolerated Jake. As I had already been doing for two and a half years. He made more than enough money to pull his own weight. And I had the added benefit of living with a man which gave me a sense of safety.

"Hey," he said, coming up behind me unexpectedly, putting his soggy cereal down on the counter next to me.

"What?" I snapped, staring out the window over the sink, bracing myself for the next unfeeling thing bound to come out of his mouth.

"Why didn't you tell me?"

Surprised, I turned, brows drawing together. "What?"

"Why didn't you tell me that you have like... issues with that?"

"Why would I?"

"Aw, love, that hurts," he said, putting a hand over his heart. "I thought we were pretty close. I buy you fucking tampons for God's sake."

"It's not something I like to talk about," I said, shrugging a shoulder. Though I had to admit, it was sort of nice that someone knew, that someone saw the whole picture.

It was getting beyond irritating to go to family dinners and be teased relentlessly about my always being single. About how much my mother wanted grand babies. Or have my coworkers got annoyed at me when they discussed their sexcapades and I never had anything to pitch in.

"Christ, I feel like a dick, Ava," he said, backing up and leaning against the kitchen island. "How many times did I pick at you about needing to get laid? If I had known you have like... problems..."

"You still would have teased me," I said, smiling slightly. He might have felt like a heel, but the fact of the matter was... that was just his personality. He was always saying things that got him in trouble. Hitting on women in front of their men. Telling the meatheads at the gym that they must be compensating for something. He seemed to have an innate ability to know just what buttons to press... and then push the heck out of them.

"Yeah, maybe," he smiled, boyish, charming, "but I would have felt bad about it after."

"You're a prince," I said, rolling my eyes.

"So, how did it go?" he asked, putting his hands at the edge of the counter behind him, completely comfortable with his half-nakedness. He always had been. For which, I couldn't blame him. He looked like he was sculpted out of clay.

"Are we really going to talk about this?" I asked, shaking my head at the cereal bowl he was totally going to let sit there on the counter to fester.

"Only if you don't want me constantly pestering you about it."

"Fine," I said, turning to strain the milk down the drain and drop the globs of cereal into the garbage. "It was weird. Uncomfortable."

"Well, I mean... you're going to be fucking the dude. So... yeah." He stayed silent as I washed the bowl and spoon, placing them in the drying rack. "Was he halfway decent looking? Please don't tell me you're fucking a gross fat old guy."

"He's probably the best looking guy I've ever seen," I admitted.

"Hey," Jake objected, eyes squinted at me.

"Aside from you," I laughed.

"That's better," he smiled, and I could see why so many women blindly followed him home. "So, he got your panties all wet, huh?"

"What? No!" I screeched, too loud, too fast. A blush crept up into my cheeks and Jake threw his head back and laughed.

"You're cute when you're all turned on by your new sex doctor."

"Oh, my God. Shut up," I said, brushing past him.

His arm swung out, grabbing my bicep and holding me in place until I looked at him. "I'm just playing," he said, shrugging. "I'm glad you're getting help. And if you need to talk about the sex stuff, well," he said, smiling his devilish smile again, "I *am* an expert too."

I laughed. "Oh, yeah? What credentials do you have?"

"Baby, I graduated at the top of my class in Pussyology at Fucking U."

I giggled, shaking my head. "You're such a tool."

"For serious though," he said, letting my arm go, "if you have any questions or want to talk about it... I know you don't have anyone else to talk to."

"I don't need a sympathy ear," I said, spine straightening.

"It's not sympathy. It's interest. Hell, maybe I should get a job working as a sexual surrogate..."

"It's good money," I said, starting toward my room.

"How much money?" he asked, pushing my door open as I went to my closet.

"Three grand for ten, well, technically eleven, sessions."

"You're paying this fucker three K to teach you how to have sex?"

"Not exactly," I grumbled, reaching for a pair of huge, baggy sweatpants and a big t-shirt.

"Ava, I'll fuck ya for half that," he laughed.

"That's charming," I snorted, grabbing my towel off the back of my door.

"I have references," he said, following me to the bathroom.

"I've met all your so-called references," I laughed over my shoulder at him, putting my clothes on top of the closed hamper.

"Yeah, so you know," he laughed. I went to push the door closed, but he grabbed it with his hand and held it open. "Seriously though, if you can't go through it with him, I am here if you need someone you know and trust to... experiment with."

"Who says I trust you?" I smirked, cocking an eyebrow, trying to push the door shut.

"Ouch," he said, still smiling. "Just... keep it in mind," he said, suddenly letting go of the door and sending me falling into it as it slammed closed.

Okay.

Weird day.

I stripped out of my clothes, running the water on hot, and stepping in. I had already showered, but sometimes I just needed the water to calm down, clear my head, get my thoughts in the right order, have imaginary conversations for hypothetical situations that would probably never take place. You know, normal stuff.

So, not only did I have stuff with Dr. Chase to think about, I had whatever the heck just happened with Jake to consider too. I mean... what the hell *was* that? Never once had he ever even come close to insinuating he would sleep with me. If he had, he probably would have been out on his ass a long time ago. It was my name on the lease, after all.

But his offer was almost... sweet.

Jesus. Did I just say that anything, literally anything, related to Jake Summers was... sweet? This was the guy who once told me that the dress I chose to wear to my work's New Year's Eve party was going to inspire a thousand flaccid penises. The guy who once announced, to an apartment full of people I didn't even know, that I hadn't gotten laid in over a year... and asked if anyone was up for ending my "drought".

He was a grade A jackass ninety-nine percent of the time.

So, seriously, why the sudden pep talk and sex offer? Just because it was a challenge? Because I wasn't, like he thought, just some uptight bitch. That I had actual issues. And, what? He wanted to try his hand at fixing them? Like the other four guys who had tried? Probably. That was very likely exactly why he was interested. Because I was an anomaly. Because I didn't make sense. Because he wanted to prove his manhood by trying to get me all hot and bothered.

Unfortunately for him, I couldn't think about him without thinking about the pile of clothes sitting right in front of the freaking hamper. Not in it. In front of it. Or the shakers full of dried protein powder smoothies from his workouts sitting on the counter. Or his steadfast refusal to take the full garbage bag out of the can and put a new one in.

I would be laying in bed with him silently seething about the water marks his beer left on my coffee table.

Like a freaking resentful, unappreciated wife.

And that wasn't sexy at all.

Now, Chase.

Chase was the poster boy for sexy. What had even led him into psychology in the first place? He could have made a fortune just posing for pictures. Or reading the phone book to women who would drool over every last number coming from between his lips.

I mean... he would have needed to go to college and then grad school. Totaling at least nine years in education. He must have had some strong interest in the psychological field, not just sex therapy. And then after graduating with such a lofty degree, and the potential to earn all kinds of money, why would he decide to become a sexual surrogate on the side? Had he, himself, suffered from some sort of sexual dysfunction at one time? Did he see a surrogate that helped him? How does someone come to work in such an odd field?

Nine years of education. Which meant he would have graduated, at earliest, around twenty-nine. He couldn't be much older than... thirty-five or thirty-six. He hadn't even been practicing for very long.

Unless...

Unless he became a sexual surrogate before he graduated. As a way to make money to get him through his schooling. And he just... continued it because he liked it. Or was good at it.

Which I hoped, for my sake.

From what I read online, there was no law stating a sexual surrogate needed to have any kind of license or certification. Dr. Hudson did. Along with his doctorate. Which made him the best possible choice for me. I had the highest likelihood of success with him.

It had to work. Because I was out of other options. And I couldn't pay to go through the program again.

"Yo," Jake's voice called through the door, making me start and slip slightly, arms flying out to brace myself. Just what I needed, to break my ass naked in the shower with only Jake around to help me. "You've been in there long enough. You're gonna have to let your surrogate get the cobwebs off that pussy with his mouth. Soap and water ain't gonna cut it," he called, making me take a slow, deep breath. The asshole was back. And that was good.

"What the hell do you care how long I'm in here?" I growled, angry that I had settled on an apartment with one bathroom.

"I have a client coming in twenty. I want to clean up."

"Fine. I'm getting out."

"Halle-fucking-lujah."

Jake, by some awful twist of fate, was a massage therapist. I got to walk into my apartment at all hours to see someone laid up on a table, their naughty bits covered (or surprisingly often, *not* covered) by one of my bath towels. I was constantly surrounded by half, or full, nudity in my own home. There was no escaping the in-my-face proof of how unusual I was. Me and my inability to even walk around the house in a pair of panties and a t-shirt.

I dried, slipped into my clothes, opened the door and gave Jake a scathing look, then made my way to my room.

In truth, yes, Jake drove me up every goddamn wall (and across the ceiling) in the apartment, but I had come to love him. Like the brother I never had. Which was probably why I was so put-off by his invitation. Because, seriously, he was an excellent male specimen. And underneath all the innuendos, foot-in-mouth tendencies, and sloppiness... he was actually a really good guy.

He totally did buy me tampons once. I had literally grabbed the last one, cursing under my breath about having to run out so late at night, when I walked out into the living room to him unloading more jugs of protein powder, then turning and holding out a box of tampons to me.

It was the small things.

And, he was right. The walls were thin in the apartment and I had heard more than my fair share of his sexual conquests night after night. The girls screamed until they lost their damn voices, talking to me all hoarse in the morning. He was good.

But he wasn't man meat material for me.

He was the only real friend I had in the world.

I prayed to whatever almighty power there might be to the universe, that he was not, in any way, harboring sexual feelings toward me. Before, or after, the day's conversation.

I sighed, walking over to my computer where noise was coming out of the speakers. A very specific kind of noise. An unmistakable noise.

And, sure enough, the asshole left the porn site up on my screen. I clicked it closed, shaking my head. I didn't have an issue with porn. I could watch it. It didn't (usually) freak me out. But it didn't particularly do it for me either. It was so cold. Devoid of something.

But, then again, I guessed, so was what I was about to do. What could be more passionless than paying someone to talk you through intimate acts?

I set a password on my computer, shut it off, and made my way toward the bed. It was early, but I felt drained from all the anxiety. I curled up on my side, staring out the window, and not... absolutely not, thinking about Dr. Chase Hudson.

Not about his dark hair. Or his blue eyes. Or his big hand on my knee. Or the fact that he was going to kiss me in three days. *Kiss me.* In all his gorgeousness. And I certainly did not think about his sexy, deep voice telling me I was beautiful. No, I didn't think about that at all.

It totally did not go on repeat in my head all through the weekend. And then the whole day at work on Monday. Nope. Not at all. I wasn't that ridiculous.

First Session

"The one that shows more of your tits," Jake said behind me, making me jump and swing around.

"Dude. Knock," I scolded for what must have been the millionth time since he had moved in.

"Like you'd hear me," he smiled, leaning against the doorjamb. "You're all lost in your little doctor fantasy dream world."

"No," I said, but I was. I absolutely was. "I am just trying to find something appropriate to wear."

"Like I said... the one with more boobage."

"What," I started, raising a brow, "in my wardrobe has ever screamed 'boobs'?"

"That's a good point," he said, unfolding his arms and walking toward my closet.

"What are you doing?"

"You obviously can't be trusted to pick your own clothes out. I mean what was that shit you wore to work?" he asked, rummaging around, making all my neatly folded piles topple. "Here," he said, producing black skinny jeans and a black tank top.

"It's cold outside," I objected, taking them because he didn't really give me a choice.

"Fine," he said, reaching and ripping something off a hanger and flinging a lightweight red wine colored cardigan at me, "But leave this open." He moved back toward the door. "Heels and put your hair down," he said, closing the door and leaving me alone.

Dressed, I had to admit, he made a good choice. Better by far than what I would have chosen. I paced my room for a good twenty minutes, messing with my hair occasionally, applying endless coats of lip balm, rubbing a small amount of vanilla scented lotion across my neck and chest. By the time I got there, the scent would be dull, just a hint on the skin. Which was the only way to wear any kind of scent, not bathing in the stuff like the women I worked with did.

"Go get you some ass," Jake said, swatting my butt as I walked past him toward the door, only twenty minutes early. It wouldn't take me more than ten to get there. But ten minutes early wasn't ridiculous.

I walked up to the doors a short nine minutes later, taking a deep breath, and pulling it open. Expecting, I guess, to see the same secretary from my last appointment. But no, there standing behind the front desk, was Dr. Chase Hudson himself, looking way too good in a gray suit, the jacket open, only one button undone on his (that time black) dress shirt.

He looked up at the whoosh of cool air, something that might be considered a smile tugging at one corner of his lips. "Ava," he said my name on an exhale.

"Dr. Hudson," I said, forcing myself to take steps into the waiting area, not stand by the door like I was seconds away from darting.

"Chase," he corrected, moving out from behind the desk and toward me, making me stiffen. But he walked past me, locking the front door, before turning to me. "You look nice."

Oh, my.

"Oh, um," I fumbled, shaking my head. "Thanks."

His hand moved to my lower back, feeling way too good, and I was wondering if he was just a touchy-feely person or if it was part of the 'trying to get me comfortable with physical contact' thing. Either way, it was nice. He guided me toward his office door, opening it and letting me step through.

"You're welcome," he said as I passed him. "How was your weekend?"

"Uneventful," I supplied, meaning I spent all my time trapped in my room because Jake had female company all Saturday and guys over all Sunday to watch some game on TV.

"Ava," he said as I walked over toward the little seating alcove. "This way," he said, holding an arm out toward me and I fell into step next to him.

And then he did something straight out of a darn spy movie. He reached into the bookshelf and opened a freaking hidden door behind it.

"Seriously?" I asked, smiling at him with raised brows.

He offered me a small smile back. "Yup," he said, pressing his hand into my back and pushing me through.

And that room was what I had sort-of been expecting on my first visit. But also, so much more. The walls were painted a deep, deep blue color. White treatments covered the window and billowed across the top of the canopy bed which was also covered in white sheets and comforter. It had the same hard wood floors. To one side was a small dark blue mini sectional in front of an electric fireplace. Beside the door was a long white sidebar with a state of the art stereo system and a collection of decanters full of, I imagined, liquor. At the end, was another closed door.

"Why don't you find some music to put on?" he suggested, letting his hand fall and moving over toward the liquor. "Would you like something to drink?"

Whatever will make this less nerve-racking. "Sure," I said, pressing the touch screen read out on the stereo and flipping through the playlists.

"Red, white? Something stronger?"

"Red is fine," I said, selecting a list called "coffeehouse music" because I figured it was the least likely to get sexual.

"I see what you did there," he said, and I turned to see a smirk toying with his lips as he held out a wineglass to me.

"What?" I asked, hoping to sound innocent as I took my drink and had a quick sip.

But he just shook his head, stepping away. "How about we go sit down?" he asked, gesturing toward the sectional.

I followed blindly behind, taking slow, deep, deliberate breaths. He placed his wineglass down on the single end table, turning his back on me as he fiddled with the fireplace and, apparently, the lights because they dimmed dramatically.

I sat down two cushions away from the cushion next to the end table, sitting back stiffly and sipping my wine. For courage. For something to do. The fireplace clicked on, the flames at once relaxing and exciting, the music got slightly louder and, finally, Chase turned back toward me, taking in my seat choice with a barely noticeable raised brow.

He walked over to his wineglass, picking it up, and drinking the entire contents, placing it back down, and moving to the cushion next to mine. He sat, slightly turned toward me, his feet next to mine, his hips pivoted away.

"Nervous?" he asked, putting his arm across the back of the couch, but not touching me.

"Yes," I admitted because, well, if I wasn't honest, the process wasn't going to work.

He nodded, then the hand that wasn't behind me, reached out and landed on top of my knee. "What, exactly, are you nervous about? Me touching you?" he asked, and I felt myself nodding tightly, watching the fake fire. "I'm touching you right now." He didn't need to tell me that. I felt like the contact was shooting right up my leg into my core. "Do you want me to stop?" he asked, his hand squeezing slightly.

Did I? I was so caught up in the 'what might happens' that I wasn't even actually sure how I felt about the contact. In the end, I decided, "No."

"Good," he said and I sucked in a deep breath, "because I don't want to stop."

The air hissed out of my mouth, my head turning quickly to find his gaze on my face, "Wh... okay," I finished, not sure what I was about to ask him.

His hand moved downward, stroking across the front of my leg, then back up to my knee, casual, lazy, but damn if it wasn't sending off sparks. My hand gripped hard at my empty wineglass and his hand reached up, "Why don't we get rid of that?" he suggested, taking it, his fingers brushing against mine as he did. He turned, placing my glass next to his, then faced me again. This time, when his arm reached out, it went to the other knee, his arm like a barrier across my body, blocking me in.

And the heart palpitations started.

That's always how the anxiety worked. First the pounding heart, the sweaty palms, the hot and cold at the same time sensation, the trouble catching my breath, then the dizziness, the nausea, the absolute certainty that if I didn't get away, I was going to be sick all over myself and then pass out.

"Ava," Chase said, making my head snap toward him. "Breathe," he told me and I realized he was right, I was holding my breath. I sucked in a shaky breath and he nodded. "Good. Now, tell me why you're anxious."

I swallowed hard. If there was one thing that people didn't get about anxiety and panic attacks, it was how much the sufferers didn't want to talk about it. How they didn't want to be perceived as weak or crazy or dramatic.

"I feel trapped," I admitted.

"Okay," he said, his hand squeezing my knee. "Are you really trapped?"

"No." Of course not, but that didn't matter. Anxiety wasn't rational.

"Can you leave at any time?"

I bit into my lower lip for a second. "Yes."

"Do you think I would be mad or disappointed if you needed to get up and walk away?"

My eyes went to his, surprised. Because, well, yes. That was exactly what made the sensation so bad, knowing that the guys I had been with didn't understand, that they'd been offended or upset. But he wasn't them. He understood. He wasn't judging me. "No," I said finally.

"Okay, so why don't we stop thinking about that?" he suggested, his hand dipping low, stroking down the front of my leg, then snaking around to my calf, before moving back up to my knee. "Do you like this?" he asked, his fingers sliding toward the outside of my thigh, snaking upward.

I looked down from his eyes, staring at his throat instead. "Yes," I whispered.

"Good, I like that," he said, and it sounded like praise... something a man had never offered me before. "I like touching you," he said, making my belly do a strange little flip flop. His other arm, the one behind me, slid downward, settling behind my shoulders, just pressure, not wrapping around me. "And I'm not just saying that because it's my job," he said, sounding closer, and I glanced lower to see he had scooted closer, his hips just an inch or so from mine. I hadn't even felt him move.

"Really?" I asked, a blush creeping up my cheeks, hot and furious.

His hand suddenly stopped toying with my leg, moving upward, stroking across my jaw, then grabbing my chin lightly, forcing my face up to look at him. "Babe," he said, sounding serious, "if I saw you in a bar, I'd have taken you home in a heartbeat."

Oh, my.

My eyes dropped self-consciously, but his hand stayed there, patient, waiting. For me to look at him again. When I finally did, "Do you believe me?"

Did I? He had no reason to lie. He didn't need to admit that in the first place. "Yes."

He nodded slightly, just the barest of movements, still not dropping his hand from my chin. "I would have walked over to you, gotten close, whispered in your ear, told you how fucking gorgeous you are..."

Oh, my God.

Was he really saying that?

Seriously?

"And then, I would bring you back to my apartment and as soon as you stepped inside, I would push you up hard against the door, and crush my lips to yours," he said, his thumb moving upward and stroking across my lips. The words settled, like a fluid sensation in my belly, sending a jolt of desire so strong I felt my panties start to get wet, and pressed my thighs tightly together to stem the chaos brewing between them. "Does that sound good?" He asked, his thumb stroking again, my lips parting slightly and his finger pressed between the crease.

"Y... yes," I admitted.

"Are you turned on, Ava?" he asked, his eyes dropping to look at my lips.

Was I turned on? Only more than ever before. "Yes," I admitted.

He made a short, low, almost growling sound. "I like that," he said, his hand moving back across my jaw, pausing, then slipping down the side of my neck. And I swear the contact felt like fireworks. I felt a small involuntary shiver shake my body. Chase chuckled slightly, leaning closer. "You're so sensitive."

Was I? I was usually so busy freaking out by this point that I was just... almost numb to the sensations. "Not usually," I said, wanting to be forthcoming.

His head dipped toward me, his nose grazing across my jaw, his warm breath on my neck. "Just for me then?" he asked and I felt my head float backward, begging for things I knew I never wanted before. Lips on skin. Hands in hair. Fingers in... places.

"I guess," I mumbled, eyes closing.

"Do you want me to kiss you here?" he asked, his nose brushing across the sensitive skin underneath my ear.

Did I? I think I did. "Yes."

"Tell me," he said, his breath causing another shiver.

"Tell you what?"

"Tell me you want me to kiss your neck," he instructed.

Damn. If the process was going to be 'I'll do things to you, but only after you ask for them', then we weren't going to get anywhere.

Because I couldn't. Literally couldn't. It didn't make sense. I knew that rationally. There was no good reason I couldn't open my mouth and force the words out. But I just couldn't. No matter how much I wanted to. The words would get caught on my tongue and some sort of crippling anxiety would keep me mute.

And it wasn't just sex. It was anything that I really wanted. Or things that I wanted to stop. The words just... wouldn't come.

"Ava," Chase said, tilting his head up to look at me. I swallowed, looking over at him, and shook my head. "No, you don't want me to? Or no you can't ask."

I brought a hand up to my face, wanting to hide. The rolling in my belly was back and I knew what was next. The need to flee. I was hoping we could get further before I needed to take steps back. "I can't ask," I admitted, my voice like a strange croak.

"Okay," he said, sounding unconcerned. "We can work on the verbal stuff," he said, looking away. "But first, this," he said.

And then his lips touched the space his nose had traced, sending a shock through my body, making me jump and my hand slam down on the top of my thigh, balling into a fist.

So, that was what it was supposed to feel like. The sweet, intoxicating sensation that had me wanting to sink back into the couch as my body came alive.

His lips pressed into the skin and I felt the hint of teeth a second before his tongue moved outward and traced a slow line down the side of my neck. I swear I felt like I was going to explode. Just. *Bam*. Shatter into a million little flecks of desire. Because that was all that I could feel. The heat. His breath on my skin. His lips planting lazy kisses. His hand on the other side of my neck, digging slightly in.

My head turned, giving him complete access as his lips landed down by the collar of the cardigan.

And then he moved away, leaving my skin feeling cold.

He sat back slightly, fingers stroking down the other side of my neck before catching in my hair. "Open your eyes," he said, his voice soft but there was an undercurrent of heat there too. I took a breath, opening slowly to land on his bright blues. "Good girl," he said, quietly. "Did you enjoy that?"

"Yes."

"What do you want now?" he asked.

I felt my eyes go wide. Because, honestly, I didn't know. I wanted whatever he wanted to give me. I couldn't just name any particular...

"Let's try this again," he said and I heard a humor in his voice. "Do you want me to keep kissing your neck?" he asked, leaning down and planting a whisper-light kiss. "Or do you want to try something else for a while?"

Choices, choices.

Both. Everything.

"Something else," I decided, knowing he said the most we would do in the first session would be kissing. There wasn't a huge chance of anything happening to fully and completely freak me out.

"Mmm," his lips vibrated on my neck and I swear I felt it... *vibrate*... somewhere else. "Okay," he said, slowly lifting his head. He sat back, the space between us seeming wider than before. "How about you turn around?" he suggested.

"Why?" I asked, straightening. His hands and lips off of me, my mind was free to race again. And I couldn't think of any good reason why he needed me to turn away.

"Because," he said, his hand moving to my arm, rubbing absentmindedly, "I am going to give you a massage."

"Oh," I breathed out, glancing at the bed, grateful he hadn't suggested we move there to do that.

"Do you think you would like that?" I looked at him, feeling my shoulder shrug. "Okay," he said, "let's find out then," he added moving back further, giving me space to move.

As soon as my back was to him, his hands went to my shoulders, close to my neck, pressing into the knots that had become so much a part of me. Jake had offered more than a hundred times to work them out, saying how unhealthy it was to walk around all tense and in pain, but I couldn't even begin to consider undressing and letting him touch me.

"Where are you?" he asked, his thumbs pressing up the back of my neck, "You're not with me."

"Sorry," I mumbled, shaking my head slightly.

"Don't be sorry. Tell me what you were thinking about."

"My roommate," I admitted.

"Why?"

"He's a massage therapist."

"Ah. I see. Have you ever let him give you a massage?"

"What do you think?" I half-laughed.

He chuckled slightly, his hands moving down toward the center of my back. "Why don't you tell me more about him?"

"Why?"

"Because you are having communication issues. I figure your roommate is a safe topic to get started." At my silence, he added, "Tell me about him."

"He's an asshole," I said, and he laughed.

"Why is he an asshole?"

"He teases me all the time," I admitted, feeling a little bit of resentment rise up.

"What does he tease you about?"

"The way I dress. How I am uptight and a little OCD about things being clean. About my needing to get laid."

"He sounds like a good guy," Chase said dryly, making me giggle slightly.

"He's actually not a bad guy all in all. It's just like... living with a teenage boy. He's a slob and has wild parties all the time. Oh, and then there's the ear-piercing screams all night."

"Screams?" Chase asked, his hands stilling around my hips.

I bit my lip, smiling slightly. "Yes... from... women."

"Ah," he said, his hands moving again. "Does that make you uncomfortable?"

"Only when I have to wake up in the morning and explain to said women that Jake is gone, he won't call, and they'll never see him again."

"Do you think that has had any effect on how you view sex?"

"Not really. Except knowing with absolutely certainty that I don't want to do it with him."

"Does this feel good?" he asked, running his hands back up toward my shoulders.

Back into the current moment, I felt my head lull toward the side. It did feel good. And that was really weird. "Yeah."

"Good," he said, one hand reaching up to brush my hair to the side, his mouth lowering toward my neck and running his lips across it again. "Why don't you turn back around?" he suggested, his teeth nipping ever so slightly into my earlobe.

"Okay," I breathed, pulling forward and turning.

Knowing what was going to happen.

He was absolutely going to kiss me.

Jesus Christ.

I wasn't ready for that. It had been so long. The last time someone kissed me... it was one of Jake's party goers: tall, brown haired, attractive, with a tattoo of a raven on the side of his neck. He had been laying it on thick to a very reluctant me for hours and he finally made a move. And I managed to yield for a total ten seconds before I started to hyperventilate and shoved hard at his chest. Then I ran, humiliated, into my room, locking the door, and crying bitter, angry, self-hate filled tears.

"Come back to me," Chase's voice said, soft and deep. He offered me a small smile when my eyes landed on his again. "What were you just thinking about?"

I let my eyes drop, making contact with his collar. "The last time someone kissed me."

His hand moved toward me, stroking across my cheek. "Tell

me about it." No. Nope. Couldn't do that. "You have to put the work in, Ava."

He was right. "Jake was having a party. There was a guy who... took interest in me..."

"Just one?" he asked, smiling a little.

"Yes. Just one. And he just... didn't seem deterred by my lack of enthusiasm. Then, hours later, he finally leaned in and..."

"And what happened?"

"I handled it for a few seconds, then freaked and ran."

"Hmm," he said, his other hand moving out toward my other cheek, cradling my face. "What did he say?"

"I never saw him again."

His head shook slightly, his eyes raking over me, "A face like this, babe, he should have been bringing you flowers and jewelry and chocolate until you got comfortable with him and let him try again."

A face like mine?

I felt that strange fluttering in my belly again.

He needed to stop saying sweet things. I wasn't prepared for it.

"Do you have any idea what men would do to possess beauty like this?" he asked, shaking his head. "And, here I am, holding it."

Holy lord.

I just... couldn't take it.

"Tell me you want me to kiss you," he urged, his words sounding almost desperate, like the suspense was too much. "Ava, tell me."

I licked my lips and his eyes went to watch intently. Did I want him to kiss me? I was pretty freaking sure I did. "I want you to kiss me," I said, barely audibly, but he heard.

"Thank God," he groaned, leaning in, pulling my face toward his at the same time.

Then his lips met mine, firm yet gentle, sending a unexpected current through my body. A soft moan escaped me. There was a second of shocked stillness before my lips started responding, pressing into his, begging for more. His head tilted slightly, taking the kiss deeper. One of his hands stayed at the side of my face, the other slid over my shoulder, down my arm, my side, sneaking around my back, pulling me close.

And then it finally started to happen.

The expected throat-constricting panic. I felt myself stiffen, my heart slamming hard like it was trying desperately to escape my rib cage. But I tried to fight it. In our intro session, he told me it was important to not push him away unless it was too much, unless I couldn't take it anymore. I could take it for a few more minutes. I could hold on. I could…

"Ava," his voice broke in, and I hadn't even realized he had stopped kissing me. He moved back, looking at my face. "On a scale of one to ten, how bad is the anxiety?"

"Six or seven," I admitted, bringing a hand to my throat like I could work out the strangled feeling.

"Okay," he said, moving slightly back, then turning and sitting with his back to the cushions. "Come here."

"What?" I asked, trying to take deep breaths and failing.

"It hasn't exactly escaped my notice that I have been touching you and you have yet to put a finger on me. Come over here," he said, holding an arm out wide. "Put your head head on my chest."

Oh, jeez.

Shit.

No.

"At least try, Ava," he coaxed, patient.

And that's what did it. The willingness to let me pull away, to be rejected, without being offended. It was so new and unexpected. He was right. I needed to try.

I scooted closer, bringing my legs up at an angle behind me, and slowly lowering the side of my face to his chest. I closed my eyes, taking a deep breath, taking in the slightest hint of a spicy cologne. Underneath my cheek, his shirt was warm from his skin, his chest hard. Which I found somehow comforting.

I moved closer, my torso leaning into his side, my knees pressing into his thigh. My hand came out and landed on the other side of his chest, in a fist, but still... touching. Willingly. Happily.

There was a long pause before his arm went around me, heavy, settling on my waist. "You okay?" he asked, his face sounding close to my hair.

"Yeah."

"What's the level?"

"Four?" I guessed, not entirely sure. Definitely better than before, but still on edge.

"Be proud of the little victories, Ava," he said, and his other hand came up, taking my hand, opening it, slipping his fingers between mine, and squeezing closed against his chest.

Holding his hand. I was holding sexy Dr. Chase Hudson's hand. I felt a strange, strangled laugh catch in the back of my throat at the idea.

His hand went from my waist, moving slowly up the center of my back. It was a slow, lazy exploration up my spine. I felt myself melt into the sensation. God, who knew it felt so good just to be touched?

I closed my eyes, feeling the anxiety slowly start to settle back down, taking grateful, greedy deep breaths.

"Ava... babe," Chase's voice called, low, gentle, like he was trying to wake someone without startling them.

Which, was exactly what happened I realized, my eyes flying open. Oh, my God. I fell asleep on him! How the hell did that happen?

"Relax," he said, his arm wrapping around my back and

squeezing slightly.

"How long was I asleep?" I asked, blinking the sleep out of my eyes.

"Maybe half an hour," he said casually, like it was totally normal for it to happen. "Ava, do you have any idea how comfortable you need to be to fall asleep with another person?"

I knew. Oh, I knew. I had never been able to sleep when another person was even in the same room. Which made for God-awful sleepovers with friends and nights over the holidays when my family would come from out of town and people would need to be crammed into all available places... like my bedroom.

"This is good, sweetheart," he said, and I could almost swear I felt his lips kiss the top of my head, but brushed that idea away. That wasn't possible.

I slowly pushed myself up, moving off of his chest, feeling unreasonably sad to do so. His hand slipped from mine and I put my feet back on the ground.

Behind me, he let out a sound that was almost a sigh, but not quite. Then he sat up next to me, his knee brushing against mine, turning his head to me. "I think this was a successful session. How do you feel about it?"

I closed my eyes, not wanting to share. Wanting to keep this memory pure, unexamined. But that was why we were there. To examine. To figure out what was wrong with me. To work on fixing it.

"I think it went really well," I agreed, not wanting to go into any more detail than that.

I could feel his eyes on me for a while before he spoke again. "Thursday, same time," he said, slowly getting onto his feet.

I followed, watching him. "Okay," I agreed. That gave me a day and a half to recover. And prepare. He led me out through to his main office, then the waiting room in silence. When we got to the front door, he paused, and I knew I had to ask or the suspense would kill me.

"Dr. Hud..."

"Chase," he corrected, his voice firm.

"Chase," I agreed, trying to meet his eyes. "What, exactly, is the next session? I know you mentioned we would be..." I couldn't even say it, dropping my eyes.

"We are each going to take our clothes off," he supplied, noting my discomfort and ignoring it. "We will kiss. You will touch me. I will touch you. But no sexual contact."

Naked. I would be naked. He would be naked. And then he expected me to touch his naked body. And to touch mine. Shit. I really didn't think that was going to go well and...

"Ava. In the moment, okay? If you're worried about it while it goes on, we will address it then. Until then, just don't think about it." He reached for the lock, turned it, and opened the door.

I stepped outside, surprised when he followed me... and locked the door.

"Okay," I agreed, knowing damn well there was no way I wasn't going to stress about it, but not wanting to tell him that either. "Well, I'll see you Thursday," I said, starting away, but he fell into step with me. "What are you doing?"

"Walking you to your car," he supplied like it was obvious. "It's nighttime, Ava. This is a good neighborhood, but even if it was goddamn Utopian, you shouldn't be walking around alone at night looking like you do."

I looked down at my clothes, simple, chaste even. My body was decent but not all that impressive beneath the material. "If you say so."

"We need to work on that," he said as we walked down the empty street.

"Work on what?" I asked, shivering slightly against the cool.

"On your confidence. Because it's fucking ridiculous that you can't see what everyone else does."

What *he* does. What *he* sees when *he* looks at *me*.

Oh, holy hell.

I walked into the parking garage, big hulking Chase beside me, his hands tucked into his pockets, and I felt his eyes on me. When I walked ahead of him, I could feel them on my ass. When I walked beside him, on my face mostly, my breasts, my legs.

"This is me," I said, waving a hand to my little blue not *too* old tiny hatchback.

He nodded, and I fetched my keys, unlocking my door before turning back to face him, feeling like I needed to offer some kind of goodbye.

"Thanks for... walking me," I said, giving him a small smile.

He nodded stiffly for a second, looking like he was thinking really hard about something. Then his eyes moved up and caught mine. "We're outside the office," he said, oddly, making my brows draw together, "I'm not supposed to do this," he said, bringing a hand up to run through his hair, like he was struggling with something. "Fuck it," he said.

His hand went behind my neck as his lips crashed down onto mine. Crashed. Not landed. Not pressed. Crashed. Hard. Bruising. Sending a shocked surge through my body, my arms going to his shoulders instinctively. He made a low growling sound against my lips, slamming my back up against my car as his teeth bit into my lower lip, drawing a groan out of me.

Then jut as suddenly as it started, he shoved away from me, rubbing a hand over his brow. "Fuck," he muttered to himself as I tried to come to grips with what the hell had just happened. My body felt electric and suddenly, with his absence, so freaking cold. "Sorry," he said, looking at me finally, moving closer. His hand reached out, running his thumb across my chin and lips, the skin feeling a bit sensitive thanks to his rough stubble. "That wasn't exactly professional of me, huh?"

"It's okay," I said, swallowing hard.

He nodded, looking down at my lips for a long second, before moving back up to my eyes. "You touched me," he said.

"What?" I asked, confused.

"You touched me. When I kissed you. Without being told or asked to. You just did it." Holy shit. He was right. I did. That was big. "Baby steps, but that's really good, Ava," he said, smiling slightly. Then he reached beside me, grabbing the handle of my car door and pulling it open. "I'll see you Thursday," he said as I slipped into the car. As he closed the door, I could swear I heard him say, "I'm looking forward to it."

Jesus.

After the Session

    The door had barely clicked closed (quietly, I might add), when Jake came walking out of his room, this time in a pair of black exercise shorts and nothing else.
    "How did it go? Did you fuck him? Did you actually come?"
    "Oh my God," I said, heat rising up in my cheeks for no good reason, "it doesn't work like that, Jake."
    "That's disappointing," he said, shrugging. "You have beard burn," he informed me.
    "What?" I asked, moving toward the kitchen, just to have something to do.
    "Beard burn," he said again, following me, watching as I

filled the kettle and put tea water on the stove. "Like when a guy you're making out with has a beard and it rubs against your skin, love. Beard burn."

Well, shoot. I was caught. I brought a hand up to my face, feeling the sensitive, almost inflamed skin. Beard burn. What an appropriate term.

"So you kissed him."

"More accurately, he kissed me," I said, turning to the fridge to look for something to eat. I had been way too nervous to eat anything substantial before I would see him.

"But you let him."

"Yeah," I said, dragging out the jelly, accepting that it was going to have to be a pb&j night seeing as I hadn't gotten around to food shopping.

"Well, this deserves a little celebration," he said, grabbing the jelly and putting it back in the fridge. "We're going out."

"Jake," I said, my tone sounding so much like a mom it was almost scary, "it is a Tuesday night."

"So the fuck what?" he asked, grabbing the knob on the stove and turning it off.

"Seriously... you know I'm not an... out and about kinda person."

"Well, until tonight, you weren't a getting kissed kinda person either. Things change. Come on," he said, his tone more serious. "I'll buy you some food. A couple drinks. What harm can be done?"

I sighed. He was right. And I was hungry. And, really, I could use a drink or two. "Okay." I agreed, and he smiled, then bounded off to his room to change into actual clothes. Though I swear he would go out shirtless if he could get into a bar like that.

Thirty minutes later, we were in a bar. There were black tables and chairs, deep reddish orange walls. There was a fair amount of people around, eating, drinking. Being normal. Jake had situated us at the bar, ordered me food and a martini, got himself a beer. Then as soon as his beer arrived, he ditched me to go flirt with a table full of young, pretty tourists.

Honestly, I should have seen it coming. I was really to blame for thinking he was genuine about celebrating my little success. Jake was all about Jake. And that was never going to change.

I sat there, picking at my appetizer sampler complete with mozzarella sticks, queso dip and chips, onion rings, and chicken strips.

"What did I say about being alone at night?"

I felt myself jump, visibly jump.

Because... what the actual hell?

My head turned as he slid into the seat beside mine, inclining his head toward the bartender who nodded and moved to make him a drink.

"What are you doing here?" I blurted out, a chip half the way to my mouth before I realized and put it back down on the plate.

He gave me a small smile, accepting his drink (something amber in a rocks glass) from the bartender. "I live across the street," he said simply.

I glanced out the window, despite myself. We were in a nice area. Leaps and bounds nicer than mine, and mine was decent. Dr. Chase Hudson had some serious cash. "Oh," I breathed the word out, looking down at my food.

"What are you doing here?" he asked, swirling his drink, but not actually drinking it.

"See the tall blond guy at the table of women behind me?" I asked.

Chase glanced over his shoulder, then back at me. "Yeah."

"That's my roommate. He was supposed to be taking me out for dinner and drinks."

Chase chuckled, shaking his head. "You were right," he said, sipping his drink, "he is an asshole."

"I really should have known better," I smiled, rolling my eyes.

"He really should be treating you better," he said, looking down at me. "That's the way you should be thinking," he told me.

I shrugged. "He's just a roommate."

"He gets the privilege of spending dinner with you and then throws it away," Chase insisted.

"I think you greatly overestimate my dinner conversation abilities," I said, attempting levity. He was so damn intense. It was disconcerting. Sexy as hell, but it put me on edge.

"Who needs talk?" he asked. "He could just look at you."

Wow. Okay. Alright. So, he just said that.

"He gets to look at me all the time. It's a small apartment."

"Lucky guy," he mumbled under his breath, but I made it out anyway, and felt a flutter accompanying it. "So, Ava," he said, his tone lighter, conversational, "what do you do for a living?"

"Oh," I said, my brows drawing together. Were we actually going to do the talking thing? If there was one thing, other than the sex thing, that I sucked at, it was the talking thing. "Um... I work in an office."

His lips twitched, like he knew what the problem was. And maybe, I don't know... found it charming. "What kind of office?"

"Oh, I work at a small non-profit. We try to help get homeless vets up on their feet, reconnect them with worried relatives. That kind of thing."

"Just a job or something you're passionate about?"

"My uncle was a vet," I said, realizing it was the first time I told the story outside of my office. "He had PTSD and ran off on his wife and baby... lived on the streets for years before one of his former platoon buddies happened upon him one day and brought him back, made sure he got help."

"How old were you?"

"Professional curiosity?" I asked, smirking.

"No," he said, shaking his head, looking down for a moment. "Can we just pretend I'm not... who I am right now? We're just two people at a bar."

"If we were just two people at the bar," I said, smiling, "we wouldn't be talking at all."

He let out a short, dry laugh. "Tell me."

"I was fifteen. He had been missing for two years."

"So you knew it was something you wanted to be involved in?"

"Yeah, I guess. My school counselor pushed me toward a career in social work. After I graduated, I tried my hand at a few different jobs. Child services, which was just... too heartbreaking. Then I worked in a drug rehab place which was... too frustrating. Then I came across this job. And it was just... a perfect fit."

He watched me as I spoke, interested, apt. His hand moved to rest on the back of my chair, not touching me, but there. "You know, you're really..."

"Hey," Jake's voice broke in from my other side. "Don't bother dude. She's not interested." What? What the hell? Was Jake actually... trying to protect me? Brushing off someone he thought was pestering me? That was so incredibly sweet and unexpected of him. "She's not interested in any one but her sex doctor."

Well, that was much more Jake-like.

"Shut the hell up, Jake," I growled, eyes shooting daggers at him. Silently trying to make sure he got the point.

"No, seriously," Jake said, too cocky or too careless to notice my silent plea for him to go away, "she's like frigid, dude. You don't want her."

Oh

my

God.

I wanted to just curl up inside myself and die. Right there. Because it was just way too freaking humiliating to live through another moment of it.

Chase leaned forward on the bar, looking at Jake, extending his hand toward him to shake. "Dr. Chase Hudson," he said, and I could sense Jake stiffen next to me.

"Oh."

"Yeah, *oh*," Chase said, glancing at me in all my embarrassment, staring down at my hands, my hair falling like a curtain around me to hide my red cheeks. "What you just did to her is absolutely fucking unacceptable," he scolded, and my head jerked up to look between them.

"Dude, I didn't mean any offense..."

"It's not me you should be apologizing to, it's her. Do you have any idea how insensitive that was? Knowing that she is struggling, to rub her face in it in front of someone you thought was a stranger? You need to take better care of her."

"I'm not her boyfriend or brother, man," Jake defended himself, but I knew he was starting to feel the guilt.

"No, but you're the reason she's here in the first place. This obviously isn't the kind of thing she's comfortable with. And then you fucking abandon her. Then make fun of her? Who does shit like that? She's in your life. You care about her at all... fucking do better," he said, throwing money onto the bar then touching my back between my shoulder blades for a brief moment. "Ava," he said, pausing, waiting for me to look at him. When I did, he gave me a smile, "I will see you Thursday."

And then he was gone. Walking out the front door, pausing to look, then crossing the street and disappearing into his apartment building.

"Damn, I feel like a chastened eight year old," Jake said, looking down at me. "Hey, sorry. I know I'm a dick. I shouldn't have... said that shit. I don't know what's wrong with me."

"It's o..." I trailed off, glancing back toward Chase's apartment building. I could practically hear him telling me not to say it was okay. *It wasn't okay.* I needed to learn to stand up for myself a little bit. At least with Jake. I put up with way too much shit from him. "Actually," I said instead, turning to look at him, "it's not okay. Nothing about tonight was okay. Taking me here only to abandon me. Then saying that stuff. It's not okay. And it needs to stop. Especially the talk about my sex life. I mean it. It stops now."

Jake's brows lowered for a moment before a smile started to play at his lips. "Damn," he said, nodding, glancing off toward the direction Chase left, "he really is helping you, huh?"

"What are you talking about?"

"That," he said, sitting down and reaching for an onion ring. "That attitude. That speech. You never would have told me off in the past. Never. No matter how far I stepped over the line. He's really helping you. That's really great for you."

He was right. He was really right. After three interactions with Chase, I felt enough confidence to stand my ground a little. Or at least try to. That was progress. That was more progress than I had made in years. "Seriously, though Jake. The talk about my sex life..."

He held up a hand, palm out. "Never again. I mean... not in front of anyone else anymore."

"Thank you," I said, meaning it.

"You should be thanking that doctor," he said, grabbing a handful of chips.

I nodded. "How do I thank a guy?" I wondered aloud.

"Guys are easy," Jake answered. "We don't need flowers and jewelry and fancy dinners. Show up wearing something sexy as fuck and we are happy men."

I looked at him, smiling a little. "You're a genius."

The next night after work I took a cab to the fanciest lingerie store I knew of. I also knew because I knew of it that whatever I ended up picking out was going to cost me a small fortune. But it would be worth it.

For two separate reasons.

One, because it might help bolster my confidence a little. Women supposedly felt sexy wearing new pretty panties and bras and all that stuff. And I was about to be getting undressed in front of someone. I could use all the sexy I could get.

Two, because like Jake said, it was a good way to thank a guy.

The inside of the store was gorgeous. The walls were a crisp, but light, gray. The floors were an immaculate dark wood. There were two large white tables with trays of lacy undies and bras on them. The walls had built-in units with racks of matching bras and panties, garter belts, nighties, even robes. There were two black chandeliers hanging from the ceiling, one over each table. Toward the back were crisp white curtains draping a doorway that led, I imagined, to the changing rooms. Beside the doorway was a discreet gray service desk, a gorgeous redhead standing behind it in a tight black dress. There was slow, sensual classical music playing through hidden speakers and the air was warm, making me shiver coming from the cool outside.

There were two other women browsing the selections. I made my way toward one of the tables, feeling unsure. I honestly didn't know what would work on me. Or what would be sexiest to a man. I bought matching things on occasion. And some could even be considered kinda hot, but I wanted something better than 'kinda hot'. I wanted something to inspire drool.

"Are you looking for something for a special occasion?" the pretty redhead from the desk asked, coming up beside me.

"Oh," I said, dropping the panties I had been looking at. "Yeah. Um... I just started..." Seeing a sex therapist? And we are about to get naked for the first time together? Yeah, no. "Seeing someone," I improvised.

"Ohh," she said, giving me a knowing smile. "Well, you don't want to be looking here," she told me, holding out an arm to follow her. Which I was all too happy to do. I could use all the help I could get. "Do you, or your... partner," she said, effortlessly guiding through political correctness, "have a color preference? Red? Pink? White?"

That was a good question. There was no way I would feel sexy in red. Which made no sense, but it just screamed sex and that would probably be too much. And I was never a fan of pink. "I think black would be best," I said, knowing myself, knowing my closet was full of varying shades of black.

"Always a good choice," she said, guiding me toward the walls where the sets were displayed. "Silk? Lace?"

"Lace," I decided, excited by the idea of the cutout peekaboo effect.

"How about this?" she asked, showing me a black floral lace balconette bra hanging above the matching panties. She reached into the rack, pulling out the panties. "These bottoms are cheeky," she informed me, flipping them to show me the back, the cut high to let the a fair view of your butt hang out, but still covered a bit, "but we also have a matching thong if you would prefer."

"Cheeky will be good," I said quickly. I wanted to at least be covered when I was still... covered.

"Great," she said, glancing down at me for a second before flipping through the hangers and handing me a pair in my size. She went back to flip through the bras. "We also have thigh-high stockings and a garter belt to go with this, if you are interested."

More layers? Sign me up. "Sure," I agreed.

Next thing I knew, I was walking out with a pretty gray and black striped bag, black tissue paper happily spilling out of the top, and a few hundred dollars poorer. But it was worth it. At least, I was hoping it would be worth it.

I let myself into the apartment, finding Jake setting up his massage table. His eyes drifted down to the telling bag, one side of his mouth quirking up. "Good choice," he said, nodding.

"Sure," I agreed, smiling, "if I can get the balls to wear it."

"I'll make sure you do," he said, nodding. "What are you wearing over it?"

"Yeah, I get it. My clothes suck," I said, rolling my eyes.

"The clothes aren't to blame. You just put them together badly."

"Even worse."

"I'll pick out something while you're at work tomorrow and lay it out for you."

"Really?" I asked, stopping short on my way to my room.

"Yeah," he said, shrugging like it was no big deal.

But for his normally selfish disposition, it was. He was going to do something just because it was nice. For me. With nothing in return. "Okay. Thank you. But nothing too crazy, okay? I don't want to look like I am asking for it."

"But you are."

"But I don't want to *seem* like it. Something modest, okay?"

"Alright," he agreed, "but only if what you have in that bag is black and lacy.

I smiled, "It is."

"Good girl," he nodded, turning back to his set up. Lotions, oils, and incense all needed to be laid out on a gorgeous silver and mirrored bar cart. "You nervous?" he asked, holding a lighter out to a stick of, what was bound to be, rose incense.

I opened my bedroom door, turning back. "Yes."

"Don't be," he said, shrugging. "He seems capable."

"Capable of what?"

"Anything you need," he said in an odd tone, but turned away from me before I could ask what he meant.

Okay.

I set the bag on my desk, stripping out of my clothes, getting into pajamas, and going to bed way too early. Because if I didn't, I was going to stress about the next night until I made myself positively sick.

And then my subconscious took over.

And I dreamed of him instead.

Second Session

I came home to find Jake lounging casually, watching TV, barely inclining his head toward me as a greeting. So much for the sweet guy I had seen the night before. Oh, well. I couldn't expect miracles. He was still Jake after all, even if he had decided to start treating me better.

After being scolded by Chase, I reminded myself.

A swift wave of nausea came over me suddenly. I had been good about not thinking about him. Well, okay, not good. But *okay*. Alright, *fine*. I had done a shit job of it. But I had tried.

I opened my door and closed it before looking up.

And there was my bed, splayed with a selection of clothes for the night, my bag of lingerie, and another unknown bag. I walked over, taking in the simple black long sleeved t-shirt dress that would be snug, but not body hugging. Effortless really. Simple. It wouldn't look slutty. It would show off my pretty sheer black stockings. It was a good choice. One that I never would have made myself.

I reached for the bag I didn't recognize, reaching inside and pulling out a pretty glass bottle of perfume.

"It's the same scent as that shit lotion you wear," Jake said from behind me, making me swing around to find him standing in my doorway.

I looked down at the bottle, taking in the label. "Jake, this is too much," I objected, knowing the general price range.

"It's no big deal," he brushed it off. I knew he made good money, way more than me by leaps and bounds, but still. It was an expensive gift. And we didn't do that kind of thing.

"Jake..."

"Just say thank you and move on," he said, shaking his head. "Christ. It's harder to give you a gift than it is to give you a compliment. Go shower and get yourself ready."

Then he was gone, and I did just that.

I felt naked underneath my dress. Which was stupid. I mean the stockings were pretty close to the leggings I usually wore under skirts. Except they weren't. Because as soon as I walked outside (after Jake insisted I show him the clasp of the garter to prove I was, in fact, wearing it) and the cold air flew up my skirt, feeling intimate and odd against my bare upper thighs.

But I kept going. Because there was no going back.

I walked up to his door a while later, taking a deep, unsteady breath. This was it. I sighed, opening the door.

"Ava," Chase said, looking up from some paperwork he was holding, leaning against the desk in another black suit, this time with a gray shirt, two buttons opened. "Can you lock the door behind you please?" he asked, putting the paperwork back into a manila envelope and sealing it.

I locked the door, thankful for an opportunity, no matter how brief, to look away from him.

When I turned back, though, he was right by me. How he moved so quietly was completely beyond me. "You look beautiful," he said easily and I felt my breath catch. At my silence, he smiled slightly. "Come on," he said, hand to my lower back as per usual, "let's go get you a drink, okay?"

"Okay."

He led me through his office into his, well, I didn't even know what to call the other room. He pointed me to the stereo as he moved to make drinks. Feeling like it was somehow a test, I flipped through the playlists, skipping over coffeehouse music, and deciding on something called "singer songwriters". As soon as it clicked on, I could see Chase nodding. And it felt like approval. And damn if it didn't give me the warm and tinglies.

He turned to me a moment later, holding out a martini to me. "I figured you might want something with a little more kick than red wine," he said, a smirk playing at his lips.

"Good guess," I said, taking it and having a large sip, a little too pleased that he had observed my drink of choice at the bar.

"One to ten?" he asked.

"Holding steady at a five for now," I admitted.

He nodded, taking his drink in one sip and putting the glass down. Which I took to mean: Alright-shit was about to go down.

So I gulped the rest of my drink and put my glass down too.

"Come on," he said, reaching down and taking my hand in his. I followed behind him, staring at our interlocking hands with a weird sense of wonder. It was so tame, but at the same time, it was so sweet a gesture. "Why don't you kick out of those shoes?" he suggested, dropping my hand and turning to mess with the firepalce and lights.

I sat down on the sectional, unstrapping my heels, then putting them at the far end of the couch, lined up.

Chase sat down a moment later, his entire body touching mine from shoulder to knee. Then he reached out, one arm going around my back, the other slipping under my knees and pulling until my legs went across his lap, his hand settling on my hip.

"Hi," he said, tilting his head, watching me.

I forced a wobbly little smile. "Hi."

"I like these," he said, running his hand down my hip, over my thigh, my calf, the sensation on the stockings so smooth and sensual that my body happily made the small leap into arousal. "Did you wear them for me?"

Hell yeah I did.

"Yes," I admitted, watching his hand continue its lazy exploration.

"You're so sweet," he said, his head leaning in, then starting to plant small kisses across my jawline. I closed my eyes, exhaling on an unexpected sigh, because the nerves were settling and all that was left underneath was the desire. There. Foreign, but familiar at the same time. "Ava," he said, softly, his kisses stopping and leaving me unreasonably disappointed.

"Yeah?" I asked, eyes still closed.

"Kiss me."

My eyes opened, finding his. Close. So close. I looked down at his lips for a second, my own opening in anticipation, then back up to his eyes. And I knew with blinding clarity that he wasn't going to let me get away with not doing it. If I didn't kiss him first, there would be no kissing. And, damn, I just... needed to taste him one more time. Just to see if it was as Earth-shaking as it had seemed the last two times.

So I leaned in. My arm moved from where it was in a fist on my thigh and reached up toward his neck, the fingers dancing across the skin at the side for a second before settling at the back of his neck. His eyes closed for a second as he took a deep breath, then opened his gorgeous blue eyes to watch me. I tilted my head up toward his, slowly closing the space between us, my lips on his softly, my eyes falling closed. Because it was barely a touch and I felt like I was freaking drowning in it.

His hand around my back dug slightly into my shoulder, but he stayed pliant under me, waiting for me to deepen the kiss, letting me have control. So I did. I pressed my lips harder into his, taking his lower lip between mine and nipping slightly.

Then he was moving, his arms grabbing my back and hips, pulling me until I moved to straddle him, lips never losing each other. Both of my hands went up, cradling the rough stubble at his jaw as I slipped my tongue between his open lips. His hands were at my hips and the second my tongue found his, his fingers dug in hard to my skin. Emboldened, I wrapped my arms around the back of his head, deepening the kiss. Trying to get completely consumed in it.

It seemed to last forever.

And I wished it would.

I would have happily kissed him until the end of friggen time.

But then his hands went to the sides of my face, pulling gently until our lips no longer touched. "Open your eyes," he said, his voice sounding husky.

I opened them slowly, the lids suddenly feeling incredibly heavy, and I watched him from underneath them.

"Jesus Christ, you're beautiful," he said softly, his thumb stroking over my cheekbone. "I want to see more of you," he told me, the idea barely breaking through the happy little fog in my head. "Take off your dress, sweetheart."

Those words broke through.

I felt myself straighten, my eyes opening wide.

"Don't freak out," he said, his hands sliding back down to my hips, grabbing the material of my dress and scrunching it up in his hands. "I want to take this off you so badly," he said, looking down at his hands, "but you need to be the one to do it." His eyes drifted back up to mine. "Please take it off for me."

Holy crap.

Okay.

Could I really refuse?

With him looking at me like that?

I took a slow, steadying breath, letting my hands reach down and land on top of his, squeezing until he let go, moving down to rest on the outsides of my knees instead. I could do it. That was why I was there. To test my limits. To push past them. To stop living in my comfort zone. Besides, I had spent hundreds on the pretty lingerie. It would be a complete waste if he didn't see it all.

I exhaled slowly, my eyes watching his face as I grabbed the material and quickly pulled it up over my head and threw it to the side. There. Done. I did it.

Chase's breath hissed out of his mouth. "*Fuck me*," he growled, shaking his head. His eyes raked over my body. And, normally, I would want to squirm, to cover, to freaking run away. But all I felt was a slow, growing heat covering my body, settling in my core. Because his eyes looked full of wonder, they looked like they were trying to memorize every inch of me.

His eyes slowly made their way up to mine. "Was this for me too?" he asked. I nodded, attempting a smile. "Baby, stand up," he told me, his hands pushing slightly against my knees until I slid off of him, suddenly self-conscious. His hands settled at the tops of the thigh-highs.

Feeling tense, I swallowed. The silence was becoming uncomfortable. "I... ah... wanted to say thank you," I mumbled.

His eyes shot back up to mine. "Babe, what do you have to thank me for?"

"Because," I said, feeling like whatever words I would come out with would be wrong. "Because... you're helping me so much."

"Oh, babe," he said, smiling a little. Then he leaned forward, shockingly, resting his forehead against my belly. "You're so perfect," he said and the words sent a shock through my system.

His praise *did* something to me.

Normally I fought compliments. I denied them. I certainly never believed them.

But I believed Chase. His words settled into my chest and belly, filling places I hadn't realized were empty. And amazing, flawless Chase Hudson thought *I* was *perfect*.

Feeling clumsy, my hand reached down, settling into the hair at the crown of his head. His face tilted slightly, planting a kiss right below my navel, before twisting his face up to look at me. He looked like he was struggling for something to say. Amazing, eloquent, confident Dr. Chase Hudson at a loss for words.

"Well, you're welcome," he said, smiling up at me.

I was so surprised I laughed. No. Not laughed. Giggled. Like a freaking school girl. Which only made him smile wider, the ends of his eyes crinkling up slightly with the motion. Then his hands moved to my hips, pushing me backward so he could slowly stand. With barely a breath of space between us, he reached up and removed his jacket, sliding it off his shoulders and arms then throwing it to the floor on top of my dress. Then, watching me, he started to unbutton his shirt.

Oh, my God.

Okay. He was getting naked.

Like... right in front of me.

And I wasn't absolutely terrified.

Stressed, sure. But more than that, I was actually... curious. I wanted to know what he looked like underneath all the clothes.

His shirt went the way of his jacket, but my eyes stayed on his. To... I don't know... protect his privacy? Which was ridiculous. "Ava, look," he said, watching me. "I want you to look."

I felt my sex tighten at that. Tighten. Hard. Like there was a coil pulled too tight for a moment, almost painful, before it released.

My eyes drifted slowly down, looking at the wide line of his shoulders. Strong. They were the kind of shoulders you knew you could always lean on. Then down to his strong chest. Lower. The lines of his abdominal muscles, strong, deep. Not the puny kind you can barely make out underneath the skin, these were etched. They were lines I could sink my fingers into. His hands were at his belt and paused until my eyes landed on them and they started working, pulling out of his belt loops and then throwing it to join the pile of discarded items on the floor. His hands went automatically to the button of his slacks, pushing it out, then sliding the zipper down. The backs of his hands pushed against my belly as he did so and I took a step back so he had room to take off his pants. They went down quickly and he stepped out of the legs, somehow pushing his shoes and socks at the same time. My eyes drifted, just a little, pausing right at his adonis belt, that deep, deep V that led into his black boxer briefs.

But I couldn't let my eyes go below the waistband, so I let my eyes drift back upward until I found his face again. He gave me a small smile. "What do you want to do?" he asked, surprising me.

What did I want to do?

Honestly, I had no freaking idea.

But what I wanted, what I needed, was a little comfort. A little reassurance.

Without thinking about it. Truly, without even knowing my real intention, I walked into him, wrapping my arms around his back and settling my face underneath his chin. There wasn't even the slightest hesitation before his arms went around me, pulling me close. And it didn't even matter that his arms were on top of mine, trapping them under his strength. For the first time in my life, I was being legitimately trapped, and I wasn't freaking out.

Underneath my ear, Chase's heart was beating faster than it would normally be. His skin felt warm and cozy. And it absolutely did not escape my notice that his hard cock was pressed into my belly. But it didn't matter. I trusted him to stay true to his word. There would be no sexual contact.

I just... trusted him.

And it was the first time I had ever fully trusted anyone.

His hands went to my arms, rubbing up and down. "I'd like to stay like this all night too, baby," he said, his voice low, "but it's time."

"It's time for what?" I asked against him, almost sleepy. I tilted my head and planted a kiss on his chest. Surprising myself more than him.

"It's time to take the rest of our clothes off."

Oh.

Shit.

Yeah. I forgot about that.

"Don't stiffen up," he urged, hands stroking as he pulled me away from him. "It's okay. You can take as much time as you need, okay?"

"Okay."

"Do you want me to finish first?"

Did I want to see his cock before I showed him my boobs and... other stuff? Um. Yeah, no. That wasn't going to work. No way would I be able to take my clothes off after seeing... that. Nope.

"Ava?"

I swallowed hard, licking my lips nervously. "Me," I whispered.

He nodded, moving away from me and did the absolute worst thing he could do. He sat down on the couch, staring up at me expectantly. Holy hell. I wasn't going to get any kind of privacy. I just had to get bare assed right there while he watched like I was some kind of stripper. Great. That was just great.

"Ava," his voice said, firm, a warning. Because he knew my mind was swirling. "Why don't you start with the stockings, okay?" he suggested.

Alright. I could do that. That wasn't that bad. I leaned forward, grabbing the clasp at the tiny slip of material holding my stockings to my garter belt. Then I slid the silken material down my legs. I paused as I stepped out of the second leg. But there was no going back. I had to do it. I had to. No matter how much I felt like I was going to vomit. Thank God I had the foresight to not eat anything all day. My hands went shakily toward my garter belt, sliding it off.

Just bra and panties left. I shook my hair so it fell forward, offering me a small amount of privacy as I bent slightly forward, half blocking myself from view as I reached behind my back for my clasp and my bra fell. I reached for the panties, snaking my fingers into the band and pressing down, my heart beating so hard in my ears and throat that it was all I could hear. As soon as I stepped out of the feet, I lost it.

I mean... *I lost it*.

"I can't, I can't," I said, going to the floor, bringing my knees to my chest, wrapping my arms around them, burying my face against my knees. "I can't. I'm sorry. I just..."

I felt like I was falling apart. My skin felt too hot. And I couldn't draw in a proper breath, leaving me lightheaded. I rocked back and forth, cradling myself, trying to give myself some sort of comfort.

"Okay, it's okay," Chase said, close, and I realized he had gotten on the ground behind me. His hands reached for me gently, grabbing my shoulder and knee and pulling me into the space between his legs until the side of my face was against his chest. One of his hands went to the side of my neck, the other to my hip. I felt his lips press down on the top of my head. "It's alright, Ava. Take a breath, okay?" I drew shaky air into my painful lungs, exhaling it quickly because it felt like it burned. "Good. Again," he said, his hand starting to stroke my hair gently. "Give me a number."

A little better.

A minute ago it was a ten, going on eleven. But it was a little better. "Eight."

"Okay. Keep breathing," he had to remind me. "What do you need from me right now?"

No one, literally no one, had ever thought to ask me that before. Which was amazing. Amazing that no one in my life who watched me suffer thought to ask that, to ask the *one* right thing they could ask.

"I need you to rub my back," I decided, thinking of how he had put me to sleep doing that.

He shifted slightly, giving him a little more access, then his fingers traced lightly up and down my spine. "Like this?"

"Yes," I murmured, turning my face in toward his chest, breathing in his scent. The hint of cologne, but mostly, just... him.

I had no idea how long we sat like that, my anxiety inching backward slowly, freeing up my lungs, slowing my heartbeat. It could have been hours for all I knew. But it worked. It was working. I was still naked, but I wasn't freaking out about it anymore.

"Okay," he said, stopping his stroking. One of his hands slid underneath my knees, the other across my back. "I am going to take you to the bed. No, don't tense up," he said, lifting my weight and getting to his feet. "I told you, there isn't going to be any sexual contact today. Okay? Do you trust me?"

For the first time in my life, yes.
"Yes."

"Okay," he said, starting to walk. "I am going to let you get under the covers so we can do this slowly. So we don't cause another panic attack. That was my fault."

"It wasn't..."

"Yes, it was," he said, bringing up a leg to balance my body on as he reached for the comforter and sheets and pulled them back. "I shouldn't have sat back like you were about to put on a show for me. That wasn't a good move. I should have known better."

He lowered me onto the mattress, still holding me, grabbing the blanket and pulling it up my body. As soon as the material was up by my shoulders, he let me go and I scooted to the center of the bed so he had room to climb in.

"I'm going to take my boxers off," he told me, reaching for the band.

"Okay."

"Do you want to watch?"

I felt that tightening again, pressing my thighs together against it. Because I did. I wanted to watch. I felt myself nod tightly.

"That's so hot, babe," he said, putting his hands in the waistband and pulling the material down.

And

Oh,

my.

I should have known. I mean the rest of him was tall and wide and strong. I should have guessed.

Because there was his cock straining out. Big. Thick. Promising to fill me more than anyone else ever had. And... I wanted to know what that felt like.

I felt a hot blush rise up on my cheeks at that thought.

"What are you thinking?" Chase asked, scooting on the bed, slipping under the blanket with me, turning on his side to watch me.

I turned too, bringing my knees up almost as a barrier. I

shook my head. No way I could say it. No fucking way.

"Ava, tell me, baby. You can trust me, remember?" he asked, his hand going to the side of my face. "Please."

I took a breath. He was right. I needed to work on the communication thing. "I was thinking about you..." Oh, God. It was excruciating. "... inside me," I finally admitted.

His eyes closed for a second, a muscle ticking in his jaw. When they opened again, heavy, he shook his head. "God, babe, that makes me happy. You have no idea how badly I want to be inside you."

"I have some idea," I mumbled, thinking of his hard cock only a few inches away from me.

Chase made a weird choked sound, then broke out laughing, a deep, rolling sound that was causing all kinds of problems between my thighs. "You're pretty amazing, do you know that?" he asked, shaking his head, still smiling.

And I was right. On my introductory session, when I thought I couldn't handle him smiling. I couldn't fucking take it. It was too perfect.

"Okay," I said, looking away. "What now?" I asked.

"Touch me."

My eyes shot up, finding a lifted brow. "You want to, don't you?" he asked, knowing I did. "Here," he said, rolling onto his back, the blanket slipping down to his waist, "I'll give you more access."

"Are you like... being playful?" I asked, my brows drawing together.

"I'm not always serious, you know," he said, turning his head on the pillow to look at me.

"Good to know," I said, pushing myself up slightly, bringing my hand out from under the blanket, hovering over his skin for a long minute, then slowly lowering down between his pecs. His breath hissed out of his mouth, his eyes watching my face intently.

Emboldened, I ran my greedy fingers down his abs, up his sides, over his arm muscles.

"So my nudity is okay," Chase observed, making my hand still guiltily.

"I guess," I shrugged.

"Okay," he said, reaching down and kicking his side of the blanket off his body. His hard, heavy cock was up toward his stomach, hovering slightly over his body. "Is this alright?"

It was fucking perfect is what it was.

"Yeah," I said, wanting, I realized with genuine shock, to touch his cock.

"Can I see more of you now?" he asked, turning the top of his body toward me, pushing up on his elbow.

Could he? Seeing as I suddenly had extremely sexual thoughts of him, there really was no reason not to let him. If I did, in fact, want him inside me... he was damn sure going to insist on looking at me first.

"Okay."

He smiled slightly, his arm reaching out to grab the blanket, but not at the top like I had expected. Instead he was pushing the material away from my legs. His hand went to my skin as soon as it was free, stroking up and down. "These are great legs," he said, looking at them.

Well, that was one thing we could agree on.

"Thank you," I said, my voice almost strong.

His eyes went to my face, nodding. "You're getting better at that."

"Well, you won't stop feeding compliments to me," I shrugged, trying to play it off a little.

"Hey," he said, his tone serious. "I don't want you thinking I am just saying shit to say it. When I tell you how beautiful you are, I mean it. I want you to know that. And I want you to start believing it too."

"I... believe you."

"Do *you* believe it?"

"I'm getting there."

He smiled slightly, bringing a hand up to my face. "Progress," he said.

"Yeah," I agreed.

Then his hand moved the material of the blanket again, and I felt the air hit a very sensitive part of me. Instinctively, I closed my thighs tight, knowing he wouldn't really be able to see anything that way. His eyes left mine, looking at the skin he had exposed. His hand pushed the blanket up further, exposing my belly. "Your choice? Or what you thought I wanted?" he asked, his hand coming down on my skin, barely touching the bare triangle above my sex.

"What?"

"Completely shaving," he supplied.

"What?" I asked again, smiling, "Did you expect everything to be all...unruly?"

"Yes, actually," he said, shrugging. "I figured you would find any way you could to hide."

"Just a personal preference," I said, watching as his hand reached for the edge of the blanket that was just barely on me then, covering only my breasts. He paused for a second, then flicked the material away.

"*Fuck me*," he murmured again, his hand landing hard on my ribs. "Ava," he said, his voice firm again as his eyes drifted to my face. "Breathe." I took a slow breath and his eyes slid downward again, coming to rest on my breasts. His hand slid upward, stopping high on my ribs, his thumb barely brushing the sensitive underside of my breast. "Babe, you're perfect. I can't wait to touch these," he said, his thumb stroking across the bottom, sending a shiver through my whole body. "Mmm," he growled. "So sensitive."

His hand drifted quickly away then, almost like he couldn't trust himself not to cross that line if he didn't force himself to focus on something else. He ran his fingers across my belly, making me arch slightly off the bed. His eyes drifted to my face, my eyes half closed in my desire.

"Okay," he said, almost like a sigh, like he was disappointed. "Why don't you roll onto your belly, sweetheart?"

"Why?"

"Please."

My eyes opened wider, taking in the pleading in his eyes. I glanced downward as I started to move, seeing his cock, seeing the wetness at the tip. He was just as far gone as I was with need. I somehow found that all the more hot.

His hand moved to the side of my hip as I started to turn, grabbing hard, before letting me finish moving. I brought my arms up, resting my head on them, facing him. His arm reached out, starting at the base of my neck and moving down my spine in a way that was becoming comfortably familiar. But it kept moving downward, up and over the roundness of my ass, resting on it.

I felt my brow raise at him and he shook his head, looking guilty. But that didn't stop him, his hand slipped lower, touching the underside of my ass and if he shifted his fingers even slightly inward, he would be touching my heat. As if sensing the thought, his hand paused there, watching me.

"Are you wet for me, Ava?"

Oh

my

gosh.

And, oh my God, yes I was.

I felt myself swallow and nod.

He drew in a slow breath. "I can't wait to touch and taste and *feel* that," he said with feeling. His hand moved to the backs of my thighs then pulled suddenly away. "Okay," he said, "come over here," he added, rolling onto his back and patting his chest. I moved to him like it was the only place in the world I wanted to be.

And I had a sneaking, nagging suspicion that that was all too true.

A while later. A long while later, he chuckled beneath me. "Your belly is growling," he said, moving to sit up. "Let's go get you some food."

After the Session

Okay. I was sure I misheard him. But then he was sliding out from underneath me and moving bare-ass naked over toward our clothes, his underwear in his hand for a long time before he finally slipped into them. Then on went his pants, socks, shoes, shirt. But he left his shirt open, bending down and retrieving the pile of my clothes and walking back toward the bed with them.

And it was then I realized I hadn't even bothered to cover up. And I certainly couldn't do so then with him looking at me like he was looking at me. Hungry. Like he was going to devour me.

But then he walked around to the foot of the bed, setting all my clothes neatly down, then getting on the bed on his knees, moving closer to me. He reached for the swatch of fabric that was my panties, opening them and reaching for my feet. He lifted one, slipping my foot into the hole, then went to the other.

Holy fucking hell.

He was dressing me.

And it wasn't weird.

It was sexy as all get out.

The material slipped up my thighs and his hands paused, waiting for me to lift my hips, then settling into place. Next went the garter belt. Then the stockings, his hands expertly sliding them up then clasping them. He bent forward, reaching for my hands and pulling me upward into a seated position. Then he slipped my bra onto my arms, settling the cups around my breasts without actually really touching them, then sliding around my back to clasp the hooks. He reached back, grabbing my dress, rouching it up in his hands, then slipped it over my head. My arms went into the sleeves.

He sat back on his heels, running a hand down my leg before it disappeared.

And then I was moving, pushing myself up on my knees to get closer to him. My hands went out, grabbing the sides of his shirt and, from the bottom, starting to carefully close him up. Damn if it didn't feel like the most natural thing in the world. Once my hands were at the top button (which I decided to leave open), my eyes rose to meet his, watching me yet again, so intensely it was hard to witness.

He took a slow breath then bounced off the back of the bed. "Alright, shoes," he instructed me, tucking his shirt and slipping on his belt. I was all shoe-d up and ready when he put his jacket on and started toward the door. "Any preference on food?" he asked, going through his office into the waiting room.

"I'll eat anything," I admitted and he nodded, leading me

outside.

Once on the street, his hand went to my lower back. And, for once, it almost seemed possessive. But that was ridiculous. That was just my mind spinning its usual tall tales. He was not, in any way, feeling possessive of me.

"Where are we going?" I asked as he just kept pushing me down the street.

As an answer, he reached into his pocket, pulling out his key and making the car a few feet from us beep and light up. "My car," he said, bringing me up to the passenger side and opening the door for me.

His car looked like it cost more than my childhood home. It was sleek, a deep charcoal color, and had soft curves. The inside was black, pristine, and still smelled new as I lowered myself in and he closed the door.

He got into the driver's side, turned the car over with a barely audible hum, then started driving.

We ended up out front of a small Italian restaurant, the deep brown walls and private black booths visible from the street. He was out and around the car before I could even reach for the door handle. "Come on," he said as I paused, looking at his extended hand, "get your pretty little ass out here."

"Well, if you're going to put it that way," I said, laughing, taking his hand and stepping out. He didn't let go of my hand, instead, interlocking our fingers as he led me to the door.

What was that? I mean, seriously. I had absolutely no idea what was going on. He was supposed to be my doctor, my surrogate. That was it, right? That was what I remembered from my research. Nowhere had I read that a surrogate takes you out to eat after a session. That seemed to blur the lines of professionalism. So what was going on?

"Ava," Chase's voice cut in, and I realized we were standing next to the table, the hostess already having placed down the menus and left. "Where are you?"

I shook my head to clear it. "Nowhere important," I said, sliding into the booth behind the table, the walls of it coming up high and closing in on the sides by several inches, like each booth was its own private little room. There were no chairs on the outside of the table, so Chase scooted in beside me.

Uncomfortable with the whole same-side sitting concept, I pivoted my hips away so I could look him in the face. He noticed, a brow raising slightly, but he didn't say anything, handing me my menu. "Doesn't matter what you order, I guarantee it will be the best Italian you've ever had."

"Oh, I don't know," I said, looking down at the options, "I have a strong preference to this little rinky dink place around the corner from my apartment. The owner came over from Italy just four years ago. His accent is too thick to understand and the only English word he knows is 'eat'. So when you go there, he just makes you whatever the hell he wants. And it is always exactly what you needed."

"That's a tall order. I'll have to try it out sometime."

The waiter came over in black slacks and white shirt, already with a bottle in his hands, "The usual," he said, showing the label to Chase, who nodded.

When he walked away, I took my glass, smiling over the rim at him.

"What?" he asked, a matching smile creeping up on his face.

I shook my head. "Not the adventurous type, huh?"

"Why would you say that?"

"You're a regular at the bar, you're a regular here..."

He put down his glass, leaning in slightly. "Maybe I am just very particular about my... pleasures."

So, he said that.

Who said stuff like that?

Apparently, Dr. Chase Hudson did.

"Oh," I said, taking a sip of the red wine, feeling the taste explode in my mouth.

"Good?" he asked, watching me.

I nodded, averting my eyes from his because we were getting way too intimate in a private place.

Besides, he was a regular. To a restaurant that was obviously meant for couples and lovers. Private. Upscale. Which meant he visited often... with women. With dates. Or clients. Or lovers.

The thought settled like lead in my belly, making the constant, gnawing hunger suddenly vanish.

I wasn't special. Where the hell had I gotten the vanity to think I was? That was what men like Chase Hudson did – rich men, powerful men, flirtatious men... they wined and dined and bedded women.

"What's the matter?" he asked, moving like he was going to put his hand on my thigh.

I scooted away, noticing his severe frown and completely disregarding it. I needed to get my shit together. I was acting like some middle school girl with a crush on the boy a grade higher because he smiled at her once. I wasn't that girl. I needed to get some space between us to remember that.

"Nothing," I said, feeling my guards slip back up. My back straightened, my nerves surfaced, not strong, just powerful enough to keep reminding me that I needed to keep my wits about me. At least if I was ever with him outside of his office.

"Don't lie, Ava," he scolded, but it was soft, almost sad. "If you don't want to tell me, that's fine. But don't lie."

"Fine," I said, snapping my menu, and turning my head to him. "I don't want to talk about it." But my sharp tone and glare didn't have the effect it usually did, and he was chuckling slightly, shaking his head. "What?" I asked, unable to stop myself.

"Kitty has claws," he murmured as the waiter came back to take our order.

Where I had originally had my eyes on the huge heaping platter of baked ziti that sounded like heaven on Earth, my little realization stole away the better part of my hunger and I just ordered a Caesar salad, knowing I was only going to pick at that too. Chase ordered my ziti and I felt unreasonably annoyed by that.

"Alright," he said, taking a sip of his wine, then turning his attention back toward me. "What happened?"

"What do you mean?" I asked, feeling on edge. Because when he got that tone, that *'I'm a licensed psychologist and you can't bullshit me'* tone, I knew I was in for it.

"Well, each step you took from the car to the booth, you got more and more tense. And then, sitting here, staring at that menu but not actually reading it, you got positively ramrod straight. Something was going on in that head of yours."

"Are we on my time right now?" I blurted out, my tone still cold.

"Your time?"

"Yes, my time. Like... is this part of the whole... experience?"

His eyes got darker, imperceptible if I hadn't been watching him so closely. "What? No."

"Then maybe you shouldn't be trying to analyze me."

One of his brows lifted. "I'm not trying to analyze you, Ava. I am trying to understand why you are looking at me like I am suddenly a different person." I opened my mouth to object, but he cut me off. "A person you hate."

"I don't hate you," I said immediately, and meaning it. I meant it. I didn't hate him. If anything, I liked him way too much for someone who I was paying to be nice to me. And that was the problem. I hated myself for liking him when I knew nothing he said was personal. He wasn't courting me. He was coaching me. There was such a huge difference that it made me sick that I had been confusing them for each other.

"There. Right there," he said, watching me. "What are you

thinking to make you look at me like that?"

"Maybe it's just my face," I said, smirking, trying to guide the conversation away because it felt like it was heading toward a confrontation, and I did not handle those well.

"No, your face is soft and sweet and gorgeous enough to launch a thousand goddamn ships," he objected. "Why won't you talk to me?"

"Do you do this to everyone?" I countered, watching him, suddenly very curious.

"Do what to everyone?"

"Try to brow beat them into telling you what they are thinking. Not all our thoughts are meant to be shared, you know."

"I'm not..." he started, looking away from me and I could see the muscle in his jaw ticking in his tension. He let out a loud, long exhale, shaking his head, then turning back to me. "Okay. We are just going to let that go. All of it. Time for a subject change."

He left it at that, making it clear it was my job to come up with the new topic. Which I sucked at, but anything was better than trying to continue that awful discussion. "Do you have any siblings?" I went with, cursing myself.

"Ten or fifteen close ones."

"Wait... what?" I blurted out, half choking on my wine.

He offered me a humorless smile. "I was in and out of foster care most of my life. One year with my mother, then they would decide she wasn't fit again and pull me out, throw me into another home with other foster kids. You cling to them when you're young and confused. I've kept in touch with a lot of them."

In and out of foster care? It was hard to imagine Chase young and powerless, but he had been. And I had been in that job, watching kids get ripped away from their families and thrown into the shitholes that were foster homes (often no better than the houses they were being pulled from in the first place). I knew how awful an experience that must have been for him. What was wrong with his mother that he needed to be taken away from her so often?

"You can ask me, Ava. I have no secrets."

"Why did you keep getting taken away?"

"My mother was bi-polar. She didn't know that. I didn't know that. The social workers didn't know that. All they knew was that she would drown it in bottles or at the bottoms of pill bottles, or even, later, in needles. And because of all that, she would forget to clean my clothes or buy food for me for days or weeks at a time."

"Oh, Chase," I said, my voice sad, my hand going out to rest on top of his.

"Don't feel sorry for me, princess," he said softly. "I wasn't abused. And the school fed me when I was there. I had it a lot better than a lot of the kids I got to know in the system."

He looked down at my hand, turning his underneath it and lacing my fingers in through his. I looked up at him, knowing without a doubt, that my heart was in my eyes, because all I could think about was poor little Chase hungry and dirty and in need of someone to take care of him. He looked back at me with what I could only describe as wonder...

And then our plates were dropped down on the table, making me automatically pull my hand away... like we had been doing something obscene. I thanked the waiter, pulling my bowl toward me and focusing on it like my life depended on doing so.

"Are you going to eat or just keep pushing the lettuce around?" Chase asked, sounding amused.

I stabbed an enormous fork full and shoved the contents into my mouth, licking my lips slightly. "Happy?" I asked, trying to chew and struggling with how much I had jammed in my yap.

But it was worth it to watch Chase throw his head back and laugh like a little kid. The sound was so happy and amused that it made my belly flip flop again.

He reached out with his thumb, brushing my lips. I imagined, wiping some stray dressing. Then he brought his thumb to his mouth and licked it off and I mean...

Panties. Soaked.

Then a slow, knowing smirk toyed at his lips. "Having some dirty thoughts, huh?" he asked.

My eyes flew down to my food. "You wish," I tried, knowing it was juvenile, but not caring.

"Damn straight I do."

I let that one slide, focusing on my salad which was great, but it wasn't what I really wanted. My eyes kept drifting over to his plate, cheesy and saucy and so good smelling it was practically orgasmic.

The next thing I knew, there was his fork in front of my face. My eyes went to his and he was smiling. "Go on. I know you want to."

And I did.

So I did.

We ended up sharing both plates, me eating more of his ziti than he did, but he didn't complain. We talked casually about his college years, skirting around the topic of sexual surrogacy. We talked about my family. Safe, tame topics.

Then, too soon, he was driving his car and parking it next to mine, getting out and opening my door for me.

There was silence, words needing to be said, but both of us reluctant to say them for our own reasons.

Chase's hand reached for my face then let his hand fall, sighing hard. "Monday. Seven," he told me, getting into his car and, once I got in my car, he pulled quickly away.

Monday. Three and a half days away. Which was good. Or, at least, I tried to convince myself of that. I needed space. I needed to get a hold of myself.

As I drove home, stopping at a red light, I had a realization that felt like a kick to the gut.

I didn't ask him before he left so I didn't know what the hell the next session was.

No fucking idea.

Which was just *wonderful*. I could spend the entire weekend freaking out about that. Now that naked was the thing, I was sure it would be the thing again. And with naked... came other things. But what other things? I had no idea. So there was no way to prepare. There was nothing I could except but work myself into knots about it. Which was just *lovely*.

Third Session

Alright. Monday was a bitch. There's really no other way to put it. After a weekend of Jake telling me to chill the fuck out, I was no more... chilled out. Actually, I was just frazzled nerve endings and sleeplessness, walking around my office jumping when anyone brushed against me, but at the same time...in a weird sleep-deprived fog.

"Yo," Shay said, snapping in my face. "What the fuck girl?" she asked, lifting up the edge of her lips in... disgust, that was really the only way to put it. Shay was a lot of things, not the least of which was blunt. She was six feet of gorgeous, flawless dark skin, with her her crazy long hair twisted into dreadlocks and pulled back into a huge ponytail at the base of her neck. Shay's father was a veteran. And her uncle. One of her brothers. Seven of her cousins.

"Sorry," I said, shaking my head at her.

Her head tilted, watching me with her bright brown eyes, way too keen for my liking. "You got a man," she accused.

"What? No! Don't be ridiculous."

"Bullshit," she said, moving to come behind my desk. Shay was the epitome of modern beauty standards. She had a thin waist, thick hips and thighs, and an ample enough natural bust and seen-from-the-front buttage. Even in jeans and a simple white t-shirt, she was stunning. Not pretty. Or even beautiful, but stunning. That was the only correct word to use when describing her.

"I swear, Shay. I'm single as a twenty-nine year old gamer living in his mother's basement."

She snorted, shaking her head. "Fine, don't tell me," she huffed, getting up and moving to storm away. "I tell you about *all* my men," she said, turning back.

Of that, I was all too aware.

"Shay, I swear... when I have a man to talk about, I will tell you anything you want to know."

"Including dick size," she said, firmly.

I laughed. "Yeah, Shay. Even that."

"Fine," she said, going back to her own desk.

I forced down half a pot of coffee (which I generally hated) which gave me the energy I wanted, with a heavy punch of, you guessed it, more nervousness. By the time I got home, I was just a mess. And with only two hours until I had my session, there was no hope of getting it together.

"Jesus," Jake hissed as I walked through the door.

"What now?"

"You look like you haven't slept in a week."

Four days. But he was close.

"Yeah, I know. I've been anxious."

"Isn't the doctor supposed to be, like, helping with that?"

"Yup," I said, slamming the bathroom door behind me and stripping, getting under the blessedly hot water and trying to let it run over me and smooth the frayed nerves. The water ran cold before I reluctantly stepped out, brushing my teeth, towel drying my hair, and taking a look in the mirror. I could have put some effort into makeup, but honestly, I was so pale and tired-eyed that it wouldn't do any good. I traveled back to my room, digging out plain black panties and a matching bra. There was no use going all out when I was sure I would be out of them quickly. I slid into a pair of black leggings and a huge sand-colored sweater that I positively swam in and came down to about mid-thigh. I slipped into a pair of tan flats, grabbed my keys, and made my way out.

"Wow, seriously?" Jake asked, eyeing me over a Chinese take-away carton.

"Yup," I growled, closing the door behind me.

I wasn't angry. Jake just brought that out of me.

I was worried. Freaked. Anxious. Beside myself.

And on top of all that, bone deep freaking exhausted.

I walked from the garage to the office with what felt like weighted feet. Each step closer felt harder, made my chest feel tighter. I grabbed the handle, going inside, and slammed back against it.

Chase's head shot up, surprised, looking way too rested and put together in a dark blue suit and crisp white shirt. One button open. "Ava..."

"Please, please," I said, holding up one hand. "Please just tell me what this session is."

His shoulders dropped; his head tilted to the side. "Oh, baby..." he murmured, closing the distance between us and quickly pulling me off the door, enclosing me in his arms. I heard the lock click and then his lips come down on the top of my head.

"Next time you're this anxious about needing to know something, you call me. I don't want you stressing over something I can easily fix. Actually," he said, reaching for my hand and pulling out my cell, "I will give you my cell so that, no matter what time it is, you can call and I can talk you down. Okay?"

"Okay," I said, numbly, closing my eyes and listening to his heartbeat, breathing in his scent. "You still haven't answered me."

"I know," he said, moving away and slipping his arm around me, guiding me through the waiting room, his office and into his other room. The door closed. I went to the stereo. He offered drinks, which I refused. The last thing I needed was alcohol to make me even more tired. I selected the same music as the night before and turned to him, and he was watching me. "Babe, how long has it been since you've slept?"

"For how long?"

He rolled his eyes slightly. "For more than an hour at a time."

"Wednesday."

He shook his head, holding my phone out. "Next time, you call me," he said, putting the phone down next to the stereo, and taking my hand. He led me over to the bed, slipped out of his shoes, discarded his jacket and belt. Then stopped. "Hop in," he said. And I really didn't need to be told twice. I kicked off my shoes and crawled under the blankets.

He slid in beside me. Not touching me. Not reaching for me. Not asking or telling me to do anything. Just lying there. His arm went out across the back of my pillows.

In the end, it was me who moved.

Shocking myself, I think, more than him.

I scooted closer, reaching for the buttons on his shirt and opening them. Then I slid my head against his warm skin, and his arms finally went around me, holding tight.

"Tonight's session," he started and I felt myself stiffen against him, but he only wrapped his arms tighter, "is about masturbation."

Oh

good

God.

Seriously?

"What about it?" I heard myself asking, needing to know everything.

"Everything about it. We will talk about it. Then we will undress. And then we will do it."

"Wait. What?" I said, my voice high and squeaky. Because... no way. No freaking way. Most women would never masturbate in front of their spouses. And neither would most men for that matter.

"Ava, calm down. I know it's an uncomfortable topic for a lot of people. Actually, this might be one of the hardest lessons. It's understandable that you feel awkward or embarrassed. That's totally normal."

"Do you?"

"No, baby."

Of course not. Because he had probably done it a hundred times before in front of someone. Meanwhile I rarely ever did it when I was alone. Not because I didn't like it or didn't know how, but because, inevitably, images of my failed sexual conquests would shoot into my mind and completely ruin it for me.

"But listen," he went on at my silence, "there is nothing at all to feel embarrassed about. A woman making herself feel good is amazing. *You* making yourself feel good, that is going to be fucking beautiful. And I can't wait to see it."

Oh, hell.

My face felt hot and I brought my hands up to cover it.

"Are you more uncomfortable with watching me masturbate or having me watch you?"

"You watching me," I said, the words muffled against my hands.

"Okay. Then I will start first," he said easily. And then he was moving me off of him, going to the side of the bed and stripping out of his shirt, then reaching for his zipper. "Don't be shy in front of me, baby."

And I knew what that meant. I knew he wanted me to start taking off my clothes too. I took a deep breath, rolling my leggings down and off before reaching to discard my sweater.

"And the rest?" he asked, sounding husky as his pants fell to the floor.

I looked away from him, reaching around for my bra and tossing it aside, then slipping out of my panties. "Beautiful," he murmured, getting into bed beside me. He didn't bother to pull the blanket up. Because we were beyond that now. "Come here," he said, patting his chest and I practically flew at him.

His one arm went around my back, holding me with firm pressure. Then his other hand slowly moved down his body. His hands closed around his thick cock and his thumb brushed across the sensitive, wet head. Beneath me, his breath whooshed out of his mouth.

Suddenly I wasn't sleepy anymore. I was apt. I couldn't look away if I tried. My own desire ignited, strong, almost painful between my thighs. His hand started to move slowly up and down his cock, holding tightly.

"Are you watching?" he asked, his voice breathy.

"Yes," I admitted.

"I want to watch you baby," he said, his arm releasing me so I moved into the space beside him, his arm around my shoulders. "Please."

Maybe it was the please.

Or maybe it was the pulsing, urgent longing for release, but my hand started to move slowly downward, pausing briefly. My legs opened just enough to slip my hand between and my fingers slid across my heat. A small, unexpected whimper escaped my lips and Chase's hand grabbed my shoulder hard.

"Don't stop, Ava," he said, sounding tense. My eyes went up to his, finding them heavy-lidded and the most gorgeous shade of blue I had ever seen in my life. "Please don't stop," he said, sending another jolt of desire. My finger moved upward, finding my clit and moving across it in slow circles. "There you go," he praised. "Just like I said... fucking beautiful."

My eyes slid from his, watching his hand moving across his length, the pace, I realized, the same as mine and I wondered if he did it deliberately. If he was trying to get used to my rhythms. Cataloging them for later. So he knew how I liked it when he touched me. When he was inside of me.

That was going to be so soon. If this was the third visit... then it went to follow that, well, he was going to be touching me at the next one. Touching me how, I wasn't sure. But touching me. And then I didn't know for the next session. But the session after that... we would be having sex.

It was going so fast. Before I knew it, it would be over.

There was a sharp pang, quick, but there, at the idea. Because a big part of me was pretty sure the only reason things had progressed the way they had was because it was Chase. Good, understanding, patient Chase. With all of his charm. With all the right things he always said. If it was another guy... if it was someone else laying next to me stroking themselves, would I be able to touch myself too? I felt my skin turning cold at the idea. The rolling started in my belly.

"Ava," Chase's voice called and I looked down to see he had stopped touching himself. My eyes went up to his, a question clear in them. "There you are," he said. And then his lips came down on mine. Soft. Passionate. Full of some kind of deep longing. And I felt the matching longing somewhere buried inside me, and I dove into it. Into him. Into whatever it was that was between us.

His tongue slipped between my lips to toy with mine, soft, a light caress that had me sighing against his mouth. Then it withdrew and his lips took my lower lip and sucked hard. And the jolt of desire had my whole body jerking. "Touch yourself, baby. Think of me doing it."

Then my hand was moving against my clit, slow light caresses like I thought he would tease me with. His big, skilled hands knowing exactly how to build anticipation. To turn desire into a delicious slow burn.

His hand moved to his cock again, stroking almost absentmindedly as he watched me. My face, my hand between my legs. Pausing in between the two to take in the view of my naked abdomen and chest.

I felt myself driving upward, my back arching slightly off the bed.

Unbidden, wholly unwanted, an image flew through the front of my thoughts. And suddenly I was seventeen again, laying on my boyfriend's futon, his hand pressed hard, painfully hard against my clit. The sensation did absolutely nothing for me. Then he got up, stroking his cock a few times, positioned his cock between my legs and shoving hard. The pain was instantaneous and searing.

I felt the bile rise up in my throat at the memory. Much like it had when I was young- making me wrench away from him and getting sick all over the floor.

My hand stopped moving, my thoughts flew around from one bad sexual encounter to another, making my anxiety bubble up toward the surface, pushing away the want and need Chase had instilled in me.

But then I felt Chase's hand come down on mine. I hadn't even realized he pulled it from around my shoulders, but there it was on top of my hand, pressing. My eyes flew open.

"Be here. With me," he said, his fingers crooking into mine, pushing against my clit, making me gasp. "Yeah, like that. Keep your eyes on me."

So I did.

And his hand stayed on top of mine, not helping, just reassuring, just connecting himself to the motion. Which was exactly what I needed. I needed that grounding. I needed him to keep me from thinking of the others before him.

He just knew that.

I was groaned quietly, arching off the mattress, my legs moving up and down, my hips rising to meet my hand at each pass.

"So sexy," he growled, tense beside me and I knew he was as close as I was.

I tilted my face up toward his and his lips came down on mine. Harder. Hungry. Desperate. And my body went up up up. My breath caught, pulling away from his face, feeling suspended in a strange nothingness for a second.

"That's it. Come for me, baby."

Then I did.

I crashed into it.

Hard.

My body pulsated, tightened, every nerve ending attuned to the sensation as it rolled through me in seemingly endless waves, cried out, my other hand slamming down on top of Chase's arm.

Spent, I shifted slightly onto my side toward him. His hand slid off of mine, resting intimately between my thighs, not touching my sex, but close. Close enough that he must have felt the heat and wetness there.

I looked up to find his eyes heavy, his breathing ragged. Then I glanced down to see his hand stroking his cock hard and fast and I suddenly couldn't decide what I wanted to watch more: his face when he came, or his cock.

But the decision was taken out of my hands as his hand stroked upward once more and he came hard. His hand dug into my inner thigh. "Fuck... Ava..." he growled out, his strokes slowing, his body slackening.

I snuggled my head underneath his chin, placing a kiss right below his throat. The silence set in then, Chase catching his breath, me too wrapped up in the afterglow of an orgasm to even consider worrying about anything.

His head tilted, kissing my forehead gently. "Let me up, babe," he said. I made a grumbling noise, rolling off of him, and he chuckled, swinging his legs off the bed and standing. He walked toward the door at the end of the sidebar and went inside. I heard water running and figured it must have been a bathroom. Which was good to know. I reached down and grabbed the blankets, bringing them up and around me, suddenly so bone deep tired that my eyes refused to stay completely open.

Chase came back a moment later, smiling sweetly down at me and coming in beside me. His arm grabbed me, pulling me to his chest. "It's okay," he said, his other arm going around me. "Get some sleep. I'm right here."

I'm right here.

That was exactly where I wanted him.

And I liked that a lot more than I should have.

I slowly drifted off to sleep with one of Chase's hands stroking through my hair and the other rubbing across my hips, his heartbeat slow and strong beneath my ear. It was the most relaxed, most comfortable I could ever recall feeling in my entire life.

And I also liked *that* a lot more than I should.

But soon, sleep claimed my overtired brain and body.

For the first time in a long time, I dreamed of nothing.

After the Session

I woke up as slowly as I had drifted off. I squinted against the dimness, swearing that it had been brighter when I went to sleep. Beneath me, Chase was dead asleep. His breathing was slow, his face so much less intense in sleep.

I watched him for an uncomfortably long time before I inched off of him, careful not to wake him, and made my way to my clothes. I slipped into them quickly, moving to the sidebar and checking my phone. My heart flew into my chest when I realized it was almost two in the morning.

Shit. Shit. Shit. Shit.

Jake was going to be all over me about it. Great. That was just lovely. I grabbed my wallet and keys, carefully letting myself out of the room and his office. I walked out front, shivering in the cold, looking at the door guiltily. I couldn't just... leave it open. There were patient files everywhere. Hell, *my* file was in there somewhere. I'd have a heart attack if someone got a hold of that information.

    I pulled out my keys, finding the one most similar to the one he would need and fiddling with the lock for a long time before I finally heard it click, then turned and hauled ass to my car, Chase's warning about being alone at night replaying over and over in my head.

    "Well well well, the hussy returns," Jake greeted me, still completely awake, on the couch.
    "I fell asleep."
    "That lie doesn't even work when you're a teenager. Try a new one."
    "No, seriously," I said, dropping my phone and keys on the table.
    He eyed me for a long minute. "Yeah, alright. There's no way you got laid."
    "Hey," I objected, not entirely sure why the hell I would be offended by that.
    "Speaking of laid," I said, looking around curiously.
    "She's taking a nap," he shrugged.
    "Then onto round two?"
    "Two?" he asked, scrunching up his face. "What is this? Amateur hour? Try round four."
    "Impressive," I said, making my way to my room, intent on finding sleep before all the noise started up again.

"You alright?"

"You know," I said, turning around in my doorway to face him, "this new and improved *'maybe I give a shit about other people'* Jake is really growing on me."

I closed the door on his laugh, turning into my closet and picking out a pair of pink and black pajama pants and a tight pink t-shirt to go with it. I crawled into bed, turning on my side, cuddling into my pillow like a lover. And I thought of him.

There was really no way I wasn't going to.

But it wasn't just his body. His magnificent, perfect freaking body. It wasn't just the way my name rushed out of his mouth when he came. It wasn't just the way he affected me. It was him. As a whole. As a person. The little bits and pieces I had gotten to get to know.

The dirty, hungry little boy watching his mother suffer and self-medicate which, eventually, led him into psychology. To understand her. To understand the life he had needed to live through because of her mental illness. The boy who clung to other kids who were damaged and forged bonds that lasted into adulthood.

Then there was Chase as a man. He was strong, capable, eloquent, sexy as fuck, and so incredibly sweet I was shocked I hadn't blubbered all over him at some point. Chase with his solid job. His appreciation for good food and better wine. Chase with his amazing suits. His occasional, and lovely spark of humor. His gentleness. His intuition.

What did he do in his free time? Restaurants, obviously. But other than that. Did he read? Listen to music? Go to concerts or museums? What were his interests and his passions?

For all I did know, there was so much I didn't. So much I found myself wanting to know.

How long had it even been since I allowed myself to even want to get to know a man? Months? A year? Longer? It always seemed pointless to even let myself get to that point seeing as I always knew it was doomed to fail.

Which was why my interest in Chase made no sense. Because what we had going on was temporary. It would be over as quickly as it started. He would become the man who changed my life. And I would be just another client in his records.

I fell asleep feeling such a strange, deep sadness that I felt tears of unknown origins slipping down my cheeks.

The slamming woke me up. Which was nothing new. I woke up to slamming at least four times a week. And that was on a slow week for Jake. I pulled my pillow over my head, letting out a groan. I was finally able to catch up on sleep and the jerk was messing with it.

Then I sat up, staring at our shared wall. And, yes, there was slamming coming from there. But that wasn't the only slamming. There was another sound, coming from the other end of the apartment. I got groggily out of bed, my heart beating a little too hard as I opened my bedroom door. And, sure enough, it was the front door. Someone was knocking. No, someone was *pounding* on the front door.

I looked at Jake's door, considering going to get him, but that would only lead to a pissed off confrontation, blaming me for cock blocking him. Or, worse yet, if it was yet another of his pissed off one-night stands coming by to scream at him, he would scream at me for not dealing with it myself. It was a lose-lose.

I inched my way to the door, going up on my tiptoes to look out the peephole.

What the actual hell?

I landed hard on my feet, going for the locks with suddenly clumsy fingers, then pulled the door quickly open. "Chase?"

"Jesus Christ, woman," he growled, running a hand through his hair.

"Chase, what are you doing here?"

"You scared the fuck out of me."

Wait... what?

"What?"

"I woke up alone," he said, looking at me like I had gone dumb. "I woke up alone and there was no note or anything. And my front door was somehow locked."

"I fiddled with it with one of my keys until it finally clicked," I supplied, unsure why he was so worked up. I mean... we weren't dating. I didn't see why I would need to leave a note.

"I called your phone... I don't know... twenty-five times."

"Oh," I said, glancing where I had left it beside the door, the indicator light flashing bright blue into the dim apartment. "I didn't have it with me," I said, shrugging. "Chase, why are you here?"

"I got up. You were gone. No note. You didn't answer your cell..."

"You were... worried about me?"

"Hell fucking yeah I was worried about you," he said, shaking his head. "What did I say about walking around at night? Not just at night. It must have been like... two in the morning. That was taking an unnecessary risk. You should have woken me up so I could walk you."

"Chase, I've been walking myself around this city alone, even at night, for years."

"Taking stupid chances," he said. "Looking like you do, you

should have someone on you all the time."

"It's... sweet of you to worry about me and I'm sorry I didn't leave a note or answer my phone. I just didn't want to wake you."

"I can always get more sleep. I can't get another you."

"What?" I asked, my heart starting to pound in my ears.

"Nothing," he said, shaking his head and looking away, making me think I must have misheard him.

"What the hell is going on?" Jake's voice called, coming out of his room. "Ava who is at the door at this... oh," he said, stopping short. "Dr. Hudson," he said, inclining his head at Chase. Apparently, Jake was still feeling very much like a chastened boy around him.

"Get back in here and finish fucking m..." a pretty black-haired girl with a diamond pendant necklace, and nothing else on, said as she came out of Jake's room.

I felt my eyes go wide, my face snapping toward Chase who took in the random naked girl (who was completely unashamed of her nudity as she just kept standing there) with a vague sort of disinterest.

"Oh, well... *hello*," the girl practically purred at Chase.

"Hi," he barked, looking back at me with a furrowed brow. Silently screaming at me. *Do something.*

"Um, Jake," I said, shaking my head and looking over at him.

"Yeah?" he asked, looking completely comfortable with the whole situation.

"I'm pretty sure we agreed to a *no naked in the main area of the house* rule," I said, nodding my head toward his bed buddy.

"Yeah, sure," he said, looking between me and Chase. "Get back in that room and get yourself started," he instructed her and I felt a blush creep up on my face, ducking my head to look down at my feet. "You sure you guys are alright out here?" Jake asked.

"Yeah, Jake, fine," I mumbled, head still bowed.

"Alright," he said, moving next to me and whispering in my ear, "Damn girrrl."

The silence hung until Jake's door slammed and we could hear moaning and slamming again. "This is an interesting place you live in," Chase said, sounding amused. "Ava," he said when I didn't look up. Then his hand went under my chin, pulling up until I looked at him. "What's going on in that little head of yours?" he wondered aloud. "You're blushing."

"I think it's polite to *not* say that to someone who is, in fact, blushing."

"Are you blushing because of that comment your roommate made?"

"What comment?" I asked.

"The one where he told her to get started without him, ah," he said, smiling a little as my face got hotter, "I thought so." His finger stroked over the apples of my cheeks, rubbing at the redness. "Are you embarrassed that I saw you touch yourself tonight?"

"Shh," I said, wide-eyed, jerking my head away to check and make sure Jake's door was still closed.

Chase chuckled. "They sound like they're going to break through the wall; they can't hear us."

I turned back to Chase. His eyes looked smaller, his brows lowered, like he was considering something. Feeling uncomfortable, I cleared my throat. "But, yeah, sorry again for making you worry..."

"It's alright," he said, shaking his head slightly. "I'm gonna go," he said, looking antsy. "Keep your phone by you. It's a safety thing. And lock your door." He paused, "What?" he asked, watching my smile.

"You're bossy."

He half-laughed, half-snorted. "Phone and lock, okay?"

"Okay." I agreed.

"Tomorrow night," he said, moving away from the door.

"Seven."

Then he was gone.

I watched his retreating form until it disappeared, shaking my head and closing the door. I slid all the locks into place, grabbed my phone, and went back to bed.

Well, that was weird.

Like... really weird.

I got it that he worried. It was a little careless of me to not leave a note. But still. I mean.. I was just a client. He'd actually freaked out enough to go through my records, get my address, and come over because I didn't answer my phone in the middle of the night?

Then there was how... odd he was acting at my door.

The man was an enigma.

I had just started to doze off when my phone started screeching, loud and insistent, from my nightstand. I picked it up, flipped it over, and sawChase's name pop up on my screen. I hit the green button and brought it up to my ear.

"Hello?"

"Take your clothes off."

I shot up in bed, wide eyed, fully awake. "What?"

"Take your clothes off, baby."

"Why?"

There was a low, chuckling sound from him. "How about you don't fight me on everything?"

"Why could you possibly want me to..."

"We are going to masturbate together again."

"Oh," the air rushed out of me. Over the phone? Why over the phone? That was, in a way, so much worse than with him next to me. At least near him, I felt the comfort that always overtook me around him. There would be none of that. And, oh God, what if Jake and his guest heard me? That would be humiliating.

"I can hear those gears turning. Just take off your clothes

and lay back down, okay?"

"Is this part of the... program?" I found myself asking.

There was a short pause. "Yeah, baby."

But I didn't quite believe him.

Still, I was slipping out of my clothes, flashing the light of my phone toward the door to make sure I had locked it, then laying back against my pillows.

"Are you naked?"

"Yes."

"So am I," he said, his voice deep and low.

So, yeah. We were really going to do it.

"Chase..."

"Run your hand down your body," he instructed and I found myself immediately following instructions.

"Okay."

"Are you wet, baby?"

"Yes."

"Mmm," he murmured. "Touch yourself. And I am going to touch myself. Just relax, let me hear you."

Oh, lordy.

Let him hear me.

I closed my eyes, straining to hear anything from his side of the phone. His breathing, anything. But soon, my body came alive under my hand even without anything to listen to. Because all I needed was to know he was there, and I was beside myself with need.

"Does that feel good?" he asked, his voice heavy.

A groan was my answer, louder than I had expected, but I was beyond caring.

"Fuck baby, you sound so sweet when you moan."

He sounded so good when he said anything. Literally anything. Everything out of his mouth sounded sexy.

I got there fast. To that point of nothingness. That

suspension. "Chase," I whimpered.

"Let me hear you come, Ava."

My orgasm tore through me quick and insistent, a fast pulsating that had me choking out a gasp as I arched off my bed, my body going tense. As the last waves crashed over me, I made a strange, gasp/whimper/sob combination as I collapsed back on the bed.

"Fuck," Chase growled in my ear and I could hear his breath hitch, then explode out of his mouth as he came. And damn if I didn't feel another rush of desire through my tired body.

There was a shuffling noise, then silence for long enough for me to pull the phone away to make sure the connection was still made.

"Ava?"

"I'm here," I answered immediately. Maybe a bit too eagerly.

"Tomorrow at seven," he said. And silence. That time a disconnect.

I put my phone back on the the nightstand and crawled out of bed, my limbs feeling heavy. I slipped back into my clothes and got back into bed.

Tomorrow at seven.

And, yet again, I had no idea what the session was about. I was starting to wonder if he wasn't doing that deliberately. Was he afraid I wouldn't show up if I knew, exactly, what we would be doing? I had to admit, that was a valid fear. It was absolutely something I could see myself doing. Even though the sessions were costing a small fortune. Even though they were with sexy Chase Hudson.

I was a flight risk.

And he needed to make sure I showed up.

I turned in bed, hearing Jake's door slam. Not shut. Slam. Hard. It was a sound I was very familiar with.

"You fucking asshole!" the pretty black-haired beauty

screamed. Not said, not called... screamed. Like a goddamn banshee.

"I never promised you flowers and candy, baby," Jake said, his tone completely unaffected.

"You also never fucking said you would throw me out on my ass at three in the fucking morning like some goddamn trash!"

Oh, boy.

I slowly got up out of bed and made my way to the door. I knew what would come next. Things would fly. And break. My things. Not Jake's. Jake didn't have much. It was all mine. And I had needed to replace so many items over the years.

Besides, Chase's words were in my head. About pretty women alone on the streets at night. And Jake's girl was gorgeous.

I got my feet into slippers and opened my door. "Hey," I said, cutting into their raised voices with my low one.

"What?"

"Jake and I are going to drive you home," I supplied, looking at the girl whose face immediately got less tense.

"Like fucking hell I..."

"Shut up," I said, looking at him. "If you are going to insist she leave in the middle of the night, the very least you can do is make sure she gets home safe. If you don't want to have to do that, let her stay until the morning. But, seeing as you screwed up the chances of her wanting to stay, go get some shoes on and let's go. I'm tired."

Jake walked back to his room, mumbling. "It sounds like you want me to *do better*," he said, using Chase's words against me.

"Yeah, that's exactly what I want you to do. Better. Because you're better than this," I insisted, grabbing my keys.

"Thank you," the girl said to me, her eyes truly grateful.

"Don't mention it," I said.

Jake shot daggers at the side of my face as we drove and waited out front the girl's building to make sure she got in. "Why did I have to come? You want to be all noble and bring her home? Fine. But don't make me come."

"*I'm* here because I care about her well being," I said easily. "*You're* here because you care about mine."

There was a long silence, Jake's anger deflating under my superior rationality. "Well, I can't fucking argue with that."

"Good, because I'm exhausted."

Fourth Session

I felt good the next day. Yes, there were nerves about the unknown, but they were taking a back seat to my good mood. I had gotten a good night of sleep, I had helped a freaked out girl get home whilst simultaneously putting Jake in his place, I had two orgasms in the course of a few hours. I was doing pretty darn well.

Shay kept looking at me sideways all day at work. Then, finally, grabbing her purse at the end of the day, she sat down on my desk.

"You get laid?"

I laughed, rolling my eyes. "No, Shay."

"You sure?"

"I think I would remember that," I smiled.

"You seem different."

"I don't know. I got a good night of sleep, I guess."

"Girl that ain't no good sleep putting that look on your face," she objected. "Good dick is what puts that look on a woman's face."

I snorted, but suddenly wanted to tell her. Shay had done everything possible to keep a foot in my life, no matter how much I pushed her away, no matter how many times I refused to go out with her. She had actively, I realized, been trying to forge a deeper friendship with me. And I had always been too wrapped up in my own shit that I didn't see it.

"Look, I know you have like some issues with guys or somethin'..."

"I'm seeing someone."

"Girl, I knew it. Spill."

"He's a doctor."

"That's right. You set your sights high. Find someone who fucking wants to take care of you."

"No, Shay. He's a shrink. But he's a special kind of shrink."

"What kind of shrink?" she asked, brows drawing together.

"The kind to help me overcome my issues with sex."

To my surprise, she didn't look confused, she just nodded. Like it was the most normal thing in the world. "Please tell me he's at least yummy to look at."

"Oh, my God, Shay..."

"Damn. That good? You'll be right back on that hobby horse in no time. And then I need dick descriptions," she said, standing.

"I promise."

"Hey," she said, going toward the door.

"Yeah?"

"Let's go out Friday night."

"Absolutely."

The smile on her face made me realize how much I let other people suffer because of my issues. "I'll meet you at your place so we can share a cab and get schnockered."

"Sounds great," I said, because, well... it did.

I left work a while later, going back to the apartment.

"What?" I asked Jake who had been following me around the apartment like a little lost puppy since I got home.

"What's up with you?"

"Nothing."

"You're making food," he accused.

"Yeah, I'm hungry. I need food to survive. I'm not an automaton, you know."

"You have a session tonight."

"Yeah," I said, turning, raising a brow.

"And you're eating."

"Okay, Jake. Spit it out. I'm short on time today."

"You've been smiling since you walked in the door. And now you're eating before a session," he mused to himself. "Shit, woman."

"What?" I asked, taking a bite of my sandwich.

"You have a crush on your sex doctor."

"What? No!"

But then it came through with blinding clarity.

He was right.

I liked Chase.

Not just as someone who was helping me immeasurably.

I just liked him.

As a person.

Especially, as a man.

Oh, good God.

I turned, spitting my mouthful into the garbage and tossing the rest of the sandwich. I brought a hand to my forehead. Because, well... shit shit shit.

"Why are you freaking out?"

"I can't have a fucking *crush* on Chase!"

"Well, that sucks... because you do."

"Oh. My. God," I groaned.

"Dude, it was bound to happen," Jake said casually. "He says nice things to you. He touches you. You don't have enough experience with men to be able to not let that bother you." He watched me for a minute as I shook my head and stared out the window. "Look, I'm sure he's used to it. I mean, in his profession. It has to happen all the time. Actually, don't they even have a word for it when a patient thinks they have a thing for their shrinks?"

"Transference," I supplied.

"Yeah. So you got transference. No big deal."

But it was a big deal. Because it changed things. And being aware of it would really change things.

"Stop freaking out. Go take your shower. Calm down. Get pretty. Go to your session. You need to stop analyzing things so much."

"Easier said than done," I said, but made my way to the bathroom anyway.

I had less than an hour and I was having to go show up there fully aware that I had feelings for him. Not just interest. But actual feelings. And then we were going to do things. And I was going to feel even closer to him.

I dressed in simple jeans and a long sleeved purple t-shirt then started on my way there before I decided to call and completely cancel the rest of my sessions.

"Hey, babe," Chase said, waiting for me outside his office

door. "You look nice."

Compliments were part of the process, I reminded myself, they didn't mean anything more than that.

"What's with the look?"

"Nothing," I said automatically, shaking my head, wondering how I had been looking at him.

His brows lowered, but he reached out for me. I walked toward him, feeling tense. "Want a drink?"

Or Ten. Or Twenty. Enough to knock me out.

"Sure."

I went to the stereo and picked out an blues play list that fit my mood. Chase turned to me, holding out a martini. "Want to talk about it?"

"Talk about what?" I asked, shamelessly taking a huge sip of my drink.

"About whatever is making you tense and play sad music."

"I knew the music thing was some kind of test," I said, squinting my eyes at him. "Sneaky."

He smiled, shrugging. "It's a good way to get an idea what kind of mental state a pat... *someone* is in."

A patient.

A patient.

He had a slip that revealed exactly what I needed to hear. That I was a patient. Nothing more.

"Clever," I said, finishing my drink and putting it down next to the decanters. "I'm assuming this is a clothes-off session again," I said, watching him watch me, his eyes dark as he considered me.

"Yes."

"Okay," I said, my strong sense of self-preservation letting me push past my normal insecurities as I reached for my jeans and slipped out of them. Then my shirt. My hands were at my bra before he spoke.

"Ava... what's going on?"

"What do you mean? I asked, shrugging, but not finishing unclasping my bra. "This is what I am supposed to be doing, right?"

"Maybe if you communicated with me instead of assuming things, you would already know the answer to that." He sighed, putting his drink down. "Talk to me."

"It's nothing. Jake said something that put me in a bad mood." And then you almost said something that confirmed the stupidity of my one-sided crush.

"Come here," he said, holding out his arms.

And, helpless to do anything but, I walked into them. He held me silently for a long time before finally speaking. "Tonight, I wanted to undress you."

Oh.

Well.

I fucked that up for myself, didn't I?

"Sorry," I mumbled against his shirt.

"It's okay. I still have some things to remove," he said, his hands moving up my back to where my bra still had two clasps holding it closed.

"Am I going to undress you?"

"Yeah, baby," he murmured against my hair.

My hands moved up between us, grabbing his shirt and pulling it up out of his pants, then moving my fingers to work on the buttons. Against me, Chase went still. Surprised, I was sure, that I was willing to take the lead without encouragement. So was I to an extent. And the motives were mixed. On one hand, I was trying to move things along. Keep things on schedule. Try not to drag it out and make myself suffer or let myself think there was more to it than there was. On the other hand, I just needed to feel him against me. His warm skin, the evidence of his strength in his muscles.

My hands at the top, I slipped my hands under, pushing his

shirt and his jacket back and he released me so the material could slide from his arms. One of his hands rested lightly on my hip, the other going to the side of my neck.

"Ava..."

I shook my head, looking down and watching as I unbuckled his belt, removed it, and started on the fly of his slacks. My hands paused, and I took a deep breath and quickly pushed them off. Then, before I could let myself think about it, I grabbed the waistband of his boxer briefs and pulled down.

He was already hard.

He really did have a perfect cock. Shay would love to hear about it. I felt a laugh rise in my throat and fought to keep it in, because, well, it would be pretty awful to laugh when you're looking at someone's junk.

"Ava," he said in *that* tone. That tone that said *look at me*. My eyes drifted slowly upward, taking in his abs then the chest I liked to rest on, then finally to his gorgeous scruffy face. "While I'm glad you're taking the lead, babe," he started, his hand going to the side of my face, "I want to make sure it's for the right reasons."

"Are there wrong reasons to undress you?" I countered, running my hands down his stomach.

He made a growling noise, taking a deep breath. "Fine. I'll let it go for now. But I will get to the bottom of it eventually. Go get on the bed."

It occurred to me as I laid down, watching him walk toward me, gloriously naked, that I still didn't know what we would be doing.

But then he was in the bed, looming slightly over me as he reached behind my back and unclasped my bra. He left the cups to cover me as he slid the straps down my arms. Then, very slowly, he inched the black material away, revealing me. Then his hand reached out, ever so slightly brushing over my breast.

So that was what we were doing.

And, also, oh my God.

There was an instant shiver, and a slow awakening of desire between my thighs. His eyes lifted to mine, heavy-lidded and beautiful, then his hand did another brush, this time he was watching my face for my reaction. I felt my lips part, my back arching into his hand. His fingers moved to my nipple, gently rolling it between them, making me suck in a shaky breath. "You okay?" he asked, looking as turned on as I suddenly felt.

"Yeah," I said, my voice sounding foreign: airy, needy.

"Thank God," I said, taking my other nipple in his other hand and continuing his slow, sweet torment. "You have no idea how hard it has been not to touch you." Under his inspection, my breasts felt heavy, my nipples more sensitive than I knew they were capable of being and it felt like there was a connection from his hands to my sex which felt tight and desperate for relief. "This is what we are doing this session," he said, watching his hands. "I am going to touch you here," he said, then one of his hands moved slowly down the center of my belly and rested the palm against the juncture of my thighs, "and here."

Oh, my.

Yes. Yes. Yes.

But at the same time, I wasn't sure how that would go.

"Look at me, Ava," he said, one of his hands still cupping my breast, the other covering my heat. "I am going to touch you. And you are going to touch me."

Okay.

I was pretty sure I could do that.

Maybe.

"Do you think it would be better for me to touch you first or..."

"Me touch you," I said before he could even finish.

"You're sure?"

Nope. Not at all.

"Yes."

"Okay," he said, removing both his hands and moving to sit next to me, upright against the headboard. "Come here."

Alright. This was it. I was going to have to touch his cock. The idea settled with both a surge of excitement and dread, making a weird wobbly feeling swirl in my belly.

But I pushed myself up and scooted in beside him, resting my head on my favorite place in the damn world. He reached across his body, taking my hand in his and holding it. "You nervous?"

" A little."

"A little isn't bad, right?" he asked, his other arm around me, stroking up and down my arm. "Give me a number."

"Four-ish," I said, breathing him in.

"I can work with four-ish," he said, sounding lazy. Like there was no rush. "How about the idea of me touching you?"

"Seven?"

"I can work with that too," he said, slowly unfolding my hand and flattening it against his chest, his resting on top of mine. "But let's not think about that yet, alright?"

"Alright."

Then his hand was pressing mine slowly down his body. I watched, my hand all but swallowed up by his as it slid down his chest, over his abs, down the small line of dark hair leading toward his cock. I felt my hand tense, digging into his skin as if I could hold on and he quickly picked it up, turning it, bringing it up and kissing the palm.

But then he was pulling it back down, much more quickly, and my hand wrapped around the base of his cock. Chase exhaled loudly and I felt my hand instinctively tighten around him, holding him "That's it, touch me baby," he said, his hand moving from mine, settling on his thigh, I guessed, in case I needed help.

Though right in that moment, I didn't. Because I wanted to

make him feel good. I wanted to hear his breath whoosh out of his mouth, curse, groan.

My hand stroked upward, my thumb brushing over the head, stroking his wet desire, and drawing my much wanted groan from his lips. Emboldened, I started stroking quickly. Up and down. Then twisting slightly with each stroke. Chase's hand on my arm was digging in painfully, his body stiff underneath me.

"That feels good, baby," he praised me and it set off a flurry of fluttering in my chest. His hand went over mine for a second, squeezing. "Just a little harder," he instructed and I did as he said. "Yeah, just like that."

I lifted my head, sitting up a little straighter so I could watch his face. His head was titled up toward the ceiling, eyes closed. Then, as if sensing me, he looked down and his eyes found mine and stayed there.

"Fuck," he hissed, his eyes getting heavier. "I'm gonna come," he told me, the words falling with a small thrill. Because I had never been able to make that happen before. Then his hand positively crushed into my shoulder, his other hand grabbing my wrist hard as he cursed, his body jerking. "Fuck, *Ava*..." he ground out as he came.

He leaned over a moment later and kissed my forehead, and I smiled up at him with my own internal victory. Maybe to most, it was small. But to me, it was huge.

He smiled back down at me, knowing, sharing it with me.

"I made you feel good," I said, a little shyly, knowing it was an immature way to put it, but it was the best I could bring myself to say.

"Yeah, you did," he smiled wider. Then his face came toward me, pressing his lips into mine, kissing me until my entire body felt like it was starting to tingle. "Okay," he said, pulling away, "I'll be right back," he said, taking off toward the bathroom. He came back a moment later, a washcloth in his hand, taking my hand and rubbing gently over it. Finished, he pulled it up toward him, kissing my knuckles and let it drop.

He came back a few seconds later, slipping in beside me, laying on his side.

"Are the nerves better?" he asked, pulling me on my side to face him.

"A little," I admitted. Because they had been. Though they were quickly coming back.

He was going to touch me.

Soon.

"Good," he said, leaning closer and brushing the hair off my neck a second before his lips went down there, making me sigh at the contact, "Because I really want to make you feel good. I want to watch you as I make you come. And just when you start to come down, I am going to drive you back up and make it happen again. Until your body can't take anymore."

Oh

my

God.

Where did he learn to talk like that?

"Does that sound good?"

I swallowed hard. "Yes."

"Good," he said, his hand sliding to my breast, taking the nipple and working it into a painfully tight point. His hand went up to my shoulder, pressing until I lay flat, then went to the other nipple until I was squirming, pressing my thighs so hard together that the muscles were aching.

His hand moved between my breasts, slowly moving a straight line down my belly, pausing, then stroking down my thigh, then back up the other one. His hand rested at the triangle above my sex. "Let me in, baby," he murmured and my legs just... spread for him. Then his hand slipped between them, quickly stroking up my cleft, making me gasp and jump at the unfamiliar contact.

"You're so wet for me," he groaned, his fingers stroking my folds. "Is this okay?"

Okay? No.

No it wasn't okay.

It was fucking incredible.

It was everything everyone had ever told me it was.

And more.

"Yes," the word came out on a moan, and his eyes quickly went up to my face, apt.

Then his fingers moved upward, stroking over my painfully sensitive clit. And I almost jumped off the bed. "Fuck," he hissed, watching my face twist, my back arch, as his finger started slow circles around the sensitive point. "Ava, look at me," he urged.

My eyes drifted to his as his finger moved across my clit and my body exploded into an unexpected orgasm. "Ah," I cried out, shocked, then groaned as my body pulsated hard over and over, my body going taut, my hand slamming down hard on Chase's shoulder.

Chase let the orgasm wash over me, fingers stilling. Then as my body relaxed, his finger started working again. Just like he promised. "God, you're so fucking beautiful when you come," he said, leaning down and taking my lips gently in his.

I turned slightly toward him, my arm going around his back, kissing him back with all the amazement I was wrapped up in, wanting him to share it. And he did, greedily.

He pulled away, waiting until my eyes slowly opened, then his finger slid away from my clit, drawing out a frustrated grumble from me. "Don't worry, you're going to come again," he said, his finger pressing against my entrance. Then his finger slid slowly inside me, making my body jerk.

Because it had been so long. Honestly, I wasn't sure I had ever really even *experienced* what it felt like to have a finger or... anything else, inside of me. I was usually too busy trying to calm myself down to feel anything but my own pounding heart. But, God, it felt good.

"You with me?" he asked, his finger stilling inside.

I smiled slightly at him. "Always," I found myself saying. Then, seeing the darkness come over his eyes, wished I could suck it back in. His finger turned inside me, stroking up against the top wall, finding the spot most men weren't even sure existed and raking his finger across it. And nothing else mattered but that feeling.

"Oh my God," I whimpered, my fingers digging hard into the skin on his back.

Chase gave me a small smile. "Does that feel good?" he asked, knowing damn well it did.

"Yes," I cried out, my hips sliding up toward him, wanting more.

But then he stopped stroking my G-spot and started thrusting fast in and out of me, making my breath catch, arching up toward his hand, crying out shamelessly as my body went up up up again. Just when I thought I couldn't take another second of the torment, his thumb found my clit as he stroked back over my G-spot and I just.. shattered.

"Chase," I cried out, grabbing at him, pulling him toward me as my body spasmed violently.

"It's okay. I'm right here. Come baby."

It felt like it lasted forever, my body completely beyond my control, shaking, writhing, being completely consumed in the sensations.

I came down slowly and Chase's finger moved inside me and I shook my head at him.

"No?"

"I can't," I said, burying my face in his chest because I felt a sudden, overwhelming urge to cry. Not sob. Not break down. Just... cry. Because it was just... too much. I couldn't take it.

His finger slid out of me, his hands moving to stroke me down my back, down my side. "Talk to me," he urged, one of his hands slipping into my hair.

But I couldn't. Because I was concentrating on my very silent little cry, tilting my face just away from him enough that the tears didn't fall on his chest.

"Babe? Ava..." he urged, then shifted, grabbing the side of my face and forcing it up to look at him. "Oh, sweetheart," he murmured, his fingers catching the tears and brushing them away. "Are these good tears or bad tears?" Not able to find the words, I turned my head and kissed his hand. "Good tears," he concluded, smiling at me. Then he leaned down and kissed my wet cheeks, kissed my eyes closed, then finally... kissed my lips. Until all that there was was him and me and the sweet, delicious feeling of lips trying to consume each other.

A while later, me sprawled across his chest like it was the safest place in the world because, for me, it was, his hand heavy on my back. "That was fucking amazing," he said, half to himself. "I'm serious," he said, turning to look down at me. "You did really well tonight."

I felt myself force a smile. Force because he just inadvertently reminded me what we were. Not lovers. Doctor and patient.

"Where are you going?" he asked, trying to reach for me as I moved off of him and slipped off the other end of the bed, away from him.

I didn't answer him because, well, what could I say?

I need to leave because if I stay, it is only going to blur these lines even more for me and I am already in so deep I can barely see the surface anymore?

Yeah, that wasn't going to work.

I slipped into my clothes faster than I probably ever had before, taking a deep breath and looking back toward the bed. But he wasn't where I left him. He was sitting off the side of the bed, his feet on the floor, his head in his hands.

"Hey," I said, feeling almost worried, "are you okay?"

He didn't answer for a long moment. "Yup," he said in a tone I didn't trust. Then, "So, ya' leaving me?" he asked in a voice I didn't even consider his. It was odd. Guarded? Distant? Something like that.

"It's late," I guessed. "I have work in the morning."

"Okay," he said, still sitting there, not looking at me. "Thursday. Seven-thirty."

Same cold, dead tone.

"Umm," I said, feeling torn. The part of me that needed to protect myself, needed to leave. The other part, the part that felt too strongly about Chase to ever want to leave, wanted to know what was wrong. To go to him. To soothe over his feelings like he did for me. But, I reminded myself, taking a breath, that wasn't my place. I wasn't his girlfriend. I was his patient. Nothing more. "Okay," I said, my voice numb as I was feeling, "I'll see you then."

After the Session

"What are you doing?" Jake asked, coming in from the gym so drenched it was actually impressive.

I saluted him with my spoon, then dug it back into the half gallon of salted caramel gelato I had stocked the freezer with, completely wiping out the deli around the corner on my way home from Chase's office.

I was situated on the couch in baggy sweat clothes and a huge gray men's robe and fluffy purple slippers. My hair was pulled back into the same messy ponytail I had pulled it into before I went to bed the night before, at least a third of it sneaking down around my face and shoulders. "Just catching up on some TV," I said, shrugging.

"It's ten o'clock in the morning."

"And *that's* what makes on-demand such an awesome invention."

"It's not a holiday."

"Nope."

"You've literally never missed a day of work before."

"That's true."

"Oh, my God. It's like talking to a three year old with ADD," he said, throwing his gym bag next to the door. "Are you sick?"

"Nah."

Well, maybe a little heart sick. But hell, I wasn't sharing that.

"Are you having some kind of fucking mental break down? Should I call one of your shrinks or something?"

"Oh Jesus," I grumbled, pausing my show. "I'm taking a day off from work, not speaking in tongues."

"Love, a normal person taking a day off is considered good for their mental health. You taking a day off is like the complete opposite."

"You're such an ass," I said, taking another spoonful.

"Alright. I'm taking a shower and when I get out, you're fucking sharing that gelato. And then telling me what is wrong with you."

"I'll bite your hand off if you try. And good luck getting it out of me," I said to his retreating form, turning my show back on.

He was actually right. I didn't take off from work. Not even when I was down with a case of pneumonia that threw me for a loop for three weeks, making me too sick to eat and losing fifteen pounds. I didn't know why I was that way, but I always had been. Every year at school, I got the award for perfect attendance. That was just how I was. Always there. Always there on time, usually early.

But, I had tossed and turned all night long, plagued with dreams about Chase. Good dreams. Him kissing me, touching me, complimenting me. Then not so good ones. Ones of him standing there sneering at me because he found out I liked him. Or out and out telling me I was never anything but a patient to him.

My alarm went off like a damn air horn in my head. And I just... couldn't make myself get up. Get dressed. Go to work. Act like I wasn't in a grumpy mood.

So, I just didn't.

I called the office to have Shay pick up. "What the fuck do you mean you're not coming in? Are you dying?"

"No, Shay."

"Good, because even that won't get you out of going out with me Friday. I'm holding you to that."

"I know, Shay." Actually, I was starting to look forward to it. I needed something else to focus on. "I'm excited to go actually," I admitted, surprising myself. I wasn't the kind of person who shared information like that.

"Me too, girl. I am bringing you an outfit because, well, I mean... you don't own a damn thing appropriate for what I have planned."

"Please don't tell me all my bits will be on display."

"Fuck yeah they will. Make the men drool so they buy us drinks."

"I think you'll be the one making them drool, Shay."

"Girl, sometimes I just don't get you. You know you're hot shit, right?"

"If you say so."

She made a weird growling objection noise. "You're hopeless. Look, I am gonna come to your apartment at like... seven. We'll get all dolled up, then hit the town. Sound good?"

"Great."

"Aight. Have a good fake sick day," she said, hanging up.

Jake came to the couch with his own container of my gelato wrapped up in a kitchen towel. For my sake, he had actually put a shirt on. Which was new. He stared at the TV until the credits rolled and I got booted back to the main screen.

"Now spill."

"There's nothing to spill, Jake. Oh," I said, thinking of Shay, "by the way, I am having a girl from work over Friday. And you are not, under and circumstances, going to hit on her."

"What do you mean you have a girl from work coming over?" he asked, looking at me like I had genuinely gone off the deep end.

"I mean... Shay, a girl I have worked with for years, is going to come over here on Friday at seven. We are going to get dressed up and then we are going to go out."

"Okay. What the fuck? Seriously. Am I on some hidden fucking camera show? Did aliens beam you up and steal your body or something?"

I laughed, shaking my head. "I'm just... branching out. Trying new things."

"Damn. I guess that sex doctor was worth every penny, huh?" At the mention, I felt myself flinch. Visibly. Hard. "Well, shit.." he said, watching me.

"So what do you want to watch next? Another show? A movie?" I asked, silently pleading for him to let it go.

"You caught feelings."

Mother fucker.

I should have known better to hope for Jake to have a little mercy. He wasn't the type.

"I have not," I objected, but my voice was too high and squeaky to hold any authority.

"You are a dirty little feelings haver," he insisted, sticking his spoon out toward me. "I should have known. Bathrobe, mindless TV, junk food. It's all the typical signs."

"Oh, what the hell do you know about feelings? You barely keep girls around long enough to catch STDs."

"Hardy har," he said, squinting his eyes at me. "I don't know anything about feelings myself. But I know about women and their feelings. I have four fucking older sisters, Ava. Trust me, I know."

I loved Jake's sisters. Their visits were worth every moment that he drove me nuts every other day of the year. Because around them, he cowered like a scolded dog. They attacked him about his stuff all over the apartment, about his meaningless pursuit of the perfect body, about his using women like they were disposable. They made him do the dishes. Sweep. Mop. Scrub the bathroom. I would come home to a pristine apartment with dinner on the damn table. Granted, they only stopped in maybe twice a year. But they were like mini Christmases every time.

"You are exhibiting all the typical signs." At my silent clicking around on the movie menu, he sighed. "Look, I know you think I am just some muscle bound jerk…"

"I don't…"

"Yes you do," he cut me off, smiling a little. "But it's fine. Because I don't really give you much reason to think otherwise…"

"That's not true. Lately…"

"But I am actually a decent shoulder to lean on, okay? I'll listen. I'll give you the advice you need."

I took a slow, deep breath, and, still staring at the TV, said, "I have feelings for Chase."

"There. Was that so hard?"

"Yes," I shot back, glaring at him. "And you're not exactly proving your case here, jerk."

He laughed, taking a spoonful of gelato and shrugging. "Hey, I'm still me. Even when I am being helpful. So, what? You just realized it? 'Cause you're a little slow. I've been seeing it happening for days."

"You didn't think that you should have maybe filled me in on it?"

"And let you miss out on the fun of finding out yourself?"

"Fun. Oh, yeah. It was boatloads of fun to figure out when I was in bed with him."

"In bed?" Jake asked, eyes bright.

"We're not having sex," I added quickly. "Not yet anyway."

"So you think it's legit feelings... or that thing?"

"Transference," I supplied. "I don't know. I think that is kind of the point of transference. The patient doesn't know whether the feelings are real or not."

"Maybe you should see your other shrink and ask her."

My head snapped to his. "Yet again," I said, thinking about his ideas for telling me to go get some sexy lingerie, "you are a genius."

Which brought me to Dr. Bowler's office. Familiar. Not near as swanky as Chase's. The waiting room had the typical, awful, brown arm chairs with red and blue pattered seats and backs. The coffee table was strewn with old magazines. I sat for a long half an hour before Dr. Bowler came out of her office, giving me a kind smile. "Ava."

"Dr. Bowler," I said, standing. "Thank you so much for fitting me in today."

"Of course," she said, letting me into her office and closing the door.

The walls were beige. She had a normal desk, a little cluttered. There was bland artwork on the walls. I walked over to the brown material couch, sitting down and waiting for her to take the chair across from me.

"So, Ava, what brings you here?"

"I think I have transference."

Her head looked up from her notes, her face trying to look impassive and failing slightly. "For me?"

Oh, ha. That was stupid of me.

"No, no. For my sexual surrogate."

"Oh," she said, looking relieved. Which was almost a little offensive. "Okay. Well, what makes you think that?"

"Because I like him. A lot. Way more than I should like my doctor."

"I have heard stories about Dr. Hudson being very attractive."

"Whatever the stories were," I said, shaking my head, "I bet they don't even come close to how good looking he actually is."

She offered me a conspiratory smile. "Alright. How about we start with how your sessions are going with him?"

"I think. I mean I know... they're going really well. And it's not just the stuff with the sex. I think just... my confidence is improving. I am agreeing to go out with coworkers and I am standing up to Jake."

"That's amazing. I'm so happy for you." There was a silent *after all these years* attached to that- a mix of pity and joy.

"Thanks. But yeah, I don't know. We are going on session five tomorrow and I just... needed to talk to someone before we go any further."

"Transference is really common in just regular psychological practices. Patients share their deepest fears and desires with their therapists. The patient, therefore, feels closer to them than they do any other person in their lives. That situation is exasperated, I am sure, by an actual physical connection with said therapist. Not only do they know you mentally and emotionally, but they also know you physically. It is, essentially, a mock relationship. Which makes it all the more confusing to be able to understand the professional lines."

"When it comes to transference, do the doctors ever..."

"Ava, no," she said, very firmly, very finally. There was no question in her mind whatsoever. Chase was the doctor. Chase understood the lines. Chase did it for a living. There was nothing in it more than that. Ever. "I know, I sound harsh..."

"Harsh is good," I mumbled. I needed harsh. I needed that smarting slap of reality across the face.

"But the fact of the matter is, transference is almost always one sided. And it usually fades as soon as the patient stops seeing the doctor, usually by force when they find out. I know this is a very confusing time for you, especially given your past. But you have to understand that while what you are dealing with is fairly common, it is still an unhealthy reaction. It is good that you are realizing it for what it is. That will help you get over it. And in... five more sessions, the feelings will likely dissipate and you will still be blessed with having the chance to have opened you up to a wonderful human experience."

"Right. Okay. Thank you so much, Dr. Bowler."

"Ava," she called as I got up and made my way to the door. I turned back. "If you need to talk, please come see me. I would really like to see this therapy work for you. So if you need another ear, I am always here for you. Even if all you need to do is tell someone about your feelings for him, to help you sort them out. It's good that you are getting to the point where you want to share. And I want to make sure you don't backtrack because of something as impermanent as transference."

"I'll keep that in mind, thank you again," I said and left.

Outside, I ran my hands over my face. Frustrated. But I had no right to be frustrated. She had just confirmed what I knew was going on.

I sighed, walking back to my car.

I needed more gelato.

Enough to fill up the hole that felt like it was growing larger by the second.

I was just given an opinion from an actual professional in the field that transference was just a phenomenon. Common. Normal. That it meant nothing. But the fact was, it didn't *feel* like nothing. That was the problem. Transference felt *real*. I felt like I was falling for him. I melted under his praise, so much so that I felt the need to do things to seek it out. I turned into his hands when, in the past, all hands made me want to do was shrink away. I felt a shiver at the way he said my name or when he called me "baby", "babe", or "sweetheart". I was sad to leave him. I anticipated seeing him again. I fretted about my outfits, wondering what might please him. I dreamed about going with him places: the Italian place he took me again, the Italian place I had suggested. I dreamed of him returning my feelings.

His chest was the safest place in the world.

"Fuck fuck fuck fuck fuck me," I grumbled, letting myself back into my apartment, ignoring Jake as I went to my room to change back into my fake-sick day wardrobe. I didn't even bother to stop changing when I heard him open my door and wait for me to face him.

"Why aren't you screaming at me to get out? I've never so much as seen you in a bathing suit before."

"What the hell does it even matter?" I said, pulling pants up my bare legs, then reaching to pull my sweatshirt over my head.

I turned back to him, his eyes curious for a long moment. "You know," he said, a trademark smirk toying at his lips, "you have some good raw materials."

"Gee, thanks," I said, shaking my head and moving past him.

"You're gonna ruin them with all that ice cream," he said, watching me take my half-finished gallon out of the freezer.

"Good."

"So I'm guessing the visit didn't go so well."

"I have transference. And I just have to grin and bear it until my therapy is over."

"What does transference feel like?"

"Like falling in love with someone, but it's not real."

"That sucks."

"You're telling me."

"You're seeing Dr. Sex tomorrow."

"Yep."

"That sucks," he repeated.

"Yep," I agreed again.

He had no idea. And it was only bound to get worse before it got better.

Fifth Session

    To say I was less than thrilled for my session was probably the biggest understatement of the year. Not because I didn't want to see him, but because I did. I like, really really really wanted to see him.
    But my stupid brain was just confused.
    And I couldn't talk myself out of it either.
    I tried.
    For hours.
    There was no use.
    I dressed in a pair of black yoga pants and a heavy black

sweater and headed out. Black suited my mood. Black was like a way to hide from the world.

But there was no way to hide from Chase.

Because soon he would have me out of my clothes again.

And it also hadn't escaped my obsessive over-thinking that our goodbye last time had been weird. Cold. Detached. Unlike anything that had ever been between us before. Which was the thought I had swirling around my head as I drove there, as I walked up to the building, as I opened the door. How things might be different. Chase might be different. And I wasn't sure I could handle that.

"Ava," Chase said, nodding at me as I walked in and locked the door.

"Hey," I managed, taking in his tense shoulders, the muscle ticking in his jaw.

It looked like my fears had been founded.

My Chase was gone.

Oh

my

God.

He was never mine to begin with.

"You look like you're ready to bolt."

"Yep," I agreed, beyond lying. It never got me far anyway. He always knew.

"Care to tell me why?"

Oh, because I'm in fake love with you. No biggie. Totally normal.

"I don't know. Care to tell *me* why *you're* so tense?"

A look of surprise crossed his face, quickly covered by a smirk. "That was... snippy."

"Yes, I have feelings other than anxiety, you know."

"I'm getting a picture," he said, smiling wider. His shoulders eased slightly, the muscle stopped ticking. "Jake on your nerves again?"

"Jake's been great actually," I countered. It was true enough. He was still leaving clothes all over and being obnoxious. Now he just balanced it out with being a decent human being every once in a while.

"Work getting to you?"

"I took off yesterday. And it was my manager's birthday today so all we did was eat cake and gab."

"You took off yesterday? Were you sick?"

I fought the urge to roll my eyes. "No. I just wanted a day off."

"What did you do?"

It hadn't escaped my notice that I was still pressed against the door and he hadn't walked out from behind the desk.

"I ate enough gelato to feed a small village and watched TV with Jake." And saw my other shrink who told me I am projecting inappropriate, misplaced feelings on you.

"Sounds like a good day."

"It was much needed."

"Are you going to stand in the doorway all night?"

"Are you going to stand behind the desk all night?" I shot back.

"Alright, smartass," he smiled, moving toward his office door instead of toward me, "lets go get a drink."

I followed stiffly behind him, taking my station at the stereo. He wanted a play list that matched my mood? Well, he could have it.

Then, coming out loud through the speakers, was a heavy dose of female fronted metal music.

Chase's brow raised as he mixed my drink, but said nothing. He handed me my glass which I didn't even go through the pretense of sipping. I gulped it down. He watched me, throwing back his drink in one shot as well.

"I get it," he said, taking my drink. "You're in a mood." He brushed past me, going to the stereo and fiddling with it, "but let's listen to something a little more appropriate for the session," he said, and some sensual r&b music started playing. "You haven't asked what tonight's session is yet."

"I know."

"Do you want to know?" he asked, his brows scrunching together like I wasn't making sense. I knew I wasn't.

But I was too busy freaking out about my fake feelings for him to freak out about what new sex act we were going to engage in. "Sure."

"I am going to go down on you. And you're going to go down on me."

Oh.

Well.

I should have seen that coming.

And that was a dirty thought when I thought about it.

Oh, my God. Seriously, what *was* wrong with me?

"Do you know what that means?" he asked, looking at me like I was daft.

"Yes."

"Oral sex."

"I'm aware."

"Okay, enough," he said, shaking his head. "What's the matter?"

"I'm fine."

"No, you're not."

"Is that your professional opinion?"

Oh, shit.

That was the wrong thing to say.

He looked almost murderous for a moment before he pushed it away.

"Are you having problems with this situation?" he said, gesturing between us.

Just big, fat, ugly, can't eat or sleep without you popping into my brain problems.

"I think things are going pretty well."

"That's not what I asked, Ava. I want..." he trailed off, looking at me. "Oh, fuck talking," he said, grabbing me and slamming his lips into mine. Hard. Full of all the frustration I had, no doubt, been bringing about. His teeth bit into my lower lip hard, making me open on a gasp and his tongue took the opportunity to slip inside.

His hands went up and under my sweater, running up my back, then swiveling around to the front, up my belly, grabbing my breasts hard, then slipping his hands into the cups of my bra and grabbing my nipples, pinching and twisting until they were hardened points. Until all my reservations fell away and there was only him. His touch. His lips.

He pulled away suddenly, making me stumble humiliatingly forward, having to put a hand on his chest to keep from falling into him. His hand went up to my jaw, stroking across my lips. "There," he said, nodding. "That's better."

Oh, the bastard.

"Don't think you can..." but the rest of my argument was muffled as he dragged my sweater up and over my head, my arms trapped in the thick material for a long moment before I got free again. "Listen..."

"Nope."

"What?"

"No, I'm not going to listen. I am going to take the rest of your clothes off and bury my face in your pussy until you are screaming so loud you forget all about being in this pissy ass mood."

Whoa.

Well then.

If he put it that way.

And he meant to make good on that because as soon as the words were out of his mouth, I was out of my bra and his hands went to my waistband, grabbing my pants and panties and tugging them down.

"Much better," he said, stepping back and taking me in. And I didn't feel the urge to cover myself as his hungry eyes raked over me slowly. "Get on the bed."

Okay.

He needed to stop being bossy.

Because I was pretty sure I was liking it way too much.

"You're still..." I started to object and he practically flew out of his jacket and started tugging aggressively at his buttons, pulling two off in the process. Naked from the waist up, he stopped.

"Now get on the bed."

Well. Okay then.

I got on the bed.

I watched him, moving toward the foot of the bed, watching me, never taking his eyes off. His hands went out suddenly, grabbing my ankles and pushing them upward until my feet were flat on the bed. He moved to rest his knees at the edge of the mattress, then reached up, grabbing my hips and dragging me to the edge of the bed, my ass almost falling off. My legs flailed out as I grabbed the sheets. He grabbed my ankles again, taking them and placing them on his shoulders.

And I was completely exposed to him. And he was looking. Like... *really looking*.

Then his hands went up the insides of my thighs, pressing them further open.

"Chase..."

"Shh," he said, glancing up at my face, then quickly away.

And before I could draw breath to think about objecting, his head moved forward and I felt his tongue slide up my slick cleft.

There was no more objecting.

There was no way I was going to fuck it up for myself.

No way I was going to miss out on Dr. Chase freaking Hudson going down on me like his damn life depended on it.

His tongue worked up and down for a long time, stroking near my clit but never quite touching it. My hands fisted harder into the sheets, my back arching, my hips rising toward him. His tongue moved back downward, finding the entrance, curling in on itself, then thrusting forward.

"Oh my God," I groaned, my hand slamming down on the back of his head, holding him there just in case he decided he was going to try to stop. He wasn't allowed to stop.

He thrust in and out of me until my body felt hot and sweaty, until the groans became choked begging. Then he withdrew, stroking upward and pressing his tongue hard into my clit.

Everything went freaking white.

My body pulsated, my thighs slamming tight around his head as I cried out his name over and over, until I felt drained. Until every last thread of desire felt spent.

Chase turned his head, kissing my inner thigh before raising his head to look at me. "Fuck, baby."

I patted the back of his head, too awestruck to think of talking.

"Hmm," he said, looking at me, "I don't think that quite cut it," he said, glancing back down between my legs.

I found my voice.

"Chase... I can't..."

"Well, we'll just see about that, won't we?"

And then we did.

And, apparently, I could.

And I screamed loud enough to forget all about my pissy ass mood.

"You taste so sweet," he said, sliding in beside me, pulling me across his chest.

Nestled in my little safe spot, I didn't care anymore. I didn't care if the feelings were fake. That he just saw me as a client. I didn't care. It didn't matter. All that mattered, like Chase had once told me, was the moment. And the moment was good. The moment was as close to perfect as I had ever known. I wasn't going to sabotage that for myself. I was going to lay with him and enjoy it. Let the memory get pressed into my skin so I could never forget it.

"You okay?" he asked, all his tension seemingly evaporated.

"Mmhmm," I murmured, kissing his chest.

"Little come drunk, huh?"

"What?" I asked, tilting my head up to look at him.

"Come drunk. Orgasm drunk," he explained like it was a phrase everyone in the world knew but me.

I giggled, laying back down on his chest. "I guess."

"You handled that a lot better than I thought you would."

"Did you expect me to start yelling and push you off?"

"Maybe. Maybe something not so dramatic. I didn't think you would just... enjoy yourself."

"I enjoyed you," I corrected, biting my lip, hoping that wasn't too wishy-washy.

"That's sweet," he said, kissing my head. "God, you're like a teensy little oven," he said, kicking off the blankets and sighing at the cooler air.

And then I looked down, seeing his cock, hard, straining against the material of his pants. My hand moved downward slowly. Very, very slowly. Still a little more unsure than I cared to admit.

"Babe," he said, grabbing my wrist, "it's okay. We have all night. You don't need to..."

"But I want to," I said, pushing up and looking down at him.

"*Fuck me*," he said, bringing a hand up to the side of my face for a second. "You're perfect just how you are, okay? Don't let anyone try to convince you otherwise." He paused. "Not even yourself."

Oh, the flood of warm and gushy that filled my chest and belly sure *felt* real right then.

I gave him a small smile, leaning and pressing my lips to his, then putting my leg on the other side of his body to straddle him so I could kiss my way down like I had been thinking of doing. "Wait," he said, grabbing me. "Let a man enjoy the view for a second," he said, smiling. His hands moved up my belly, over my ribs, then gently covered my breasts, running his thumbs over my nipples. "Perfect," he said again.

I slid down his body, going down onto my forearms as I kissed his neck, between his pecs, down the center of his abdominals, the muscles jerking slightly underneath the contact. Chase reached down, taking my hair and brushing it toward one side of my head, then holding it in his hand, not pulling, just keeping it out of the way so he could watch. My mouth reached his waistband and I pushed myself up to balance on my knees as I worked his belt off, then unfastened his slacks. My hands went underneath the waistband of them and his underwear, pulling up and downward until they slid and revealed what I was looking for.

Up close, it somehow managed to be just as perfect as I had thought. Thick, long, smooth.

"Ava..."

"Let a *woman* enjoy the view for a second," I said, smiling, and was rewarded by a long, appreciative laugh.

My hand reached out, taking his length and stroking down to the base, pulling him upward toward my mouth.

This was new.

Not in the way that I had never given oral sex before, but in the method. Usually (and I guess it said a lot of the guys I dated), I was freaking out. So they just... took over. They held the back of my neck hard and just... slammed their cocks into my throat. No finesse. No desire to please them. Just being used.

This wasn't that.

This was me wanting to taste him, to hear his groans. This was me wanting to know what he tasted like, just as he wanted to know how I tasted. This was just as much for my pleasure as it was for his.

And that made me feel powerful.

And it was new and exciting.

I leaned forward, stroking my tongue over the smooth head, his hand pulling involuntarily at my hair. Encouraged, I closed my mouth around him, stroking slowly downward, taking my time to get to know every solid inch of him. I felt my gag reflex object, swallowing against it, letting it settle, and moving further down. Until I felt him press up hard against the back of my throat.

"Holy... *fuck*... Ava..."

I let my eyes drift upward, finding his and he exhaled his breath sharply. Watching him, I moved slowly back upward, sucking hard, then running my tongue over the head again. His mouth parted, cursing under his breath, watching me so intensely that I knew I was doing a pretty damn good job. I starting moving up and down, faster, sucking harder, twisting my mouth around, letting his cock hit my throat at every downward stroke. My hand slipped away, unneeded, and stroked gently over his balls.

I could have done it forever. Despite the neck ache, despite the sore jaw. I would have happily sucked him into the next year, listening to his breathing get more and more ragged, watching his eyes close, then open because he didn't want to miss the show, feeling his hand dig into my neck hard enough for there to be marks in the morning. I was so absorbed in him and his desire that there was nothing else in the world.

"Ava..." his voice held a warning. "I'm gonna come, if you don't want..."

But I did want.

Oh, how I wanted.

I flicked my tongue over the head quickly then took him to the hilt and he came hard, his body going rigid, his hand grabbing my neck, the other one slamming down on the top of my head. The taste of his desire filled my mouth and I swallowed greedily until there was nothing left. I held him deep for a moment, then moved ever so slowly back upward, sucking at the tip, then kissing my way back up toward his neck.

His hands reached out to stop me from scooting to my favorite spot, cradling my face and pulling it up. "Ava..."

"I did good, didn't I?" I asked, a proud smile toying at my lips.

"No, baby," he said, shaking his head. "That wasn't good. That was fucking phenomenal," he said, stroking my cheeks, running his finger over my lips. Like he couldn't get enough of touching me.

There was a swelling in my chest, strong, unmistakable. Even if someone had never felt it before, they knew it when it happened. It was a warmth, a fullness. It was foreign, yet somehow familiar. Love. It was love. I was sooooo in *fake* love with Dr. Chase Hudson.

But it didn't feel fake.

And I wasn't going to ruin it.

So I moved to lay in the center of his chest, next to the heart I felt so attached to, my legs on the outer side of his, and just... drifted into the feeling.

His arms went tight around me. And we both were just... there. Awake. Lost in our own thoughts, holding onto one another like it would be the last time.

Eventually, I fell asleep.

I woke up later to Chase's hands swatting my ass. That was my wake-up call. I started, pushing up off his chest with sleepy eyes. "What?" I grumbled.

"Nothin'," he said, looking almost... coy. "I just wanted you to wake up."

"What for?"

The slow growing devilish grin made me wish I hadn't asked.

"I'm going to taste you again," he said casually, but the grin didn't go away.

"Why do I feel like there's a hitch?"

"This time you're going to ride my face."

Oh, hell no.

No.

That just didn't even *sound* sexy.

"And at the same time you're going to suck my cock again."

Well, that made it moderately better.

"Chase..."

"You don't like it, we stop. No questions asked. Let's give it a try, okay?"

Was it really even possible to say no to him?

"Okay."

"Alright," he said, scooting down on the bed a little. "Why don't you turn and straddle me. Get started. I get the feeling you'd be more comfortable with that."

"Yeah."

So then I swiveled, straddling him facing his feet, letting him guide my legs back until I was where he wanted me (and trying really, really hard to not think what he was face to face with). His hands went on my hips and I quickly leaned down and started to take him in my mouth. It wasn't long until his hands pressed me down and I felt his tongue find my clit.

And any original objections to the position flew away.

I was shrugging back into my clothes later. A lot later. Sometime after two AM. Chase was back in his slacks and was in the process of buttoning his shirt.

"I need to see you tomorrow."

"What?" I asked, sure I misheard him.

"For the next session. Tomorrow."

Right. Session. Because I was a client.

Back to the real world, Ava.

And also...

holy

fuck.

The next session was the sixth session.

The sixth session was the sex session.

He was going to be *inside* me.

I felt my head shaking.

"No?" he asked, brows drawing together. "Why? What's the matter? Are you nervous? Because we should talk about it then, babe."

"No... I, ah, I have plans to go out with a coworker. Shay," I added, not knowing why I needed to make it clear she was female. "She's been pestering me and I finally agreed."

"That's great," he said, but looked almost... disappointed? "Okay. Monday night. At seven."

Monday at seven. Okay. No need to freak out. Yeah, that was a joke. I was gonna freak.

After the Session

Alright. I went to bed. I tried not to freak out. I woke up. I tried again. I showered, dressed, left the house. I tried again. All day at work, I kept freaking trying.

And it didn't work.

It was going to be the longest weekend of my life.

But, I reminded myself as I showered and prepared some dinner, I was going out. I was going to get a distraction that would, hopefully, pull me out of my anxiety-fueled funk. Hell, I was going to drink until I forgot about if that needed to happen.

"Are you eating a salad?" Jake asked, crossing his arms over his, yet again, bare chest.

"Are you scoffing at me? You're the one always picking at me to eat better."

"Yeah, on a day to day basis, not before a night out."

"What the hell difference does it make?"

"Oh, my poor poor nightlife virgin," he said, shaking his head, moving to take my salad bowl and put it in the fridge.

"How about tell me what you mean without being so condescending?"

"You need to put something in your stomach for the booze to settle on. Hamburgers. Fries. Pizza. Something greasy and filling. I know you. You'll be on your ass after two drinks if you go in on an empty stomach."

He wasn't wrong. I had a twelve year old's tolerance for alcohol. Two drinks and I was super buzzed. Three and I was on the verge of being a mess. Four... I was home in bed because I could never get past four.

"Alright. How about you order food?" I suggested, shrugging. "Use my credit card. I am going to go dry my hair. Shay should be here in like... half an hour."

When I walked out of the bathroom, the kitchen counter was full of food. And I mean full. Like he intended to feed an entire freaking high school football team instead of two people.

"What is..." the knock at the door interrupted me and I rushed over to answer it.

In sashayed Shay, her face bare for the first time since I had known her, dressed in a loose t-shirt and leggings. She had an enormous makeup kit in one hand, a yellow food store bag hanging off her wrist, and four dresses in her other hand.

"Oh, is that grease?" she asked, pushing in like she had been in my apartment a hundred times before. "Good thinking. We need some lining... oh," she said, spotting Jake. "Well... hello," she said in the most overtly flirtatious tone possible.

"Don't bother," I said, taking the dresses from her and draping them across the back of the couch. "He's pretty but he's an asshole."

"Oh, girl, but those are the best kind of men. I'm Shay," she said, walking over to him. "Nice adonis belt."

"You should see what's below it."

Oh my God.

They were not flirting.

That was only going to end in violent, awful flames.

"All talk," Shay said, smirking.

"You want a little preview?" he asked, reaching for his waistband.

"Regardless of what she may want, there will be no nudity in my kitchen," I said, shaking my head at them.

"You're literally being a cock block right now," Jake complained.

"Don't worry. Shay will be here for a while. You can flash her when I'm not looking," I said, going to the bags of food. "So what did you get?"

"Everything," Jake said, shrugging. "Burgers, fries, mozzarella sticks, onion rings, fried chicken..."

"I'm not gonna be able to fit in any of those dresses," I complained, reaching for plates.

"Better a little bloated than passed out on a bar floor," Jake said and I silently agreed.

We ate for a long time, Shay insisting it would be absolutely ridiculous to show up at a club before ten anyway. Then she dragged me into the bathroom, laying out makeup and hair products all over the sink counter, taking out a straightening iron and leaving it to heat up in the sink. "Not for me, obviously," she said, gesturing toward her dreadlocks. "I want to see what your hair looks like real straight."

I dragged a stool from the kitchen and sat down. "Alright,

do what you will," I told her, closing my eyes slightly.

Apparently, what Shay "willed" took over an hour and a half of primping. My hair was straightened, then straightened again, then a third time just to make sure. My face was dabbed, patted, brushed with... God knew what. My eyelashes were curled then had endless coats of mascara applied. Lipstick was put on, blotted, then taken off to try a different shade.

"Alright," she said, stepping back, the tube of lipstick in one hand, the top in the other. She squinted at me. "Yeah," she nodded, smiling slowly. "That's good."

"Let me look..." I started to say, getting off my seat which had been killing my butt for the last half hour.

"No," she said, pushing my shoulder back down. "You don't get to see until you are dressed."

"Fine," I grumbled, sitting back down. "What about your makeup?"

"Oh, yeah, give me five," she said, turning to the mirror.

Then she literally took five minutes. Five. After all she put me through. She applied a little powder, lined her eyes, and put on a coat of lip gloss and she was done. Flawless as per usual.

She grabbed the dresses off the door, finding the one she wanted: a bright eye-grabbing red number, sleeveless, skin tight, short, with a visible zipper running up one side. She confidently stripped out of her clothes, standing in front of me in her thong and strapless bra for a long moment before slipping into her dress. And she was nothing short of billboard worthy.

"Okay, I brought a few for you, but I know the one you should wear. Now," she said, her voice getting serious, turning down the music like what she was about to say was super important, "I know you usually have a very... um... conservative style. So you are just going to have to take a deep breath, put on your big girl panties, and get over it. Though," she said, grabbing the dress, "you're probably better going panty-less in this."

"That's not gonna happen."

She rolled her eyes dramatically. "Get your clothes off."

Oh. So I wasn't going to get to change in private. Well, okay. I mean... I could do it. She did it. I tried not to think that she did it because she was literally perfect as I reached to take of my shirt and pants.

"Okay, thong works," she said, nodding at my near-nudity. "Okay, I want to be surprised," she said, handing me the dress and clapping her hands. "I know it's going to be perfect, but I want to see the big reveal so I am going to wait in the living room. Be careful not to get your makeup on it," she warned and was out the door.

I looked at the dress. It was electric blue and looked like it was going to fit like a second skin. Two small straps. The bust slightly scalloped so that it would dip a bit between my breasts. I turned it, finding a huge cutout in the shape of heart in the back. So, apparently, I wasn't allowed to wear normal panties... or a bra.

I took a deep breath, deciding to try to go with the flow, taking off my bra, and sliding in. Luckily, there was a small shelf bra inside, providing a bit of support and keeping my nipples out of sight. I shimmied the dress up, slipping the straps into place, finding the hem didn't even come half way down my thigh.

I took a deep breath, moving the remaining dresses off the back of the door so I could get a look in the full-length mirror attached to it.

And... damn.

I wasn't one for vanity (in fact, it was usually crushing insecurity), but Shay had worked some kind of magic. My hair fell in straight sheets around my shoulders. And the makeup that seemed like it was going to be caked-on and over the top, was actually pretty understated. My lids had cat-eye liner, my lashes darkened to make them pop, a tiny bit of pink to my pale cheeks, and some bright red lipstick.

The dress looked great, hugging of bust and hip, making them the highlights, rouching slightly so you couldn't see every movement of skin underneath.

"I'm growing old out here," Shay called and I shook my head, turning off the straightener, squirting a spray of the perfume Jake had bought me over my chest, and opening the door.

"Daaaaammn," Shay said, smiling and nodding.

"Holy fuck, Ava, that you?" Jake asked, walking to stand next to Shay, fully dressed in slacks and a button-up.

"Why are you dressed?" I asked, suspicious.

"I'm coming with."

"Oh, like hell..."

"Hey," he said, holding up a hand. "I was told that if I am in your life and I care about you, I have to do better. So I think that means being a chaperon to make sure you don't get stupid drunk and go home with some sleezebag."

"Oh, bullshit. You just want to convince Shay to come back here with you."

"Yeah, well, that too..."

"You're impossible."

"Hey it works out better," Shay insisted, grabbing her purse and pulling out two wallets, one small and one normal. She took out cash, and ID, a condom, and two sticks of gum from the big one and put them in the small one. "He can hold our wallets," she said, handing hers to him and he easily tucked it in his pocket.

"Fine," I said, going to find something small to put my stuff in. Minus the condom. Add in a single serve packet of aspirin. "We ready?" I asked, reaching for a coat.

"No coats," Shay and Jake said at the same time.

"It's cold out!" I objected. "I don't want to stand in line in the middle of fall in glorified underwear."

"Oh, honey," Shay said, shaking her head, "we won't be waiting on any lines."

And we didn't. As soon as we got out of the cab, Shay grabbed my hand and pulled me to the door, giving the security guard a soul sucking smile... and in we went. They didn't even bother to check our IDs.

"First is first," Jake declared, a hand at each of our backs, guiding us toward the bar. "Drinks."

And then I was plied with liquor.

The night was a bit of a blur after the first two drinks. A shot (Jake insisted we take before anything else, toasting to a good night), then a martini. Jake disappeared and Shay dragged me to the dance floor, promising to keep the creeps away.

Which, to her credit, she managed to do.

Jake showed up on occasion, handing Shay and me drinks. First something pink and fruity. Then something blue and fruity. Then something green and melon-y.

And I danced.

Now, to be perfectly honest, I had never been much of a dancer. Okay. I had never been *any* kind of dancer, period. Except in my room while I was getting dressed. Never in public. Never in a huge crowd of bodies crushing in on me. But the music was throbbing, hard and sexual, vibrating through my feet and upward until I felt it reverberate in every cell in my body. That, mixed with the gloriously swirling feeling in my head... and, well, I was dancing.

Time got lost. All that mattered was the music and Shay

laughing and spinning around with me, and the floating feeling of my soul. Everything felt light and unimportant outside of our little circle.

Some time later, late enough for me to start to feel my shoes biting into my feet, Jake showed up with another drink. Orange and citrus-y. Then he was dancing with Shay, talking into her ear from behind and she turned her head to answer.

Two minutes later, I was being pulled out to a cab and driven back to my apartment. Where, apparently, we were having some kind of after party. Ten people I didn't know, men and women alike, were crowding around, drinking liquor Jake pulled out of the cabinet, dancing to the music Shay had put on.

I kicked out of my shoes, going to the couch because the world was doing some spinning thing that made me feel like I couldn't stand on my own two feet anymore. I sat there, looking around in a weird sort of detached entertainment for a long time.

Then I was reaching for my phone.

And I dialed Chase.

I got the machine.

Drunk and undeterred, I listened to his outgoing message and waited for the beep. "I don't care what Dr. Bowler says. It feels real," I said, my words coming out in a voice that was mine, but wasn't... slower, slightly slurred. "And you can be as mea... stop pawing at me!" I growled to some random guy who sat down next to me and put a hand on my hip. "I'm talking to Chase's machine, leave me alone," I said to him, thinking my voice sounded super stern, but the guy only laughed. "So, anyway, Chase... I don't care if it's fake, you know? It's okay. I'll deal with that... okay, buddy," I said, slapping his hand hard enough to make my palm smart despite the alcohol, "get off my couch. Off. Get off. You ruined my message!" I accused, ending the call, unnecessarily angry at the stranger.

"Come on, baby, you look ripe..."

"I'm not a piece of fruit," I objected, then broke off into a fit of giggles.

He was attractive. He was around my age with brown hair and big brown eyes, and a sharp jaw. He was dressed in a blue button up and jeans. He was attractive in a very ex-frat boy kind of way.

A quiet settled then, me looking around, swatting his hand away when it kept reaching out to touch me. Then, what felt forever later, but couldn't have been more than a ten minutes, I broke the silence.

"Listen, I know you like my blue dress," I said, shaking my head. "It's very nice. But it's not mine." In my drunk logic, that was somehow supposed to deter him.

"Well then maybe you should take it off," he suggested.

"I can't."

"Why not?"

"Because I only have a thong on," I admitted, completely unaware how bad a thing that was to say.

"That sounds sexy. Why don't you show me?"

"Why do you keep touching me?" I asked, looking down at his hand on my thigh.

"Do you like when I touch you?" he asked, his hand snaking upward.

"I don't even know you."

"Makes it even hotter, don't you think?"

I squinted at him, "I don't think I work that way."

"Oh, baby, I can make you work that way."

"You're not allowed to call me that," I objected.

"Why not?"

"Because Chase does."

"Who the hell is Chase?"

"I am," Chase's voice said from in front of me.

I turned my head and there he was, in a blue suit and white

shirt. From my angle, he looked like a giant: strong, intimidating. It didn't help that he was glaring, positively glaring at random frat guy.

"It's Chase!" I declared, pointing, as if it wasn't obvious. "You're here!"

"Yeah, baby," he said, giving me a short glance, then turning back to frat guy. "Get your hands off of her," he said, his voice low, scary. "Take a look at her. Does she really seem like she is any condition to consent?"

"She's fine, man. Who the hell are you?"

"He's Chase," I supplied, un-helpfully.

"Get lost," Chase said, reaching down to grab the front of the guy's shirt and hauling him up.

"Alright, alright. Fuck. She ain't worth all this trouble."

"Hey!" I objected, lowering my eyes at him.

"So," Chase said, sighing a little, "did you have fun tonight?"

"I had a *lot* to drink," I said up to him.

"Seems like it," he agreed, moving down to take the space the ex-frat boy had vacated. "So where is your friend?"

"Shay?" I asked, looking at him, his dark scruff, his bright eyes.

"Yes, Shay."

"Oh, look for the most beautiful girl in the room. That's her."

"I'm looking at the most beautiful girl in the room," he countered, reaching out to touch my silky hair.

"You need to stop saying things like that."

"Why?"

"Because I like it."

"Isn't that even more reason that I should say it?" he asked, reaching down for my knees and pulling my legs over his lap.

"I don't know," I said, shaking my head like I could clear the fog there. "I feel like no."

"Hey," Shay's voice broke in, glaring at Chase. "She's wasted.

Back off."

Chase smiled up at her. And I knew her protectiveness had already won him over.

"That's Ava's..." Jake broke in, touching Shay's lower back, "friend," he decided, looking at us. "It's fine. She's fine," he said, leading her away.

"I like Shay."

"She's good people," I murmured, feeling tired. I scooted closer to him, resting my head on his chest.

"Who is Dr. Bowler, babe?"

"She's my shrink. My other shrink. She's good people too," I said, eyes getting heavy. "Even if she's right."

"Right about what?"

"But I think she might be wrong. But maybe not. That's how it works, I guess."

"How what works?"

I shook my head, taking a deep breath. His arm went around my back, keeping me close. I snuggled my face against his shirt. "This is my spot," I declared, tapping his chest with my hand.

His other arm went around me, his lips kissing the top of my head. "Yeah, baby, it is," he agreed.

"Safest place in the world," I murmured, drifting slowly off to sleep.

I woke up to banging noises, having the same effect as

bombs in my aching brain. I groaned, opening my eyes to find the apartment painfully bright.

"Hey there sleeping beauty," the voice attached to the chest I was laying on said.

I shot up, disoriented, looking up. "Chase?" I asked, blinking at him.

"Yeah, babe."

And then it all came back. Shay. Getting dressed. The club. Dancing. Music. The alcohol. Oh, the alcohol. Then being back at the apartment. Picking up my phone...

"Oh, God..." I groaned, burying my face in my hands. "Please tell me I didn't say anything stupid."

"No, babe... you fell asleep almost as soon as I got here."

But the message. The phone message. What the hell had I said? Something about Dr. Bowler being wrong. It didn't feel fake. Okay. That wasn't too bad. I could live with that. Blame it on the booze. Pretend I had no idea what he was talking about if he brought it up.

"Why did you come?" I asked, looking up at him. I was pretty sure I hadn't invited him. Or even said where I was.

"I heard you yelling at someone to stop touching you. He didn't seem to get the message. So I just wanted to make sure you were okay. If I had known what a guard dog Shay is, I wouldn't have been so worried."

"Hey, we gals got to stick together," Shay called.

My head snapped up to find Shay standing in my kitchen, makeup cleaned off, looking fresh and somehow rested, wearing one of my tank tops and a pair of my pajama pants. And what was even more shocking, was that Jake was next to her... helping her... cook.

"Okay, I think I woke up in some different dimension," I grumbled. I looked around, expecting to find a mess everywhere, but all was neat. Neater than I had left it even. Someone had actually... cleaned?

"Jake and I got up early to clean for you. I know you like things neat," Shay supplied, noticing my inspection.

"That was really sweet," I said, meaning it. "Wait... did you say *Jake* got up early and... cleaned?"

"Yeah," she said, shrugging like it was no big deal.

"Did you have him at gun point?"

Shay snorted. "Girl, all you need to handle a man like him is a sharp tongue and a withering stare. Boy got sisters. He's trained to obey."

"She's not wrong," Jake agreed.

"Then how come you never do what I ask?"

"Because," Shay answered for him, "you can't *ask*. You tell."

"I'll have to keep that in mind," I said, getting up slowly, pulling the dress down where it had ridden up high on my thighs. "Alright. I need to go get some less... binding clothes," I said, taking off to my room. I had just dragged some clothes out of my closet when I heard my bedroom door open and close. "I'll have the dress cleaned for you and bring it to work on Monday," I said, expecting Shay.

But then I turned and saw Chase looking gorgeously disheveled in his wrinkly suit. "Hey baby," he said, leaning up against the closed door.

"Hey," I said, feeling uncertain, grabbing my towel and piling it with my clothes.

"Turn around," he said.

And there was the little flip-flop feeling in my belly.

There was nothing hotter than bossy Chase.

So I turned around.

And then I felt his fingers tracing the heart shaped cutout in the back of the dress. I shivered under the sensation.

"You look so sexy in this dress."

Oh.

My.

"Thank you."

His hands moved up my back to my shoulders, pressing into the muscles, aching from sleeping in such an odd position. I melted back into him, my head rolling to the side. And then his lips were right underneath my ear, kissing a line down the side of my neck and across my shoulder. "Okay, you should stop that," I groaned.

"Why? Are you getting wet for me, baby?"

Fuck yeah, I was.

"Yes."

"Good," he said, moving upward and biting my earlobe. "I want you thinking about me every minute until Monday night. And every time you think of me, I want you to be wet."

So, he said that.

And it was fucking hot as hell.

"Think you can do that for me?"

Not a problem.

"Yes."

"Good. And when you get to my office," he said, his nose grazing my neck, "you are going to be wearing a dress."

"Why?"

"Because I am going to push you up against the wall, rip off your panties, lift your skirt, and lick your clit until you are begging for release."

Well, that was certainly a good reason to wear a dress.

I swallowed hard. "Anything else?"

"You're not allowed to touch yourself at all until then."

So he wanted me to walk around unbearably horny with no relief?

"Okay."

"Good girl," he murmured, then moved suddenly away from me, making me stumble. "Now go get showered. Shay and

Jake are almost done with breakfast."

Oh jeez.

He was staying for breakfast? With me? And my friends?

Oh, lord.

Jake was bound to say something completely inappropriate. Actually, for that matter, so was Shay. And Chase was going to be there to witness it. I made my way to the shower, nervous at the entire prospect. Would he find them funny? Offensive? Would he try to, like, analyze them?

At the same turn, would they find him stiff and calculated?

I scrubbed off my makeup, took a few aspirin, brushed my teeth mercilessly, then hopped in the shower. There was really no reason to be freaking out about how they would get along. What did it really matter? He was my shrink. They were my friends. Soon he wouldn't even be in my life anymore.

I tried really hard to ignore the pang that came with that thought as I toweled off and got into my jeans and white t-shirt.

I opened the door to seeing all three of them sitting at the table, laughing.

And I felt the most ridiculous surge of relief that it was almost embarrassing.

Chase's head turned, as if sensing me, and smiled, patting the chair next to him.

Oh, my poor heart.

He was really going to hurt me.

And soon.

Sixth Session

I knew I was going to be confronted. Shay kept looking at me all day, but we found ourselves unusually busy, having to work through lunch and not getting a moment to even think about gossiping.

Breakfast had gone well. Too well. Everything was light, funny. Shay told her wild stories; Jake pitched in. We all discussed how we met, all but me and Chase. Jake had expertly turned the conversation right when Shay was about to ask. Thank God for him, because I had no idea how I would handle that. Jake and Shay jumped up to clear the plates and do the dishes and Chase excused himself, touching my hip at the door and whispering, "Monday. Seven. Dress," before he left.

And I knew Shay had been dying to ask since the second she saw him show up and cuddle me on the couch.

I planned to freaking book it out the door the minute the clock struck five. I already had enough on my plate with my session later. I didn't need her stress on top of it too.

"Not so fast," she caught me as I rounded her desk, head lowered.

I could have pretended I didn't hear her. Or didn't know she was talking to me. But that seemed petty and childish. "What's up, Shay?"

"Who was that *di-vine* man you were all lovey dovey with this weekend?"

"I was not..."

"Oh, girl. Who do you think you're talking to? I know a woman who is all tied up when I see one. Who is he?"

Oh, hell.

Normally, I would have sidestepped the issue. Or even lied to save face.

But Shay was quickly becoming a close friend and while I didn't have too much experience with close friendships, I was pretty sure lying wasn't part of the equation to a successful one.

I looked around, watching people mill out, some still sitting at their desks. Some chatting.

"Aight," she said, standing, "let's take a walk and you tell me."

"Actually," I said, looking at her, "I need to buy a dress. Want to help?"

"Only if I get a dick description."

"Fine," I grumbled.

"Girl, I knew it!" she accused, shaking her head at me as she put on her jacket.

A few minutes later, trapped in a store I had never been in before, but Shay had insisted on, I took a deep breath.

"Have you ever heard of a sexual surrogate?"

"Ava," she said, her tone dead serious, "there ain't nothing about sex I don't know about. What about sex surrogates?"

"Chase is one."

"Oh," the breath whooshed out of her mouth.

I turned, so shocked to see Shay speechless that I couldn't help but laugh. "Surprised?"

"No. I mean, yes. But no. That man oozes some sexual confidence. So it makes sense. Ava," she said, leaning closer and I felt my stomach clench, "why are you seeing a sex surrogate?"

I glanced around quickly. "I can't have sex. I've tried. But I like... have massive panic attacks and completely zone out during the whole thing. I honestly couldn't even tell you what it feels like," I admitted, and felt like a weight got lifted.

Shay nodded, looking kind and accepting. "I'm glad you're seeing someone then. Sex is way too good to miss out on." She flipped through a few dresses, scrunching her nose up at all the ones I was silently considering. "Wait," she said, turning back to me with a hand on her hip. "Why the hell is he showing up at your apartment if he's just a surrogate?"

"I called him," I admitted.

She gave me a sly smile, shaking her head, moving to a different rack of (much sluttier) dresses. "So why do you need a new dress?"

"I've been with him for five sessions and they like... grow in..."

"Intimacy?" she supplied.

"Yeah," I said, swallowing. "Tonight is the sixth session."

"And what is the sixth session?"

"Sex."

Her head snapped to me, brow raised, mouth opening slightly. She looked like she was struggling to say something for a minute, then thought better of it.

"Well," she said, pulling out a tight, pure white, tube top dress, "then this is what you need."

"Really? White?" I asked, laughing. "I'm not a virgin."

"Aren't you, though?" she asked, turning her head to the side. "I mean... if you've never really experienced it, does it count?"

I shrugged, but I took the dress up toward the service counter.

"Hold up," Shay said, running up, something white and lacy in her hands. "I got you some pretty panties to go with.

"He said he was going to be ripping those off."

"Even better," she smirked. "The dress has the built in cup things so you don't need a bra. You can be fully clothed to fully naked in five seconds."

I smiled over at her. "You know what, Shay?"

"What?"

"I think you and I are going to be really good friends."

She smiled, hitting my shoulder with hers. "Dick description. Now."

I took my time getting ready, making a sort of ritual out of it. To take up time. To soothe my nerves. I took my usual long shower, carefully dried my hair, then pressed it with the straightening iron Shay had left behind. I applied my vanilla lotion to every inch of my body. I put on a small amount of makeup. Brushed my teeth. Then finally, close to my time to leave, I slipped into the lacy white panties and the white dress. Simple. Tight. Short. But perfect.

I decided Shay was going to pick out all my clothes in the future.

I put on white patent leather ballet flats, grabbed my keys and wallet, and walked out of the bathroom with the biggest knot of tension in my stomach.

"Shit. That'll do it," Jake nodded.

"Do what?" I asked.

"Whatever you are planning to do," he said, shrugging.

I nodded, taking a steadying breath. "I'll be late tonight."

"I bet you will," he smirked. Then the smile fell and he walked up to me, touching my shoulder briefly. "Everything is gonna be alright, okay?"

"Okay," I agreed numbly.

"Go on," he said, nudging me toward the door. "You're gonna be late."

I was right on time. I practically ran from my car to the office door because Shay had threatened to flay me if I showed up covering the dress with a jacket. I stopped outside the door, oblivious to the cold seeping into my skin, taking a few deep breaths, settling my hair back into place, tugging the bodice of the dress up slightly. Then I reached for the knob and went in.

Chase was at his usual place beside the desk, in a black suit and white shirt. His head drifted upward slightly as he tucked a piece of folded paper into his pocket.

"Oh, baby," he said, his head tilting to the side, watching me.

The heat in his eyes was enough to have the knot inside slowly unraveling. But he just stood there, looking at me, taking me in. And I started to feel squirmy under his gaze.

"I, ah, believe I was promised something that involved being... um... pushed against a wall," I said, feeling like a bumbling child.

A slow, devilish smile spread across his face. "That you were," he agreed, closing the space between us. His hand went to the back of my neck, pulling me to him, and his lips pressed hard on mine. Then my back was slamming against the wall, but all I felt was him. His tongue slipped into my mouth at the same time his hand pushed between my thighs, finding my clit through my panties and making me groan into his mouth.

"So wet," he murmured against my lips.

"Chase..."

But I didn't get to finish my thought because his hands grabbed a hold of my panties and ripped them off of me. Just like he promised. And then he was down on his knees, looking up at me with hungry eyes, his hands inching my skirt up my legs until it clung around my belly.

"Tell me it's for me."

"Always. It's always for you," I agreed.

And I had the sinking feeling that it always would be.

"Fuck, baby," he said, grabbing my leg and bringing it up over his shoulder. Then his tongue was stroking up my cleft, finding my clit and lavishing over it.

My hands went down on the back of his head, holding him against me.

It wasn't long until I felt my orgasm threatening to break, digging my hands into his hair and groaning out his name.

But just when I was sure I was going to come, he pulled quickly away, kissing the triangle above my sex and sitting back on his heels.

"Chase..."

"Don't worry, babe, I am going to make you come tonight. Just not yet. First," he said, getting up on his feet and taking my hand, "we need to go in the other room."

So, he made drinks. I searched through music. What music did I want to have sex to? I felt my stomach clench at the idea and tried to think past it. What music did I want Chase to hold me to? That worked better. I settled on a play list of bluesy music and turned to take my martini.

"Come on," he said, taking my hand and pulling me toward the seating area. I followed behind, curious, finishing my drink quickly and placing it on the end table before sitting down next to him. "I figured maybe tonight we should do some talking first."

"Oh, okay," I said, sounding as hesitant as I felt.

"First of all," he said, setting his drink down on the floor and reaching into his pocket for the paper I had seen him stuff there when I walked in. He unfolded it and handed it to me. "I should have given it to you a while ago, but I kept forgetting."

I took the paper, looking down at it, finding his name under the title "patient name" and then there was a read out of tests. It was a results of an STD test. All, of course, negative.

"I wanted you to feel completely comfortable with me. We will be using condoms, of course," he added quickly, "but this was just for your peace of mind."

"Okay," I said, folding it back up and putting it on the seat behind me. "Thanks," I said, looking down at the hands in my lap

"I know you're nervous."

Nervous didn't even begin to cover it. This was *the* big deal. This is what I had decided to pay so much money to fix about myself. This was my biggest insecurity.

"Talk to me, babe."

"I don't know what to say."

"Say anything. Say that you're nervous. Say why. Just talk."

"I'm nervous," I admitted.

"Okay," he said, his hand landing on my thigh, just resting there, an anchor.

"This is the thing I am most insecure about."

"What makes you so insecure? That you can't enjoy it? That you're worried about being a disappointment?"

"Both."

He nodded, reaching for my hands and putting his on top of them. "Ava, nothing you could ever do would disappoint me," he said, so much sincerity in his tone that I actually believed him. "And I promise you that, no matter what happens, I will show you that you can enjoy it. No matter how long it takes." He paused, squeezing my hands. "Okay?"

"Okay."

"Look at me," he said, then waited. "Do you believe me?"

"Yes."

"Good. Now come here," he said, patting his chest.

I didn't need any more encouragement than that.

Once I was settled and his arms encircled me, he took a breath. "So, let's talk about sex."

Fuck.

"Okay."

"In the past, have you ever had an orgasm during intercourse?"

"No."

"Ever been close?"

"No."

"Can you tell me what sex has been like for you in the past?"

Crap.

"Terrible," I supplied easily. "As soon as clothes start coming off, the anxiety builds."

"And when someone has their hands on you, how does that feel?"

"Like I want to scrape off my skin."

"Do you know why?"

"No. I mean, yes and no. I think the anxiety just makes me so uncomfortable and then angry because I can't control it, that the touching feels wrong. Like it hurts instead of feels good."

I felt his cheek come down on the top of my head. "And what about when they are inside of you?"

I closed my eyes tight, not wanting to think about it. "I feel nothing."

"Nothing?" he asked. "Not even the skin crawling sensation?"

"I mean, the first time..." I started.

"When you lost your virginity," he supplied.

"Yeah."

"That hurt," he guessed.

More than anything I had ever felt.

"Yes. A lot. I got sick."

"Okay," he said, squeezing me tighter. "And since then... just numbness."

"Pretty much. Sometimes I can quiet the anxiety enough to feel, but just for like a couple seconds because it doesn't..." I shook my head.

"Because you were stressed out so you weren't turned on," he guessed, "and it felt rough and uncomfortable. And then the anxiety came back, stronger."

"Yes."

"Alright," he said, kissing the top of my head. "Thank you for sharing that. That is helpful." He rubbed my back for a few seconds. "I'm sorry it's always been like that for you."

So was I.

"It's okay."

"No, it's not," he said, shaking his head. "Baby," he said, pulling me away and looking down at me, "it's not okay. That should never have happened. Those guys..." he said, grimacing, "they should have seen that you were struggling and they should have stopped and tried to help you through it."

"Not all guys are like you, Chase," I said, shrugging.

"No, but they should fucking try to be," he said, sounding angry. He took a breath, putting his hand to the side of my face. "Look, at any point tonight you feel anxious, you tell me. This isn't like the past when I told you that you should power through it and only push me away when you couldn't take it anymore. This is different. If you get above a four on that scale, you tell me. And if you don't feel like you can say it, all you have to do is say the word 'red' and I'll stop. And I'll try to talk you down. If that doesn't work, we can be done for the night. I will not be upset. I will not be disappointed. Understand?"

I nodded. "Yes."

"Good. What is the safe word?"

"Red."

"Good. Anything else?"

There was. There was something else. Something that had been nagging at me, albeit only slightly, but there. It wasn't my business. And I wasn't a jealous kind of girl. At all. But there was a part of me that wanted to know.

"Ava... just ask," he said, watching me.

I took a deep breath, letting it out slowly. "How many..."

"Twelve," he cut me off.

"Twelve?" I repeated, more than a little surprised.

"Men are more likely to seek help for their dysfunction. Women, due to society sex standards and often their upbringing, many women who are suffering simply won't seek help. Surrogacy is a very small part of my medical practice. I have been doing this for about a decade and I have only had about one surrogate patient a year."

Okay. That was good to know. For some reason. Maybe a part of me had been worried he had been seeing other surrogate patients at the same time as me. Not that it should have mattered. He was a doctor. I was a client. That was all.

But that wasn't all.

At least it didn't feel like that.

"Okay," I said, nodding.

"Okay," he repeated.. "Come here," he said, pulling my face to his and kissing me until I felt it down to the base of my spine. Until it was all there was. Until I had moved to straddle him, to get closer, my hands on both sides of his face, my teeth biting into his lips.

His arms went tight around me and he slowly got to his feet. I wrapped my legs around his waist, my arms around his neck, holding on as he led us toward the bed. Chase turned, sitting down on the edge of the bed with me on top of him, simply kissing me back for a long time before his hands went to the hem of my skirt and pulled it upward. Over my ass, up my stomach, bunching up by my breasts, waiting.

I slid backward, watching his eyes, then put my arms up over my head. Material gone, he looked down at me, his eyes closing as he took a deep breath. "Perfect," he said, his hands moving up to cover my breasts. He leaned forward, planting a kiss between then. "Thank you for sharing yourself with me," he said quietly, making the insides of my belly feel wobbly.

    My hand moved to the back of his head, slipping into his hair. "Thank you for being so patient." I slid further down his legs, giving me access to his chest. I slid off his jacket, then unbuttoned his shirt, running my hands over the skin underneath.

    Because, in that moment, he was mine.

    Maybe only for the night.

    Maybe only in my mind.

    But he was mine.

    And I wanted to memorize every inch of him.

    He lifted me, placing me down on the bed and standing next to it, removing his shoes, his belt, his pants, then finally... his boxer briefs.

    At the sight of his hard cock, I felt the tension coil slightly. Nerves. Not quite panic, but hinting at it.

    Then he moved in beside me, slipping under the covers, pulling me onto my side, then running his hands over me. Lightly. Just barely touching. And it felt like every one of my nerve endings was reaching out for him, trying to grab him, hold him closer.

    He pressed me back onto my back, leaning over me and kissing down my neck, over my breasts, taking the nipples gently in his mouth and sucking, then continuing down over my ribs, my stomach, down each of my thighs. Until I was writhing. Until my hands were grabbing at him, trying to pull him back up to me.

    He smiled, turning away into the bedside table and coming back with a condom foil, opening it and pulling it on. "This doesn't mean anything," he said, kissing my lips softly. "You can take as long as you need."

    But I didn't need a long time.

    I didn't even need a minute.

    I needed him. All of him.

I reached for his shoulders, pulling him until he followed and came over me, holding himself up my his forearms. My hands drifted down his back, over his muscles. Then my thighs parted, letting his body slide between. I felt my sex clench hard at the contact. Anticipating. Wanting it so badly.

Chase shifted his hips and his cock pressed against me, hard, just stroking up my cleft in the most excruciatingly slow pace possible.

My hands settled on the backs of his shoulders, my hips grinding against his. "Chase..." I murmured, his name full of all the need.

"You're sure?" he asked, eyes heavy, the muscle in his jaw ticking.

I had never been more sure of anything in my life. "Yes."

He leaned forward, kissing me until my lips felt fuzzy. Then I felt his cock press hard against the entrance, feeling my body tense slightly. His eyes watched me as he slowly pressed forward. And he was so big. And it had been so long. There was pain, a pinching, a burning that I winced against as his head pressed in.

"You okay?"

I nodded, my legs widening, trying to relieve the ache a bit as he kept pressing forward, one thick inch at a time, so slow that I could feel my body making room for him. His cock hit deep and my head jerked off the pillow and hit his arm. "Ow."

"Okay," he said, stilling inside me. "Baby," he called. "Look at me." I took a breath, putting my head back down and looked up at him. "I'm inside you." I knew. Oh, I knew. The pain was receding, leaving only the tension. The desire. "What's the number?"

"Three."

"I can work with three," he said, leaning down and taking my lips.

My legs moved upward, my feet flat on the mattress as my

hips started rising up, trying to stoke the desire, trying to get what I needed.

Chase chuckled against my lips, pulling back, sliding slightly out and pressing forward, making me whimper. "So fucking tight," he groaned, shaking his head.

"So... big," I corrected, smiling.

He smiled back, shifting inside of me slightly. "You ready?"

Hell yeah I was.

"Yes."

He exhaled slowly, then slid half way out of me, then fully back in.

And if that was what sex was supposed to be, Shay was right, I was as virgin as the fresh fallen snow.

Because this was other wordly. This was the closest to heaven I had ever been.

"You're so beautiful," Chase said, leaning down toward my ear, his breath ragged as he kept his intoxicating slow pace.

My legs went up, wrapping around his back, pulling him closer. My hips rose up to meet each thrust, arching into it, taking him as deep as possible.

"Oh my God. Oh my God," I whimpered, my hands grabbing into his back, digging in.

"That's it, baby," he said, pulling upward to look down at me. "Come for me. I want to feel your pussy grab me."

I drove up to meet him and just... splintered apart.

"Chase!" I cried out, pulling upward and burying in his neck as my muscles pulsated hard around him, the sensation of him filling me making the orgasm feel stronger than I had known before.

"Fuck, beautiful," he growled, pushing into me again, his body jerking. "Ava... *fuck me*...."

His body came down on mine hard, and I wrapped myself completely around him, my body jerking through the aftershocks.

"Baby, let me look at you," he said, trying to pull against my hold. I shook my head, pulling him tighter. "I'll hold you, okay? Just let me look at you." My arms slackened slightly and he pulled up. "Are you okay?" I shook my head. "No?"

My eyes opened slowly. "Okay isn't even close to how you make me feel," I said, because it was true.

"Oh, babe," he said, shaking his head, rolling to his side and bringing me with him. His hand went to the side of my face again. "I'm so glad you feel that way."

Not 'I feel the same way too'.

No.

He was glad *I* felt that way.

Because, for him, it wasn't personal.

I was a patient. A client. Nothing more.

"What's the matter?" he asked, watching my face with drawn-in brows.

"Nothing," I lied. Outright lied.

Because everything was wrong.

"I need to go to the bathroom," I said, moving away from him, sliding toward the other side of the bed, dragging the sheet with me, staying wrapped up. Hidden.

I closed the door, sinking almost immediately down the wall, wrapping my arms around my legs. What the hell did I get myself into? What made me think I would be prepared to take something like this situation on? I was so out of my depths. There was no way I could have gone into that arrangement and not developed confused feelings. I didn't have enough experience with the opposite sex, with intimacy, to not confuse sex for something deeper.

I buried my face in my hands, feeling the tears coming, hot and unstoppable. They just needed to get out. I needed to purge the misery.

I looked up.

But not there.

Not in his bathroom. In his office.

I got up, dropping the sheet, and went to the shower, flicking it on and climbing in. If the water was hot enough, it might be able to melt away a few layers of the feelings before I had to face Chase again. Before I needed to put on a brave face and act unaffected.

I could do it.

But then the shower curtain moved and Chase was stepping in with me.

"You should have told me you were taking a shower," he said, coming in behind me. "I would have joined earlier."

The anxiety rose, settling heavily toward anger and I felt myself straightening. I stayed under the spray, staring at the wall in front of me as he slid in closer. His hand moved out, landing right under my breasts and moving down.

I couldn't take it.

I just... couldn't.

I was done.

"Red," I said, my voice firmer than I thought it would be.

His hand froze for a second, then moved quickly away.

"Ava, babe... what's wr..."

But I wasn't listening.

I reached for the only towel, drying as best I could as I rushed out into room, grabbing my dress and slipping it awkwardly up my still damp skin, dropping the towel. A naked Chase came storming sopping wet into the room, eyes worried.

"Ava, please talk to me..."

My boobs wouldn't settle into the bodice right, but I wasn't wasting time with that. I grabbed my keys and wallet, reached for the door to the office and went out.

Chase had grabbed the towel, wrapping it around his waist, following me out. "Ava!"

Then I was running, in through the waiting room, unlocking the door with clumsy fingers, then throwing myself out into the street.

He might have been willing to do a lot of things, but he wasn't going to haul out into the streets wearing only a towel. I had been counting on that as I took off at a dead run toward the parking garage, bare feet slapping on the pavement.

I shoved my key into the ignition with shaking hands, pulling out of the garage as quickly as possible, taking the back road so I wouldn't have to pass by his office.

Shit.
Shit.
Shit.

After the Session

I turned the heat on full blast, my wet body shaking violently against the cold.

Oh, my God.

What the hell did I do?

Fuck.

I had acted like a damn maniac.

But I just... I couldn't let him keep touching me and pretend it didn't mean more than that to me. It meant more. Even if I was just dealing with some psychological condition. It was real. It was as real as anything. And it fucking hurt. And I just couldn't keep subjecting myself to that.

It was over.

I was done.

I wasn't going back.

He could keep the money.

Even though I was more screwed up than when I first went in.

Because I couldn't imagine anyone else ever laying a hand on me again.

I ran into my apartment building, hauling the door open and...

"Congratulations!" Jake's and Shay's voice chorused, sitting on the couch, a big spread of food and booze in front of them.

One look at my face and wet, disheveled body, and Shay was jumping off the couch. "Ava, what happened?"

"I can't..." I said, helplessly, shaking my head.

"Did that fucker hurt you?" Jake asked, jumping up in all his testosterone-driven masculinity.

And I wanted to say yes.

Yes.

He hurt me.

But not that way.

I shook my head and the anger deflated, leaving only worry.

"Ava," Shay's voice snapped

"I'm not going back," I said simply, moving numbly toward my bed.

The pretty white dress fell to the ground and I reached in my closet for sweatpants and the biggest, warmest sweatshirt I owned, escaping underneath them and climbing into the warmth my bed promised, buried deep under the covers despite my dripping wet hair.

Buried, I let it out.

And I mean... let it out.

Loud, ugly sobs, making my body shake and my breath hitch. I buried my face in my hands, rocking my body for comfort. But there was no comfort.

Not only was I unable to have a normal sex life. No. On top of that, I was freaking head over heels for my goddamn doctor. A man who didn't return my feelings. A man I was hellbent on never seeing again. A man who held the only piece of comfort I had in the whole world and would just continue living, letting other women rest their heads on my spot, offering them what should belong to me. But never would. And it never had. Not really.

Shay came in a while later, when the sobs subsided, the tears still streaming ruthlessly, and offered me tissues and a cup of tea. I took the tissues and let the tea become cold on my nightstand.

I didn't sleep. I stayed up, staring at the wall, letting the misery bury into my marrow.

"I don't think that's a good idea," I heard Jake's distinct voice say.

Then there was mumbling.

"Jake, I dunno," Shay's voice said, sounding like she was trying to reason with him. "You haven't seen her. She's like... bad. Maybe it will help."

"Or it could make it worse."

More mumbling.

I stopped listening, sniffling hard as a new round of tears started. My cheeks felt raw from them, my eyes swollen and painful.

My bedroom door opened and footsteps came forward.

Not Shay. She walked quieter.

Jake then.

Come one, come all... look at the pathetic mess that is Ava Davis.

"Baby..."

No.

No, please. Anyone else. Literally anyone else but him.

No wonder Jake was arguing with Shay about it.

I brought my legs further up into my chest, burying my face in the sleeves of my sweatshirt.

"Sweetheart," he crooned, grabbing my arms and prying them from my face. "Don't hide from me." I kept my eyes downcast, too embarrassed by the tear-stained mess I was. "Why did you run?"

But I wasn't talking. I couldn't. Like all the other times I couldn't. Like I was mute. There was no use trying. The words would just get stuck in my throat.

Besides, what could I even say?

"You can't talk to me right now?" he asked, his hand reaching out to rub some of the tears off my cheeks, only to be replaced by new ones. I felt my head shaking slightly. "Okay. That's okay," he said, infuriatingly patient. "I want to be here for you. Can I be here?"

No.

I needed to stay away from him. I needed distance. I needed to not rely on him. I needed to stop having flip-flopping in my belly when he talked so sweet to me. It just all needed to stop.

"I don't feel comfortable leaving you if you can't even answer me," he said, his voice sounding very professional. "So I am going to stay right here, okay?" he said, lowering himself onto the ground beside my bed. "If you need me, I'm right here. If you don't, I'm here anyway."

His hand fell from my face and I curled back up, hiding.

Eventually, sleep came.

I woke up later, my eyes half swollen shut, my face stinging. But not as bad as my heart. I looked down to see Chase still there like he promised, sitting on the floor, watching me like I might explode.

"Hey," he said, softly, like a small animal that might dart.

And then I was reaching for him, grabbing him, pulling him

toward me. He stood up, kicking out of his shoes and climbing into the space beside me. "Come on," he said, putting an arm out, "come rest on your spot."

Then the tears came again even as I moved to lay on his chest. His arms went hesitantly around me.

"I didn't know something was wrong," he murmured, mostly to himself. "I would have helped you. You seemed fine. Happy even. I knew you were in there too long. I should have guessed something was up."

I wanted to tell him it was okay. I wanted to ease some of the tension I heard in his voice. But I couldn't even comfort myself, how could I ever comfort him?

His arms tightened more. "I'm proud of you for using the safe word. I know that wasn't easy for you. Especially when you were so upset. I wish you would have stayed. I wish you would have talked to me about it. And not let yourself go to this place."

I was okay with that place.

That place felt real.

No more trying to pretend I wasn't in love with him.

Or in fake love with him.

Whatever it was.

No more forcing myself to experience things that I, by nature, didn't seem inclined to do.

Just no more faking it.

I was a mess. Case closed.

The door creaked open, sending light from the living room in. Shay walked up to the bed, sitting down on the foot, reaching out to rest a hand on my leg over the covers. "Is she gonna be alright? I've seen her panic before, but this is different."

"She'll be okay," he said in a tone that didn't sound entirely convincing.

"What happened?"

"Honestly?" he said, sounding tired. "I don't know."

"Did you guys..."

"Yeah, but she was fine. I swear, Shay. I was paying attention. In my professional opinion, she was handling it really well."

Professional opinion.

Ouch.

Like, really, *ouch*.

I shrank away from him, moving away from a place that didn't quite feel so safe anymore, and turned from him, curling up to face the other wall.

"I guess she didn't like something you said," Shay said, standing.

"Yeah," he said, tired. He sounded as tired as I felt. "But, fuck if I know what it was."

"Figure it out," she said, sounding so stern I almost wanted to smile. "I mean it, Doc. Fix her. I want her back to how she was before. She was doing so good. Going out, being more open with me and Jake..."

"I know."

"How many more sessions are you supposed to have?"

"Four."

"What are they?"

"More... intimacy. For... two more sessions. Then on the ninth session, I take her out."

"For what?"

"To teach her how to handle herself around men. Flirt with them. Shut them down if she doesn't want them. Prepare her for her new life after therapy is over."

"And the last?"

"Patient's choice. We can do recaps of everything. We can try a fetish if there's one she is interested in. Threesomes. Or even just some talk therapy."

"Pretty sure she ain't into threesomes."

"I know. Honestly, I hate those sessions anyway."

"Too much work, huh?" Shay asked and I could hear a smile in her voice.

"I think the only men who want them are men who have no idea what they are getting into."

That's right. Just have talk about all your other sexual conquests while I am lying right there. I was just dying little by little. No big deal.

"Well," Shay said, sounding further away, like she was going back to the door, "like I said… fix her. She's the best."

"I know."

Luckily, Chase didn't reach for me again. I got to cry in semi-privacy, then pass back out.

I woke up when the sun was streaming in the windows, bright on Chase's face. He was fast asleep.

I crept out of the bed, tip-toeing my way toward the door and going to take a shower. I felt more human. Especially under the hot water.

I was still broken. My edges felt sharp, like if someone touched me they would come back bloody. But I was all cried out. There were no more tears. I had used them all up.

And it still hurt. It was a sharp sensation that seemed to worsen if I focused on it. So I didn't.

But I would be okay.

I wiped the condensation off the mirror, looking at my puffy eyes. "You'll be okay," I said to my reflection, willing myself to put my faith to rest in it.

I was going to move on.

I was going to get over it.

Take my feelings for Chase and lock them in a vault somewhere deep inside, to be dealt with at a later time.

Because, well, I wasn't a quitter.

And I wasn't quitting.

I was going to go back to Chase's office. And I was going to learn everything I could learn from him. I would have more sex. I would learn about flirting. I would take whatever he could give me.

Then I would - Move. The. Fuck. On.

That was the plan.

But first- damage control.

I slipped into jeans and a black long-sleeve t-shirt, pulled my hair back into a ponytail, and went out into the living room.

Shay was still there and I had a moment of pure panic at the idea that I hadn't called out of work. And she was there too. That left the office so short...

"I said we both got the stomach flu from some bad take-out," Shay supplied, somehow knowing where my head was. "You aight?"

But then a motion to the side caught my attention. I turned my head to see Chase standing in my doorway, wrinkled, exhausted looking. How long had he stayed up after I passed out?

"Ava..." he said, the same concern clear in his voice.

I turned back to Shay, who nodded at me, then walked toward him, waiting for him to step aside so I could step in and close the door.

I took a deep breath, staring at my bed for a minute. Trying to get up the nerve. Then I turned back to him, raising my chin a little. "I'm sorry."

"Ava, you have nothing to be sorry for," he said, shaking his head. "Can you tell me what happened?"

"I... had a panic attack." That was true enough. "After. Which was different and I just... didn't handle it well."

"Okay. Why didn't you tell me?"

Because you're the one who caused it.

"I just... needed some space." Also true.

"Alright. I understand. I wish you would have felt comfortable enough to share that with me though. So we could work it out together."

He didn't meant together together. Not that way.

Squash that thrill of hope.

"I'll try harder next time. It just kind of... snuck up on me. I was zero to ten in like two minutes."

He nodded stepping closer, his arm raising like he was about to touch me. Which I couldn't let happen. I skirted past him, going back toward the door.

"I think Shay is making breakfast," I said, switching topics and his brows drew together. "You are welcome to stay."

"Oh, um... I have to go home and change. I have a client at ten."

"Okay," I said, taking a deep breath. I was doing well. And he was almost gone. "What time is our next session?"

"Ava... are you sure you're alright? You seem..."

"I'm fine," I forced a smile, the movement almost painful it was so fake.

He watched me for a long time, like he didn't believe me. Like he was thinking about bringing it up. "Okay," he said, finally. "Tomorrow at seven."

"Alright," I said, opening the door, "I'll see you then," I said, walking him toward the front door. "I'm sorry you needed to come out."

"I didn't *need* to come. I *wanted* to come. And it's nothing.

I'll... see you tomorrow," he said, looking uncomfortable.

"Yup, see you then," I agreed, then shut the door.

"Girl, that was good."

"What?" I asked, turning and walking toward her.

"That act. That was gooood."

"It wasn't..."

"Oh, please. Girl, that shit might work on the men but we girls know better. You are all torn up."

I debated just shrugging it off, but thought better of it, taking a stool and dropping down on it across from her, watching for a minute as she added veggies and cheese to an omelet she was making. "My other shrink says I have transference."

"That thing where you like your shrink?"

"Yeah."

"Girl, you ain't got no transference. You got real feelings."

"That's what transference feels like though. The only way I'll know it's not real is when it ends and suddenly all the feelings go away."

"Mmhmm," she said, her lips pursed like she wasn't buying it.

"And last night... after..."

"After you did it."

"Yeah, after we did it... I just realized how weird our situation is. How I feel like I am in love with him... but he just sees me as a client. And I freaked out and hauled out of there without saying anything."

"Then he showed up here with huge, worried eyes looking like he just lost his damn baby in a mall, fighting with Jake to let him in. That he needed to see you. He needed to make sure you were alright."

"Right."

"Yeah, that totally sounds like something a shrink does," she said dryly.

"It is," I insisted. "They can't just watch a patient in crisis and wash their hands of it because it is after hours."

"Of course not," she said, again... dryly.

"Shay..."

"Alright, alright," she said, holding her hands up. "You gonna help me eat this? I made it way too big."

"Sure," I said, hopping up to get plates. "Where's Jake?"

"Gym."

"Where did you sleep last night?"

"Jake's bed."

"Oh," I said, glancing over at her.

"No," she said, not looking at me.

"No what?"

"No I didn't fuck him," she said, taking the spatula and cutting the omelet in half and letting the pieces fall into the plates I was holding out. "His ass slept on the couch."

"What?" I sputtered, eyes wide.

"Yeah. He was a good boy and changed the sheets 'cause I ain't laying my ass down on those sheets lord knows how many skanks have been all over. And then I gave him a pillow and a blanket and sent him to the couch."

"What is this witchy power you have over men?" I asked, digging a fork into the omelet.

"Girl, it ain't as hard as all those women's magazines make it sound. Men are simple. They respond best to direct orders and rewards. They don't like all that thinking and feeling. That's for us. We project that shit on to them. No. You tell a man to clean the garage and you'll suck his cock while he watches the game on Sunday... girl, you'll have a clean fucking garage."

"You're like the man whisperer," I said, smiling. "So... what was Jake's reward for sleeping on the couch?"

"That I didn't pick up the phone and call his mama," she said, smirking. "I stole his phone. Idiot doesn't even keep it locked.

It was two in the morning, she woulda been piiiiised to get a call from a woman saying her son was being less than gentlemanly."

"Oh, my God, Shay. I love you."

"I love me too," she said, winking. "And you."

"I should kick Jake out and have you move in."

"Girl, in a heartbeat," she said, nodding. "Hell, just stick me up a murphy bed on some wall and get me a big chest for my clothes... I'll be here."

I watched her for a second. "Oh, my God... could you imagine the look on Jake's face?"

"When I move in? Or when I make him put together my murphy bed?"

I laughed. "Never change, Shay."

"Promise," she smiled through a mouthful of food. "So when are you going back to see Doctor Sex?"

"Tomorrow at seven."

Shay nodded, then pointed her fork at me. "You're gonna need steel fucking balls to get through another session with him without losing your shit again."

I nodded.

She was right.

"That's the plan."

Seventh Session

    Alright. I could do it. I had a lifetime of experience shutting myself down. I could do it to any situation that I knew would make me anxious. Going to the dentist? Shut down. Going to jury duty? Shut down.
    Going into the arms of the man I had feelings for... Shut. Fucking. Down.
    I showered, forewent makeup because I wasn't going to try to impress him anymore, and slipped into a long sleeved dress because, well, it would make less of a project out of getting naked. And I *was* going to be naked. And we *were* going to be having sex. I

was going to let myself experience the act of sex, enjoy it, have an orgasm. But I wasn't going to let myself think about it, try to mine feelings out of it.

It was just sex.

Besides, it was only another two sessions of intimacy. The he was going to take me out and teach me to flirt with other men. That was good. I needed that. I especially needed *him* to be the one to throw me at other men. That would just further cement the fact that he was not into me.

The last session was my choice.

Could my choice be to *not* have a session? I doubted it. Talk therapy would be hard. He would want to know what had flipped a switch, why I was so different. And while I might be able to brush it off when we had other things on the plate, I doubted I could fool him when talk therapy was the main course.

Oh well.

It was just going to have to be a refresher course then.

He could fuck me goodbye.

"What the fuck is Shay talking about?" Jake asked, standing in the doorway to my bedroom.

"What do you mean?"

"Something about a damn bed in the wall."

"Oh, that," I said, smiling a little.

"What do you mean 'oh that'? You two bitches can't be serious."

"I can assure you," Shay said walking behind him, "this bitch is dead serious. I'm sick of my roommate. And I am needed around here."

"Fuck you are," Jake said, lowering his eyes at her.

"What's the matter, Jakey?" she asked, leaning against the doorway, making him squish back or move into the room. He stood his ground and squished. "You afraid of what it will be like to have a roommate you can't walk all over?"

"I don't walk all over..."

"You kind of do," I said, shrugging.

Unable to defend himself on the topic, he quickly changed it. "We're too fucking old to be living like a bunch of poor college kids."

"Oh, what the hell does it matter?" I asked, sitting down on the edge of my bed to slip into my shoes. "I'll let her crash in here. It's not like I need the privacy."

"There," Shay said, smiling. Victorious. "It's all settled. Sorry you're going to have to start washing out those nasty ass protein drink shakers. Oh, and dig out your old tools."

"I don't have any tools."

"Then you better go buy some," she shrugged, pulling a nail file out of her pocket and starting to shave some of her nails.

"Why the fuck do I need to buy tools?"

"Because you're building my bed."

"No, I'm not," Jake said, folding his arms over his chest, trying his damndest to stand his ground while it was crumbling underneath his feet.

"No? Would you like to tell my brothers that?" she asked, pulling out her phone and searching through her contacts. "I have three. One is a cop, the second is a marine, and the third is a cage fighter."

"She's fucking with me, right?"

"Actually, no," I said, thinking about the huge towers of muscles that had visited her at work on occasion.

"Fuck it all to hell," he growled, charging past Shay.

"Where are you going?" I asked, my voice sickeningly sweet.

"To the goddamn hardware store," he grumbled, slipping into a shirt.

"Hey, Jake," Shay called.

"What now?"

"I walk around naked a lot," she told him, smirking.

"You fucking better."

And that was how Shay came to live with us.

Okay.

I took a deep breath, reaching for the door handle.

I could do it.

No, I was *going* to do it.

"Ava," he said, sending me a sweet smile. Light gray suit, black shirt. Two buttons. I really needed to stop realizing little things like that.

"Chase," I said in return, locking the door.

"How are you feeling?"

"Can't complain," I said, moving across the room. I wasn't going to let him walk to me. I was the one in control now. No matter how much I was shaking inside.

"You sure? You seem a little..."

"My roommates are at each other's throats," I said, moving into his office, leaving him to follow behind me for a change.

"Roommates? Plural?" he asked as we stepped into the other room and I went to the stereo.

"Yeah. Shay is moving in," I told him, trying to figure out what playlist would work. No more slow, sexy songs. No more metal. I was beyond that. And while what matched my mood was the "heartbreak" play list, I wasn't going to let him know that. I looked under the 'sex' title and found 'love making' and 'fucking'. Then I chose 'fucking'.

I turned, taking my martini from a very perplexed looking Chase.

"What?" I asked, feigning innocence as a very raunchy song came on through the speakers.

"Nothing," he said, shaking his head, watching as I drained my drink.

"So session seven," I mused.

"Yeah," he said, shaking his head again and gesturing toward the nightstand.

There, settled in a pretty white wicker basket, was what looked like a supply of sex toys. I walked closer, curious, and found packaged vibrators, feathers, floggers, handcuffs, and butt plugs. Yes, butt plugs. Apparently, we were at a kinky point in my training.

"These are just here in case you want to experiment. There is no pressure. Some of the items in there are things that some people will never have any interest in and that's fine. But I like to bring it all out because it can be easier to point out something instead of telling someone that you want to try it."

Right. He knew that from experience. From his other clients.

I reached in, grabbing the lilac purple vibrator and tossed it on the bed.

"Yeah?" he asked, smiling.

"Sure, why not?" I said, stepping out of my shoes and quickly reaching to haul my dress up over my head.

Chase's breath hissed out of his mouth.

Because I took the whole 'easy access' thing to a new level and forewent a bra or panties as well.

"You were just... walking up my street pantyless in that dress?" he asked, his eyes hot, a smile still playing with his lips.

"Yes. Now why are you still dressed?" I asked, proud of how

sure my voice sounded.

Chase's brows drew together, his head tilting to the side for a moment, considering me, trying to figure out why I was so different. But then he started slipping out of his clothes and I sat down on the edge of the bed, grabbing the vibrator and working at opening the package. Anything to keep my focus off of him for a moment.

There was just *something* about watching a good looking man undress for you. It did things to your insides.

And I couldn't let him have that kind of impact on me anymore.

Out of the corner of my eye, I saw his pants fall to the ground just as my fingers finally broke through the thick plastic. I put my full focus on what I was doing, prying the plastic apart and releasing the uber smooth vibrator. Before I could even close my hand around it, Chase's hand was grabbing it from me.

Surprised, I looked up, watching as he twisted the cap off, inserted batteries, and closed it in seconds. Like a pro.

Which was exactly what he was.

"Lay back and spread your legs."

Oh, bossy Chase.

Damn it.

I took a deep breath, scooting back on the mattress, looking up at the billowing white canopy material, and letting my legs fall open.

The vibrator came down on my heat. Already wet. There was no denying my body's reaction to him. And that was one thing I didn't want to fight. I flinched away from the cold. And then he flicked it on and my entire body shuddered, hard.

Holy shit.

Holy shit.

Why did women need men when those things existed?

He moved it slowly up to my clit, pressing hard against it

and holding there.

My hands grabbed hard at the bed sheets, my back arching painfully, my inner thigh muscles shaking slightly at the completely overwhelming new sensation. The groans came out wild, wretched from some primal part of me buried deep inside.

Then before I could even get used to the feeling, an orgasm ripped through me. Hard. Violent. Unexpected. Making me cry out loudly, my body wrenching away, curling up on my side and being helpless to do anything but let it roll through me.

"Jesus Christ," Chase hissed, the buzzing sound clicking off. I felt the bed give under his weight and his hand settled on my naked hip from behind. "Baby?"

Ugh.

No.

The pet names.

Someone didn't tell my belly to stop doing the flip-flopping.

"I'm fine," I said, before he could say anything else.

"You sure?" he asked, and I knew he was looking at me like he was afraid I was ready to bolt.

"Yep. That was just... intense."

"Yeah, I know," he said, his hand starting to stroke up my spine. "Just watching you through that... *fuck me.*"

I rolled back onto my back. "Go ahead."

"What?" he asked, his brows drawing together, his hand snaking up my belly.

"Fuck me," I suggested, making sure I kept my eyes on him.

The surprise on his face was worth the wobbly feeling I had in saying it.

"What?"

"I said go ahead and fuck me."

"Jesus," he said, shaking his head.

I sat up quickly, moving to the end of the bed.

"Babe... what's the matter? Where are you going?"

I turned back, holding out a condom from the nightstand. "Just getting something," I said, handing it to him.

He eyed me again, breaking open the condom. No doubt, still trying to piece things together.

Good luck, Chase. It was my life's mission that you never find out.

He slid the condom on, watching me. I moved to lay back down, but his arm shot out, his hand grabbing my arm. "No. We did that already. Time for something new."

"Okay," I shrugged.

"Come here," he said, patting his thigh.

Oh, my.

Okay.

I moved slowly, unfolding my body then going to straddle his waist. "Like this?" I asked, letting one hand rest on his shoulder.

"Yeah, baby," he said, his hand sliding between our bodies to grab his cock, sliding it between my slick folds. I groaned, biting hard into my lip. "You're going to ride me. Show me how you like being fucked."

Oh

good

lord

Alright.

"Okay," I agreed and felt his cock slip downward, pressing against the threshold, and waiting.

"You're in control," he said.

Damn right I was in control.

I took a slow breath, lowering my hips down, feeling him press inside me, spreading me. My eyes closed on a groan.

"That's it, baby, take me in."

Fuck.

I pressed lower, taking him in, taking him in as deep as my body would allow, the new angle making him hit places he hadn't the last time. My forehead went down on his shoulder, taking a deep breath as he filled me completely.

"You're so fucking tight. You feel how your pussy is squeezing me?"

Oh, I felt it alright.

"Find what feels good, Ava," he told me, his hands going to my hips.

Everything. Everything felt good when he was inside me.

But I shifted my hips upward, letting him slide halfway out of me, before pressing back down on a moan.

"That feel good?" he asked.

"Yeah," I whimpered, doing it again.

"Try this, baby," he said, taking my hips when I took him to the hilt again, and moving them toward his body, then away, his cock pressing up against my G-spot in the process.

"Oh, my God," I groaned, grabbing his shoulders.

"Make yourself come, Ava."

And then I did.

A slow, rolling, pulsating that had my fingers digging in hard enough to draw blood.

I collapsed against him, shaking slightly.

His hands moved up and down my spine and as I came down, I could feel him... still hard inside me.

I moved lazily backward, looking at him quizzically.

A smile toyed with his lips. "Yeah, I'm not done with you yet," he said, his voice deep and sexual. And it sent a stab of desire right where our bodies met, making me clench around him. His smile spread wider, "You like that idea don't you?"

I pursed my lips. "Eh, maybe."

He chuckled, grabbing my hips and hauling me off of him, throwing me none-too-gently onto the mattress.

And fuck if it wasn't one of the hottest things in the damn world.

"All fours," he said, going up on his knees.

I rolled over, a thrill of excitement settling in my belly. The bed shifted and I looked over my shoulder to see him standing at the edge of the bed, in all his naked glory.

When I didn't immediately move to do what I was told, his hands reached out and grabbed my ankles, pulling them hard until my knees teetered on the edge of the bed. "I said all fours," he growled.

My belly fluttered, my sex clenched, and I fucking got up on all fours.

"Good girl," he murmured, his hands going to squeeze my ass. Then they went away to slide down the backs of my thighs. And then his hand reached out and slapped hard. Hard enough to make me cry out and jump. "Now spread your legs."

Oh

hell.

Bossy *and* dominant Chase? I just... couldn't. It was too much.

I spread my legs.

I felt his cock slide between my thighs, moving to the entrance and holding there. "I am going to fuck you," he said, his hand sliding up my back toward my neck, then gliding into my hair. His fingers closed, grabbing my hair hard and jerking me upward by it. "Hard," he added.

Jesus

Christ.

Then his cock slammed into me, burying deep. "Elbows on the bed," he instructed and I moved downward, the position making his hand pull harder on my hair. My ass angled up toward him and his other hand settled right above it.

Then he was fucking me.

Hard.

As promised.

His cock withdrew almost completely each time, plowing in

so hard my body jerked as he hit so deep it pinched. In the most intoxicating, delicious way imaginable. His fingers twisted harder in my hair, his hand moved to my hip, pulling me backward with each thrust forward.

It was wild, primal.

And I felt myself fall away into it.

All that was left was the feeling of him in me, making me claw at the sheets, burying my face in them to keep the screams muffled.

"I want to hear you come," he scolded, yanking my hair until I lifted my head.

His cock slammed forward.

And I came.

And the entire freaking neighborhood could hear me.

"Fuck, fuck fuck fuck," I ground out as the waves just kept coming as he kept thrusting. "Chase..."

He thrust deep, "Fucking perfect," he ground out as he came as hard as I did.

I collapsed forward on the bed. Spent. There was nothing left.

He walked away to the bathroom and came back, getting into the bed next to me, staring up at the ceiling. He patted his chest, "Come here."

But I couldn't. Even if I wanted to.

Which I absolutely, positively did *not* want. Nope. No way.

All I managed was a strange garbled sound.

He chuckled, turning his head to look down at me. "A little come drunk, huh?"

"Shut up," I grumbled, my body thick and heavy.

He laughed, shaking his head, his hand landing on my ass cheek, squeezing quickly.

"That was fucking amazing."

Is that in your professional opinion, doctor?

I was getting bitter.

Which was good.

It kept things in perspective.

I made an acknowledging noise, because it *was* amazing, then tried to will my body to lighten up, to let me be able to move it.

But I stayed infuriatingly numb.

Chase shifted, moving upward and leaning over me. Then started planting kisses from the base of my neck downward.

And I suddenly wasn't numb anymore. I was definitely feeling that.

I knew I should take the opportunity to get up, to get dressed, to leave. But it felt too nice to walk away from.

It felt like worship.

He kissed down my spine, shifting slightly, kissing one of my ass cheeks, then down the leg to my ankle, then up the other leg, across that ass cheek, then up my spine again. Every inch of my body felt tingly. Light. Loved.

Oh, no.

Okay.

Shut. It. Down.

I wasn't loved. I wasn't worshiped. I was kissed. That was it. It wasn't anything other than that. Just kissing. Just more training. Coaching. Because I was a client, not a lover. Not a girlfriend. I was no one to him.

His lips moved across my shoulder then off.

Too soon.

And yet not soon enough.

When he settled back beside me again, I pushed myself up on all fours, then landed back on my heels.

His hand reached out for me, but I was out of reach.

"Wait. Where are you going?"

"I promised Shay I would help her set up the room tonight."

Lie. It was a bold-faced lie.

"Ava..."

I moved off the bed, reaching for my dress.

Sensing my determination to leave, he moved off the side of the bed and grabbed his pants.

"What are you doing?" I asked, pulling my dress over my head.

"I'm walking you to your car," he said, standing, reaching for his shirt while simultaneously slipping into his shoes. "You're not walking around at night with no fucking panties on."

I rolled my eyes. I had walked to his office just fine with no panties on. But, whatever. There was no use fighting him. I grabbed my wallet and keys, and walked out, leaving him to follow behind, still buttoning his shirt.

We walked in stony silence. And it *was* stony. Chase was stiff as marble beside me, but I pretended to ignore him, walking to my car and unlocking it, throwing my wallet on the passenger seat.

I was moving to turn back to him, when his hands grabbed my shoulders tight and slammed me back against my car, holding me there.

"Chase... what the hell..."

"What is wrong with you?"

Oh, boy.

"Nothing," I said, scrunching my face up like he was crazy.

"Bullshit, you've been off since you woke up the other morning and kept giving me that fake ass smile. What is going on with you?"

I took a breath, willing my voice to sound convincing. "Nothing is wrong with me," I said. "I'm good. I've been... learning a lot."

Mostly about how to pretend not to be in love with someone even when they are inside of you.

"What the fuck..." he growled, then shook his head, taking a deep breath, calming himself. "You're not being you."

"You've only seen me for a couple hours here and there, Chase. You have no idea who I really am."

Which was master liar and a royal bitch when I am on the defensive.

"I know you," he said, his words tight, his jaw ticking. "I fucking *know* you. *This*," he said, savagely, "is not you." And then he cursed, leaning forward and taking my lips in his.

I had been expecting angry. Bruising. Hard.

But his lips were soft and teasing; nipping at my lower lip, sucking it. Sweet. It was so damn sweet I felt my head tilting back, my lips parting, a whimper escaping them. His tongue slipped inside to mate with mine. Light. Full of promises. Then he pulled quickly away, stroking my cheek.

My eyes opened slowly and his eyes softened. "There. That's my Ava."

My.

My Ava.

Shit.

I needed to leave.

He didn't mean it. Not that way. It's just a phrase.

"And she's gone," he said, looking impossibly sad.

"So sorry to disappoint you," I said, my tone cold.

His eyes closed for a long moment. "Tomorrow. Seven."

"Fine," I said, wrenching away and dropping into my seat. "I'll see you tomorrow."

He slammed my door, stepping back, and watching me intently until I was out of sight.

My Ava.

I sighed, shaking my head.

Shut it down.

Three more sessions.

It was almost over.

And then I could open up that locked chest deep inside and let the pain slide out raw and wet all over the floor.

Until then, I just had to endure.

After the Session

Shay's bed arrived the next afternoon. By the time I got home from work, Jake was already halfway done putting it together. My room was the bigger of the two, but it wasn't exactly meant to have two full sized beds in it either. Jake had moved my desk and computer to one side of my bed, leaving me with maybe a foot and a half to be able to walk between. But it was tolerable. He had the back of the murphy bed attached to the wall and was working on getting the actual bed together.

"Wow, Jake," I said, leaning against the wall, "I didn't know you were so good with your hands."

"My hands," he said, sounding surly, "are meant to be good at other things." I was about to roll my eyes when he added, "Like playing with pussy or stroking my own cock. Not this manual labor shit."

I laughed, moving to sit on my bed. "You know... I've seen Shay naked."

His hands stilled, looking over his shoulder at me. "Yeah?"

"Yeah," I nodded. "It's worth that hard work."

"Fuck, I knew it," he grumbled, going to grab a screwdriver, then stopping and turning to look at me.

"So, you still have that freshly fucked glow about you."

"Yes. That tends to happen when you are working with a sex surrogate."

"It's getting good, huh?"

"There was a basket of toys on the nightstand," I confided, surprising myself.

Jake nodded. "Sounds pretty fucking good. What's the plan from now on?"

"Tonight I think it just more sex. The next session after that, I believe, is him taking me out and showing me how to flirt or something like that. And then the tenth one is the final one. We can do anything."

"I think this has been good for you. You know... aside form the whole transference thing."

"Yeah," I agreed. It had been good for me. "Alright," I said, jumping up, trying to make my mind think of anything but Dr. Chase Hudson. "Shay is going to be by with some of her stuff in like an hour. I am gonna go get us some food," I said, grabbing a jacket and making my way out the door.

Once outside, I took a deep breath. Three more sessions.

I felt a simultaneous stab of pain and wave of relief.

Almost there.

I had no idea what was on the table for later that night. And, frankly, I didn't want to know. It was easier to just... go with it. Which was, in and of itself, a completely new concept for me. I had never been a 'go with the flow' kind of person. I was a 'freak the fuck out and fight change tooth and nail' kind of person.

But I had to admit... even my generalized anxiety had been doing a lot better.

It was working.

I was getting better.

And if that meant I had to break my heart to keep going, well... that was just fine.

Sort of.

But not really.

The door chimed as I walked in, the black and white checkered floor worn and old. The walls were a bright red; the counter was an old wood that matched the few small tables and chairs inside. I was hit immediately with the scent of freshly baked Italian bread, rich red pasta sauce, and cheese. I took a slow, deep breath, enjoying it.

"Eat?" the owner asked, coming out from the back room in a white apron. He was a middle aged man with a ruddy face and thick mustache, his belly spilling happily over his waistband.

"Yes," I smiled, holding up three fingers so he knew he wasn't making food just for me.

"Hey there, *stranger*," a very familiar voice said, making me jump and turn. It hadn't escaped my notice how much of an inflection there was in the word 'stranger'. Like he really meant it. Like I wasn't me anymore.

"What are you doing here?" I asked, my heart hammering hard in my chest.

Because, sure enough, there was Chase in a black suit and gray shirt, sitting at one of the tables in my favorite rundown Italian restaurant.

"A girl I know," he said, the inflection still there, "told me this is the best Italian. I came to see for myself."

I swallowed hard against the lump in my throat, recalling it for exactly what it was- anxiety. The second I acknowledged it, I felt it sweep over my body, making my palms sweat, making my chest constrict, making me feel like if I didn't escape... I was going to pass out. My hand went to my throat, holding, like I could force the lump away.

"Ava?" Chase asked, starting to stand. "Ava... hey... take a breath."

But I couldn't. I just couldn't.

I needed to go. I needed to get out of there. Away from him.

I turned, storming out the door, and running.

I slowed in front of my apartment, looking up at it. Knowing Jake and Shay were inside. Not wanting them to see me having a panic attack. Not when they both thought I was doing so much better. I didn't want to be a disappointment. Again.

So I kept going.

But with nowhere to actually escape to, I sat down on a street bench, burying my face in my hands and breathing through it. It seemed to go on forever, my rapid heartbeat making me feel queasy and I was glad for my empty stomach.

"It's okay," I murmured to myself, rocking back and forth.

But it wasn't okay.

It wasn't getting better.

I dug in my purse for my phone, scanning through my contacts and finding the only number that could maybe help.

"Hello?"

"I need to talk to Dr. Bowler," I said, my voice high and hysterical.

"Okay. Alright," the secretary said in a soothing voice. Used to, no doubt, the occasional emergency call. "I will get her for you. Who is calling?"

"Ava Davis."

"Okay, Ava. Hold tight."

It was less than a minute later when the line switched and Dr. Bowler's voice reached out to me. "Ava. What's wrong?"

"I. Can't. Breathe."

"Alright," she said, calm. "You're having a panic attack?"

"Yes."

"Can you tell me what set it off?"

"I went to get food. My therapist was there."

"Dr. Hudson?"

Even his name hurt to hear.

"Yes."

"Ava, why would seeing Dr. Hudson trigger a panic attack? Has something happened with your... sessions..."

"I love him."

The was a beat of silence. "Alright, Ava. I understand that you feel that way, that it feels real to you, but it isn't. I need you to remember that." That was why I needed to call her. Because she would ground me. She would remind me. "How far are you in your sessions?"

"Tonight is eight."

"Okay. That's good. That means in two more days, everything will be a lot clearer. Your feelings will lessen and then, very suddenly, they will be gone. And think of how much you will have gained from the experience."

That was true. But it wouldn't be two days. Unfortunately. The next session would fall on a Friday. And then I couldn't have my final session until the following Monday. But still. I could live through it. It was the home stretch.

But I had just freaked out in front of him again.

And he was going to want to talk about it.

"Ava, what are you thinking right now?"

"I don't know what to say to him about this."

"The panic attack?"

"Yeah, he won't let this go."

"Well, because he's a good therapist. He wants to make sure you're in a good place before you two... progress. Honestly, honey," she said, sounding very much like my mother did when she was going to give me advice she wasn't exactly proud to be telling me. Like how if I just hauled off and hit the girl who kept teasing me in school, she would never bother me again. Great advice that worked, but as a mother she knew she wasn't supposed to tell me to raise my hand to people. "You are just going to have to do what all women have to do on occasion."

"What's that?" I asked, sitting back, my heart settling into a more normal rhythm.

"Fake it."

It was so unexpected, I laughed. Loud. Loud enough for the people on line at the hot pretzel stand to look over.

"I know that is probably not good advice for a therapist to give- to lie to your other therapist, but this is an unusual situation and sometimes unorthodox approaches must be tried."

"I've... tried. I mean, sort of. I kinda just attempted to shut everything down. Just be receptive to like... the actual... sex."

"And he saw right through that."

"Yeah."

"It's because it's not you. Yes, you can be very shy and reserved, but there is always a warmth about you. So if you were shutting down, and all he felt was the cool, of course he was going to tell the difference."

"So I just need to fake it better."

"Pretty much."

Okay.

Alright.

I could try that.

"Ava," Dr. Bowler said, her voice serious again. "I want to see you the day after your last session with Dr. Hudson. No excuses. I think this experience has had a lot more impact on you than either of us had anticipated. I want us to sit down and hash things out so you don't fall back into old patterns out of habit."

"I think that's a good idea," I agreed, thankful I had her in my life. I could use all the support system I could get. "I will let you know when that is."

"How's the anxiety?" she asked.

"Better."

"Okay. Ava, I know this process has been extremely difficult for you. If you are having issues, before or after sessions... no matter the time, you can call my service. I will tell them that calls from you should be considered emergent and sent through."

"Thank you so much."

"Anytime, Ava."

Okay. Game face on.

I got up off the bench and made my way back to the apartment. I only had maybe forty-five minutes left until I needed to be at Chase's office. I needed to shower and slip into another easy access dress. Then I needed to be me, but not me.

Which was going to take a lot more work than it sounded like.

"Well, finally," Jake said, his mouth full. "Just leaving us here to fucking starve. Luckily, Chase here cared enough about our..."

I stopped listening after "Chase".

My head snapped up to find him leaning against the kitchen counter next to Shay and Jake who were eating out of take-away containers from the Italian place. Chase had gotten the food I ordered and brought it over.

"Are you okay?"

Of course he had to be worried about me.

That was totally helping the confused feelings inside and I couldn't just... shut them down anymore.

"Better," I agreed, putting my purse down.

"Yo where did ya go?" Shay asked, gesturing with her garlic bread.

"I had a phone session with Dr. Bowler," I said, feeling tense.

I didn't like him in my space. Talking to my people.

Well, actually. I *did* like him in my space. I *did* like him talking to my people. That was the problem.

"Ava..." Chase said, his voice almost sad. "Why didn't you talk to me?"

I shook my head. "I don't know. I just... panicked. I needed to get out of that place. Once I got somewhere, I picked up my phone and..."

"You could have called *me*," Chase said, crossing the room toward me.

"I just... wasn't thinking," I said, looking up at him from under my lashes, letting the vulnerability show. But not from the aftermath of the anxiety, from loving someone who didn't love me back.

His face fell a little, his eyes sad. "It's okay," he murmured, reaching for my cheek, stroking over it gently. "As long as you're alright."

I wasn't sure I would ever be alright again.

"I am. That was just a bad one."

"Okay," he nodded, moving his hand to my shoulder. I glanced past him, seeing Shay and Jake watching us intently. As if sensing what I was seeing, he dropped his hand. "I'll see you in forty minutes, okay? Or I can wait here if you're still not feeling well."

"I'm okay," I said, forcing myself to look in his eyes. "I'm just going to shower and change and I'll be over."

"Okay, baby," he said, his voice dropping so only I could here. "I'll be waiting for you."

He walked out and I closed the door behind him, turning and leaning against it like my legs wouldn't hold me anymore.

"Come eat something," Shay suggested.

"No," I said, shaking my head. I didn't think anything would stay down if I tried. "I'm just gonna go shower and get dressed. Can I borrow another of your dresses tonight?" I asked.

"Girl, I'll lay some on your bed while you're getting your scrub on."

"You're the best," I said absentmindedly as I walked to the bathroom.

I primped as much as my time would allow. I did my hair. I put on makeup. I made it look like I wanted to look nice for him. Which, a part of me still did. A part of me still wanted him to call me beautiful and perfect, to look at me with wonder. So I let that part of me take the lead when it came to getting prepared. The other part of me was inwardly calling it "war paint" because fighting my feelings for him was feeling like a never ending battle.

"Aight," Shay said as I walked in wearing my robe. "I didn't know what color. So I picked out a few. But I'm thinking that the eighth session means *red*."

"Red sounds great," I nodded, going to my dresser to grab underwear.

"Thong or g-string, this material ain't too forgiving of panty lines."

I nodded, grabbing a black thong and slipping into it under my robe. "Bra?"

"Really?" Shay asked, sounding cynical. "A bra? At this point? Let the nips show, girl."

I snorted, shaking my head and turned to see what she had

planned for me. "Oh," I breathed out, looking at it.

It was red. Bright red. And the material was cut in the shape of an hourglass, covering the breasts, the center of the belly, and hips and thighs. The sides were covered in a red semi-sheer mesh. The same mesh went up as straps and then covered the whole back right down to the very lower back where it met the red material again.

"Yeah, this is a 'fuck me' dress," she said, nodding.

That was exactly what Chase was going to say when he saw it: *fuck me*. In that half-groan, half-growl he did. I felt a thrill just thinking about it. "Alright," I said, grabbing it, "the 'fuck me' dress it is."

Shay eventually convinced me to wear her black peacoat over it, buttoning only one button so I could reach for it as soon as I was in the door and surprise him.

"Here, put these on. I think we're the same size," she said, producing a pair of black patent leather, red bottom heels.

"No," I said, holding up a hand, knowing how much those shoes cost.

"Why not? You have the 'fuck me' dress. Now you need the 'fuck me' heels."

"They're too much. What if I snap a heel off or something?"

"Oh, so what? I'll make my brothers all chip in to buy me a new pair for Christmas. Come on, put them on."

So I did.

And I felt way too tall and unsteady in them. But, at the same time, kinda sexy and powerful. I could use all the confidence boosters I could get.

Jake walked in, eating my take-out Italian, nodding. "Going for the 'bend me over and take me' look tonight, I see."

I smiled, looking between then. "You know... you two are so alike," I said, watching their shared look of skepticism. "No. Seriously. You think exactly the same. It's crazy."

I didn't miss the look they gave each other, like they were trying to size the other one up.

"Alright," I said, spraying on some of the perfume Jake got me, "wish me luck."

"Go get it," Shay said, swatting my ass.

"Give it to him good," Jake added, pinching my butt as I passed.

"Seriously," I said, shooting them a look. "Twins."

Eighth Session

Alright. One button buttoned. Heels on. Bright red matte lipstick that was supposedly kiss proof. I was ready. I took a deep breath, making my way from the garage. Each click of my heels brought on more nerves. It felt like the first session all over again somehow. But I was determined to get through it.

The door opened, and I shut it behind me, locking it.

But Chase wasn't in his usual spot.

I felt a rush of uncertainty, strong enough to make me seriously consider turning and leaving.

Then his office door opened and there he was. In a blue suit and a lighter blue dress shirt. The combination made his eyes positively hypnotic. Two buttons.

"Ava," he breathed my name.

My hand went to the button, pushing it through the hole, then grabbing both sides of the lapels and dragging the material quickly off of me.

"*Fuck me*," he said. Just as I had been anticipating. He shook his head slightly and I let the jacket fall to the ground. I took a step forward, then turned in a slow circle. When I faced him again, his arm was out, inviting me to him.

So I went.

His arms didn't go around me though, they slid down my arms, taking both my hands. "You are... So. Fucking. Beautiful."

Oh

my.

Okay.

I swallowed hard. "Thank you."

His hands squeezed mine, pulling them upward, and placing them on his shoulders. One of his slid around my hips, pressing into my lower back and pushing my body against his. The other went to my jaw, tilting my face to his. "There she is," he said, nodding. "I missed her."

Fuck.

His head tilted and his lips found mine, soft, but deep, full of the passion I knew we were going to pull into the bedroom. So I sank into it. My arms wrapped around the back of his neck, my hips pressed into his, and I let him kiss me like it was the last time.

It very well might be.

"Okay," he said, pulling away, "Bed. Now."

We made out way through his office, his hand holding mine like a vice. He pulled me past the sidebar, leaving our usual ritual behind as he pulled me to the bed. He turned, sitting down at the edge of the bed, opening his legs and pulling me in between them. His hands went to my hips as he looked up at me, his eyes soft.

"Do you want to know about this session?"

Unable to stop it, my hand moved to his hair, brushing a strand that had fallen forward, back. "Sure," I said, running my hands down the side of his head until it landed on his shoulder.

"This all depends on your limits, okay? Just because this is the way it is planned out, doesn't mean it is the way it has to be. If you're not into it, we move on to something else. Okay?"

My brows furrowed slightly. "Okay."

"How do you feel about anal sex?"

Oh.

Well then.

Okay.

Somehow my overactive mind had never even thought to consider that as a possibility. And I hadn't really ever considered it outside of therapy either. I could barely tolerate normal sex. There had been no reason to think about it.

Did I have some kind of mental block about it? I knew a lot of women who did. Women who swore they never had and never would try it. I also knew some women who swore by it. And I knew Jake raved about it.

"Ava?"

"I'm thinking," I said, rolling my eyes.

"Alright," he said, his hands moving down to slide my skirt up slightly. "Then why don't you come here and think about it?" he suggested.

I climbed up on the bed, straddling his waist, resting my head on his shoulder.

"It's okay if you're not into it."

"I don't know if I am into it or not."

"That's alright," he said, his hands sliding up my back and through the thin material of the mesh, I could feel his body heat. "Do you think you want to try it?"

Did I?

Honestly, I wanted to try anything and everything with

him.

I wanted all that I could get before it was over.

"Yes," I found myself saying, kissing his neck.

"Good girl," he murmured, kissing the side of my head. "We'll start with regular sex first though, okay? Get you all warmed up."

"Okay."

"Okay. Now get a condom," he said, slapping my ass playfully.

I laughed, jumping off of him and going to the nightstand. I came back to him with one, which he took and laid on the bed next to him.

"Arms up," he instructed and my arms went up above my head. He inched the material off of me, making a game of it, enjoying each inch of flesh revealed. Finally free, I went to step out of my shoes. "No," Chase said, stopping me. "The shoes stay on."

Ten points to Shay's 'fuck me' heels.

He stared.

For a really long time.

Making me feel squirmy.

Finally, nerves starting to surface, I lowered myself down to my knees in front of him. He watched, apt, as I reached to remove his belt and pulled his zipper down. He watched as I reached into his pants, dipped my hand under the waistband of his boxer briefs, and grabbed his cock, bringing it out. Then he watched as I lowered my face down toward it, as it disappeared into my mouth, and his hand slammed down on the crown of my head.

"Fuck, baby. So sweet," he murmured, sounding out of breath and I had barely tasted him. I sucked him slowly, taking him deep, then working my tongue over his head, for a long time. "Okay. *Fuck*. Okay, baby. Stop."

I sat back on my heels, my hands on his thighs, smirking up at him. Because I knew I was the one in power. However briefly. I

THE SEX SURROGATE

had him eating out of the palm of my hand.

"Panties off. On the bed," he said, shaking his head at me.

Yes, sir.

I got to my feet, flicked my panties down my hips, moved next to him, and crawled in, lying on my back. He stood, watching me, as he removed his clothes. "Legs straight up," he said, and up they went. "Cross your ankles." Absolutely. "Fuck *fuck* me," he said, dropping his shirt. "This view, baby... fucking perfect."

His hand reached out beside me, grabbing the condom. Then I felt his finger slip between my thighs, moving slowly up my cleft until he was circling my clit. I felt my legs start to shake, moving them down. "I said legs up, ankles crossed," he instructed. Then up my legs went again. His finger moved away and he stepped closer, grabbing my legs and resting them against one of his shoulders.

Then, in one thrust, he was buried inside me.

"Oh, my God," I cried out, my thighs clenching.

"You can hold me as tight as you want like this, can't you, baby?" he asked, turning his head to kiss the inside of one of my ankles.

He was right. I pulled my thighs even tighter together, feeling each thick inch like never before.

Then he was fucking me. Not hard. Just fast. BangBangBangBangBang. His arms wrapped around my knees, holding me still as my body started bouncing with each thrust.

I felt my muscles grab at him, greedy, needy. Feeling closer faster than ever before. I was going to...

"No!" I cried out as he pulled out of me.

"Up on the bed, baby. All fours," he said, softly, letting my legs fall.

Oh.

Right.

I almost forgot.

I moved slowly, nerves rolling around in my belly as I got into position for him. He moved in behind me immediately, his knees pushing my legs wider. I felt something roll against my leg and looked down to see the lilac vibrator next to me.

Well, there was that to look forward to.

"It doesn't always feel good right away," he told me, his hands stroking across my ass. "If it hurts, tell me. I don't want to hurt you," he said, leaning down and kissing my ass cheek. "I'll be gentle until you tell me otherwise."

Yeah, I was pretty sure I was good with gentle.

"Okay," he said, and I felt his cock press against me. His other hand grabbed the vibrator and flicked it on, but didn't bring it to my clit. "Just breathe, babe," he said, and started pressing forward.

There was pain. Enough for my body to jerk, tense. But there was something else too. Something just beyond the pain, teasing me. "Ava, breathe," he said, his voice husky. I sucked in a breath and felt the vibrator touch me, my thighs shaking at the feeling. "Is it too much?" he asked, stilling. "I just have the head in, if it hurts too much..."

"It's okay," I said, focusing on breathing.

His cock pressed forward, a sharp twinge with each inch that quickly subsided. I arched my ass up slightly, adjusting away from the pinch. Then I felt his balls press up against my heat, knowing he was all the way in. I reached for the vibrator, taking it out of his hands, and turning it off.

"You okay?"

"Yeah?"

"Does it hurt?"

"No."

"Does it feel good?" I felt my face blush slightly. Because it did. And I felt like that made me some kind of freak. "Baby?"

"Yes."

There was a rumbling sound in his chest. "I want it to feel good," he said, rocking his hips into me, just the barest of movements, but... I felt it. His hands slid around me, stroking up my belly, grabbing my breasts. Then he was pulling me backward, until my back was against his chest. His arms went around me, one low on my hips, one just above my breasts. Tight.

His hips dropped downward, sliding out, then moved up, sliding all the way in. I could feel his chest moving up and down my back with each thrust and my hips started to move to meet him.

"Tell me it feels good," he said in my ear.

Oh, my God... it felt good.

"It feels good."

"No one has ever been in here before, have they?"

"No."

"It's all mine," he growled.

God, yes.

It was all his.

Everything was all his.

"It's all yours," I whispered back.

"Fuck," he hissed, kissing my neck. "*Fuck*, I like that."

It was too much.

It was too slow.

And sweet.

And intoxicating.

It felt like we were making love.

But it wasn't love. Not for him.

Not really for me either.

And it was just... too much.

"Chase?"

"Yeah, baby?" he asked, his hips still rocking gently into me.

"Harder," I said, my hands digging into his arms. I wasn't sure I actually wanted it harder. All I knew was it couldn't keep being so gentle.

And then his hips started jerking upward, hard, his cock burying deep and fast. Driving me unexpectedly upward. "Chase?" I heard my voice ask, unsure.

"You're gonna come for me, baby, and I don't even need to touch your pussy. You can come for me just like this and I will feel it."

That was all I needed to hear as his thrusts got faster, wilder.

And I let go.

And... fireworks.

My body felt like it had sparked. Like there was fizzling on all my nerve endings as my body pulsated hard.

"Fuck, baby yeah, just like that," he said in my ear, his own voice losing its cool. "I can feel you coming. Fuck... *Ava*..."

Then we sparked together.

And it was magnificent.

It lit up the whole fucking world.

Chase's hands stayed around me for a long time, holding me painfully tight, and I wouldn't have had it any other way. His mouth kissed a trail up the side of my face, resting at my temple and staying there. I brought my arms up and wrapped them around the back of his neck, trying to hold onto him the only way I could.

"So sweet," he said, lifting his head and kissing my arm. Then he released my body, reaching up to pull my arms from around his neck as he ever so slowly moved away from me then walked toward the bathroom.

I moved up onto the bed, pulling back the sheets and crawling in, rolling onto my side, away from where Chase usually rested, pulling my knees to my chest. I knew I should have been getting up and getting dressed. I should have been getting out of there. But I couldn't bring myself to go.

I heard the water run and then the door open and close. The mattress bent under his weight and, almost as soon as he got in, he was behind me, his legs coming up under mine, his arm draping across me and taking my hand.

There was a silence for a long time and then, "Are you okay?"

"Yeah."

And no... at the same time.

"That was..." he paused, looking for the right word. But there weren't any right words. Words to describe what just happened didn't exist. "Spectacular," he finally decided.

"Spectacular" didn't even come close.

But it was all there was.

I wiggled back into him and he pulled me tighter.

I let that moment hang. I wanted to let myself get lost in it. Just one more time. The last time. I wanted to feel his arms around me, his strong body holding me like I was fragile, like I was precious. I wanted his breath in my ear and his heartbeat against me. I wanted to wrap the comfort around myself like a blanket to fend against the cold days ahead.

"What are you thinking about?" he asked, nuzzling my neck slightly. "You're tense. Talk to me."

Alright.

Game face on.

No more playing at love.

Back to the real world.

"I was wondering about the next session." And then his body went tense behind me. "Chase?" I asked, snuggling back toward him because he had pulled away enough for there to be space between us. It was a literal metaphor for the emotional space we would soon we feeling.

"Tomorrow is Friday."

"Yeah."

"Tomorrow I will take you out to a bar or club. You will dress for it. Whoever helped you with the dress tonight, if anyone, that's what you need to wear."

"I can do that."

"You'll meet me here and we will drive to the destination together. You can have a drink or two, but no more than that. And then you will do what I tell you to approach men, or what to say when they approach you."

"And where will you be?"

"There," he said, more space between us. He was barely even holding me anymore, his hand on my hip, his body completely disconnected from mine. "Watching."

"So the purpose is..."

"To get you comfortable interacting with other men, not just me. But having me there to be a support system if you need it." He paused for so long I thought he was done. "We will go in together, sit down and discuss how to go about... flirting," he said the word like it was dirty. "After you get comfortable doing so with me, I will excuse myself to the bar. Then you will go to the other end of the bar."

"By myself?"

"Yes, by yourself. Men get intimidated by women with their female friends, and won't approach a woman there with a man."

"Okay."

"When a man comes up to you..."

"If," I corrected, thinking how many men had managed to avoid coming up to me in the past.

"*When*," he said more firmly, "a man comes up to you..."

"What? Is this some positive thinking nonsense? If I believe in it enough, suddenly hoards of men will find themselves flocking to me?"

Chase sighed, a long-suffering sound. He scooted further back, grabbing my shoulder and pulling until I moved onto my back. He shifted, rising up on his forearm and looking down at me. He watched me for a second, shaking his head. "How is it possible that you don't see how gorgeous you are?"

Oh

freaking

butterflies.

My belly was a traitor.

"Chase, really... I'm not..."

"Shut up. Don't you dare finish that sentence." His hand went to my face, cradling my jaw on one side. "How many times have I told you how beautiful you are?" he asked, to himself. "And you still don't believe me."

"It's not that... it's..."

"It's what?"

"It's twenty-some odd years of not feeling that way. Of no one saying that to me. It's not like I am going to transform my thinking overnight. But I'm getting better. I mean... could you picture the me who walked in here for my introductory session wearing the dress I wore tonight?"

"That's a good point," he said, nodding. "Do you believe I mean it when I say you're beautiful?"

In his professional opinion?

"There," he said, his fingers digging gently into my face. "That look. What is that look? You've been giving it to me a lot lately."

It was a distinct look? That was great. Just lovely.

"What look?"

He released my face, rolling onto his back, and raking his hands over his face. "You're killing me, woman."

Ditto.

Times about a million.

"I'll go," I said, moving to slide off the opposite side of the bed.

"That's not what I want."

I took a deep breath, my back to him, my feet on the floor.

Every ounce of me was screaming at me to go back to him, to curl up on my safe spot. For the last time. But maybe I had already gotten too many 'last times' for one night. I would just have to move on.

"I know," I said, my voice small as I finally forced myself to stand. "But it's late."

"Baby..."

The soft pleading in my voice felt like someone was grabbing my heart in their hands and twisting it.

I grabbed my dress, turning to him with a small, shaky smile. "Yeah?"

But he had nothing to say.

And I was tired of pretending I didn't.

So I slipped into my dress, then reached out and touched his foot from on top of the sheet. "I'll see you tomorrow."

"Seven."

"As usual," I nodded, grabbing my keys and wallet.

He wasn't even going to walk me to my car.

I guess we were beyond those kinds of pleasantries.

I grabbed my jacket and slipped it on, buttoning it all the way up, and walked outside.

The slamming door had such a hint of finality to it that I jumped.

It was ending.

Soon.

After the Session

"Shay?" I called, closing and locking the apartment door.

It was late. But it wasn't that late. She would still be up, primping, checking social networking sites, taking selfies.

But the apartment was suspiciously silent. Not even the sound from some random late-night show. I don't think I had ever walked into my apartment and found all the electronics and most of the lights off.

I kicked out of the heels that were making my ankles feel like they were about to splinter and hung up Shay's jacket on the back of the door.

Then I heard laughing, and Shay came dancing out of Jake's room, swatting his hands as he reached for her. And she wasn't exactly... dressed.

I looked down at the floor, clearing my throat.

The laughing stopped and I could swear I heard Jake curse under his breath.

"So *that's*... happening," I grumbled.

I could practically *hear* them looking at each other, having a silent conversation with their eyes.

"Ava," Jake's voice said, surprising me. I had expected Shay to step up. "It's nothing. It's..."

"Congratulations on the sex," I said, going into the bathroom and stripping.

It was going to be a three showers kind of day.

Things were going to be bad enough in a couple days when my therapy with Chase was over. One of two things was going to happen. Either I got over my transference right away, and felt a little bit embarrassed for being such a fool. Or it would linger and I would be feeling what I was feeling right then: hollow.

And on top of that, my roommates... the only two people in my life I had learned to trust and let in, were fucking around. Knowing them both as well as I did, I knew it was doomed to fail. The question wasn't *if*, it was *when*. Then what? I was in the middle? Trying to break up their fights, trying to reason with them? Being the bad guy who has to say 'you should have known better'?

Wonderful.

I was *totally* going to be in the mood for that.

"Look," Shay said, coming into the bathroom and slamming the door, making me jump and stare at the shower curtain like it was going to be pulled back at any moment. "Don't be getting your knickers in a bunch," she said and I could just picture the scowl she was giving me. "This was all your fault anyhow."

"Mine?" I exploded, peeking my head out from behind the

curtain. And there she was, still bare ass naked. And completely comfortable with it. "How the hell is it my fault you two are doing something so stupid?"

Her brow rose slightly at my choice of words. "You're the one who kept going on and on about how similar we are and shit."

"Which you took to mean 'you two should have sex'?"

"No, but I mean who would turn down the opportunity to play around with their twin in opposite sex form?"

"That sounded... awful."

"Alright. Whatever. You know what I meant."

"Well, I, for one, would have no interest in having sex with my male equivalent."

"Yeah, but only because you're in a unique situation. Shy girls are hot. Shy guys are boring as fuck."

I felt myself shrugging and slinking back behind the curtain. "Have you given any thought to how bad an idea this is?"

"Oh, please..."

"No, don't 'oh please' me. You live here now. He lives here. And I know you don't know him like I do, but he is a whore. No girl lasts more than a night."

"And who ever said I wanted more than that?" she asked, then paused. "Look, I'm a grown woman who has been around the block a few times. I can spot a man like Jake a mile away. I know exactly how he operates. That doesn't mean he wouldn't be worth a ride, ya know? Not all fuck buddies need to last a lifetime. Or even the weekend. We had fun."

"And you really think you're going to be able to walk around like nothing happened?"

"You know our delivery guy at work?"

"Yeah..."

"We used to fuck on every surface of that damn delivery van. You see us acting like a bunch of bitches over that shit?"

"No." In fact, they acted like polite strangers.

"Exactly."

"Alright," I said, sighing. "Fine."

"What's the matter with you?"

"Nothing. I'm fine."

"Don't," Shay said, her voice firm.

"Tomorrow is the ninth session," I said, turning the water to cold. "He's taking me out and teaching me to pick up guys at a bar."

"And you don't want to do that because you're in love with him."

"Fake love."

"Yeah, sure. Whatever you want to call it."

"Shay..." I said, my voice cracking slightly.

"I know," she said, her voice sounding soft. "Girl, I know. But you'll be alright. I'll be here."

I took a shaky breath. True. That was true. I had more than I ever had before. Even if I was losing what felt like everything. I wouldn't be alone again.

"I need a dress for tomorrow," I said, shivering against the frigid water. "Something like the one tonight."

"You've come to the right place," she mused, handing me a towel when I shut off the water. "How slutty do you want to take it?"

"Pretty damn slutty," I decided. If I was going to do it, I might as well do it up right. "But I'm not wearing those red bottoms ever again." In fact, they should have been burned. Anytime I saw them, I would think of my legs straight up in the air with Chase admiring the view.

"Shay," I said, the next evening standing in our bedroom, trying to make my voice sound reasonable. "Please tell me that is the shift, not the actual dress."

"A shift? What are you eighty? No one wears freaking shifts anymore. This is a dress. And it is designer, it ain't no cheap swatch of fabric from the club hoe store in the mall. You said you wanted slutty."

True. But apparently our views on what constituted slutty varied greatly. Because what she was holding looked like something someone would wear to the beach, not a club... in a very cold spell of fall.

It was black. And, essentially, just a bra and a super ridiculously short mini skirt with sheer black mesh connecting them.

"You can wear like semi-opaque stockings with them. But... I mean... full stockings. Thigh highs ain't gonna cut it. What club is he taking you to?"

"He didn't say."

"Well, I mean.. dressed like this, you can really get into anywhere good in the city. I've worn it a bunch of times. Plus, you'll stand out. Everyone is wearing those cut-out dresses now. Men like this peek-a-boo effect. They can see stuff, but not really see stuff. But with this one... they'll all want to unwrap you like a present."

"Alright, fine," I conceded, taking the dress from her.

"Nervous?"

"Yeah."

"When is the last time you talked to a random guy in a bar?"

Never. That would be never.

"I haven't."

"Shit. Well, it ain't that hard. Don't try to be someone you're not. Be you. But giggle more. Make eye contact. Touch them if they're close enough. Men can be a little dense on picking up on signals so you need to be a little obvious. Oh, and here..." she said, grabbing a pen and a piece of paper, scribbling something down.

"What is this?" I asked, looking down at the numbers.

"A phone number. Memorize it before you go out."

"Why?"

"To give to the guys you don't really want calling you. I'm sure your shrink will try to teach you how to let guys down gentle. But that shit don't work. So just give them this number instead and excuse yourself from them."

I nodded. That was a good idea. I couldn't see myself being able to reject people. I knew how awful that felt. "Whose number is this?"

"Oh," she said, laying out makeup on my desk, smiling wickedly, "my ex best friend from a few years back. Bitch stole my man right out from under me. She gets a lot of phone calls from random creepers. And, I'm sure, more than a few late night dick pics. Best revenge ever."

Shay pulled me to my computer chair, sitting me down, then going through the hour long process of getting me ready to go out. She went a little more crazy with the makeup than she had the last time, working tirelessly to get the perfect smokey eye. Which apparently took four tries. I had fake eyelashes applied and something called "all night spray" squirted all over my face so nothing smudged. A light shade of matte lipstick was put on my lips. Then she went through the process of straightening my hair.

"Aight," she said, standing back. "Club ready."

"I'm almost afraid to look," I said, smirking.

"It ain't that different. Your eyes just really pop now."

And she was right. The fake lashes (as weird as they felt)

looked great. And my face didn't look as caked on as it felt, just even. Foundation and powder would probably help with the blushing issue if it crept up.

"Get yourself dressed," Shay said, making her way to the door. "If you're not careful, you won't be ten minutes early."

"Ha ha," I said, squinting my eyes at her.

She was right.

I was always at least ten minutes early.

But I didn't want to be early. I wanted to be right on time. Or even a few minutes late. I didn't want to have to spend extra time alone with him. The car ride would be bad enough.

The dress slid on and I adjusted my boobs into the tight bodice that seemed intent on shoving them up as high as possible. The skirt was going to be the bane of my existence the entire night. I tried pulling the clingy material down, but it just slid right back up again. With a sigh, I sat down to strap myself into the black heels Shay had provided, tiny straps criss-crossing over the top of the feet and the heels not nearly as high as the ones from the night before.

"Are you decent?" Shay called, knocking on the door.

Not really, nope.

"Yeah," I called and the door opened.

"Dayum," she said, nodding. "That will do. Alright, here, let me spray you with some perfume."

"I have the stuff that Jake..."

"No," she said firmly, grabbing for one of her bottles. "Not that vanilla stuff. Not tonight. You need something with a little punch. Here," she said, spritzing the air, "walk through."

I did, wrinkling my nose slightly against the scent. I wasn't a huge fan of perfume to begin with and Shay's seemed to scream sex. "What is this?"

"Just a perfume... mixed with pheromones."

"Oh for God's sake," I groaned, shaking my head.

"Hey they'll come charging at you."

"Like deer in rutting season," I grumbled.

"What smells so good?" Jake asked, coming into the room, making Shay and I throw our heads back and laugh.

"Alright, you got this," Shay said, walking me to the door. I grabbed her coat from the night before, not willing to be walking around alone in glorified underwear. "You got the number memorized?"

"Yep."

"Aight. Try to have some fun with it, okay? This isn't just an assignment. It's practice for your dating filled- future," she said, handing me my wallet and keys.

My dating-filled future.

Oh, joy.

Ninth Session

Fake phone number rolling around my head on an endless reel, I walked quickly toward Chase's office, driven mostly by my desire to get the whole damn night over with as soon as possible.

I made it to his door five minutes after after seven, almost a little proud of myself for not freaking out about my punctuality. As soon I was in the door, there was Chase in a dark gray suit and white shirt.

"You're late."

"Yeah," I agreed, reaching to lock the door before I remembered it wasn't that kind of session.

"Good for you," he said, nodding. Oh, not the praise. Literally anything but the praise. "Let's see that dress, baby." Okay. Anything but the praise... *and* the endearments.

I reached for the buttons of the jacket, then pulled it off quickly. I was rewarded by the sound of his breath exhaling hard.

"Is this too much?" I asked, feeling uncertain. "Shay told me it would work for like... all the bars and clubs, but I am seriously starting to question her fashion sense."

His lips quirked up a bit as he moved across the room toward me. "It's a nice dress. But it looks extraordinary on you," he said, his hand going out to touch the mesh across my belly. He took a breath, his face crinkling up. "You don't smell like you."

It sounded like an insult.

"Shay's perfume," I supplied.

"Your eyes," he said, his voice almost sounding sad.

"Fake eyelashes. Apparently they make my eyes pop or something."

"They popped just fine on their own," he murmured, his hand moving to stroke my cheek.

I swallowed hard, trying to focus on anything but the feeling of his hand on my skin. "Should I take them off?" I asked, thinking of how weird it would be for my eyelids to not feel heavy anymore.

"No," he said, shaking his head, dropping his hand. "They're fine. Most guys will appreciate the effort."

Most guys.

Not him.

"So, um," I said, looking down at my feet, feeling a huge wave of insecurity, "where are we going?"

"You're nervous."

"Yeah."

"Why?"

"I've never been good with the whole... flirting thing."

"That's what I'm here for- to teach you."

Right. Patient/doctor. Keep those reminders coming.

"We're going to start at a restaurant. Get some food in your stomach to help with the anxiety..."

He was taking me to dinner?

My eyes shot up, curious.

"I'm assuming you have, once again, not eaten before coming here."

"No."

"Alright," he said, reaching behind me to pull the door open. "Let's go. It's getting late," he said.

Then he *didn't* put his hand at my lower back.

In fact, he didn't touch me at all. Not even by accident. He kept a safe space between us.

I sat in tense silence in his car, my heart starting to beat a little faster than usual in my chest. I held onto the door handle, crushing it into my palm, trying to focus on that and not how cold he was being. He swerved in and out of traffic, not even glancing my way once.

Then we were at the restaurant and he was opening my door, not even bothering to extend his hand to me to help me out. When I looked up at him, curious, he was pointedly looking away.

Okay.

So that was how it was.

Why the hell even bother to take me to dinner if he didn't even want to look my way? He could have easily just taken me to a club and gotten the God-awful session over with already. But, no, he had to drag it out. And not only did he need to drag it out, he needed to suddenly become another person while he was at it.

I got out of the car, trying to push the negative thoughts away. They weren't going to help. Looking up at the restaurant, my mouth fell open slightly and then I laughed, a full, rolling laugh, making me bend slightly forward, holding my belly. "Seriously?" I asked, looking up at him.

He was looking down at me, smiling wide, his eyes crinkling up at the edges. "Don't judge it by how it looks," he said, reaching out and putting a hand at my hip.

Okay. It was hard to not judge it by how it looked. Because how it looked was downright seedy. There were bright blue tables, awful faded, discolored white paint on the walls, and painfully fake looking foliage hanging from the ceiling. The people inside were all in jeans and t-shirts. And I was dressed like I was trying to find a sugar daddy.

There was a big wooden sign hanging over the door with the name of the establishment hand written poorly across it:

A Restaurant.

"So, what does A Restaurant serve?" I asked as he pushed me through the door. Chase let out a low snicker. "I don't trust that laugh," I said, watching his profile as we were told to 'just plant ourselves anywhere'.

He picked up two menus, walked us to a table in the back, and handed me mine to look over. As soon as I opened it, I knew what was so funny. "Really?" I asked, looking up over the top of my menu.

"Really," he said, smirking.

Apparently, my choices were : chicken, cow, pig, or green stuff.

"So is food poisoning a part of the plan or just an added benefit?"

Chase opened his mouth to answer, when a waitress walked over. She was tall and pretty, thick of thigh but small of waist with huge ice blue eyes. She was wearing a pair of hot pink leggings and a t-shirt that said 'Fuck Your Beauty Standards'.

"What do you want?"

I smiled again at Chase, shaking my head.

He shrugged. "Two chickens," he decided for us, handing

her the menus.

Then, without further conversation, the waitress walked away.

"Truly a charming little establishment," I observed, drinking my water.

"You'll understand when you try the food," he assured me. "So, Ava," he said, slipping back into his therapist tone effortlessly and I felt myself tense. "When was the last time you had a date?"

Oh, fun.

Let's pick at some old scabs.

Always a good way to get me in the mood to flirt with strangers.

"Over a year ago," I said simply. "Probably closer to two."

"How did that go? Where did you meet? Was it just one date?"

"Online dating site," I admitted, feeling a blush creep up. Was there anything more embarrassing to admit? "We went for dinner. It was forced and awkward."

"And?"

"And we went back to his place."

"Even though it felt forced and awkward?"

"Yeah."

"Why?"

Because I couldn't bring myself to say no.

I shrugged. "I figured I would give it another shot."

"It didn't go well."

It felt like I lost a little piece of myself in his bed. The little piece that was still willing to *try*.

"No."

"Ava..." he started in that tone. That tone that was half-scolding because I wasn't giving him what he wanted.

But by some wonderful coincidence, the food arrived, dropped down in front of us loudly. I dug right in, trying to make it clear I wasn't in the talking mood.

"No more online dating," he told me, making my head snap up.

"What? Why not?"

"Because it's too easy for you. You get to hide behind your computer screen and find the match who is the least threatening. You'll slip right back into your shell. You need to get out and experience things, Ava."

"Well," I said, uncomfortable. I felt like I was getting a lecture, not a lesson. "I am experiencing the best chicken I've ever had in my life," I said, gesturing toward my plate.

"Ava..."

"I don't want a lecture, Chase," I found myself snapping, surprising myself and Chase, whose brow lifted ever so slightly.

"I wasn't..."

"Yes," I said firmly, "you were. And you were being a condescending ass about it too."

"Good for you," he said, nodding.

"Good for me, what?"

"Standing up for yourself. Even if you're wrong," he said, smirking.

"I'm not wrong. I don't know what is up with you tonight, but you're kind of being a jerk and it's annoying."

"Annoying?"

"Yes. Annoying. And frustrating." I lowered my eyes at him. "Why are you smiling?"

"A couple weeks ago, do you think you would have been able to call me an ass, a jerk, annoying, and frustrating... to my face?"

Well, shit.

No.

"Probably not."

"Definitely not," he corrected.

"So... what? This was some kind of test?"

"Not really, no."

"So you're just in a foul mood for no good reason?"

He watched me for a long minute, his eyes intense, then looked down at his food. "I have a good reason, but it is inconsequential. Anyway," he said, pushing his plate away, all but uneaten, "we are going to Chaos from here."

I nodded, thinking about the long lines wrapped around the building and down the street, the thumping music I could hear in my car with rolled up windows as I passed, the endless parade of long legs in short skirts.

Yeah, I was *totally* going to fit in.

Suddenly, the chicken felt like lead inside and I pushed my plate away as well, taking a drink of water, then looking up at Chase. "I'm ready when you are."

He nodded, throwing money on the table, and getting up.

Ten minutes later, we were walking up to Chaos.

And I mean walked up to it. Passing all the people who had probably been on line for an hour, the girls dancing around and rubbing their bare arms to try to fend off the cold. Chase walked me right up to the doorman, saying something close to his ear, and then we were let in. Just like that.

The inside was packed. Immediately inside and downward was a dance floor and to both sides of the room were staircases that led up, one open to the public and leading to a bar, one private with a security guard at the bottom.

I was led to the private one, the security guard inclining his head to Chase and offering me a small smile as I moved past him to climb the steps. The music was thumping so hard, I could feel it through the soles of my feet and upward.

The area in the private lounge was spacious and, blessedly, not crowded. A few men sat at tables with several attractive (no doubt considering themselves lucky) women accompanying them.

Chase led me to the bar, ordering a scotch for himself and a martini for me. Then I was instructed to sit at the bar and wait.

For what... I wasn't told.

So, I sat and waited.

Listening to the music, ignoring the eye-contact some guy at the far end of the bar was trying to give me.

Then Chase slid in beside me, turning in his seat so his legs blocked me in. "Hi," he said simply and I felt my brows drawing together.

"Hi..." I said back, eyeing him.

"My name's Chase," he said, holding out his hand.

Oh.

So we were doing that.

Okay.

I could play along.

Sort of.

"I'm Alexandra Feodorovna," I said, smiling sweetly.

Chase's eyes flashed for a second, a smile tugging at his lips. Then, without missing a beat, he nodded, "You look damn good for someone who died by firing squad almost a hundred years ago."

"I moisturize," I nodded and he burst out laughing.

"This isn't going to work if you don't take it seriously," he said after a minute.

"Sorry. It just... feels weird."

"What does? Flirting with me? Baby, I've been inside you."

Oh,

lord

Jesus.

Okay.

My lady bits needed to give it a rest. One sentence from him and I felt like I was ready to drag him into the bathroom and have my way with him.

"Sorry," he smirked, "I didn't mean to get you all hot and

bothered."

"I'm not," I insisted, trying to save at least a shred of my pride.

"Really?" he asked, his hand landing really high up on my thigh. "I could... check that out for you. Just to make sure."

I really, *really* wanted him to check.

And, damn him, he knew it.

His fingers toyed with the hem of my skirt which was indecently high when I was sitting down. One of his fingers slipped upward and almost made contact with my panties.

I nearly fell off the seat.

"Okay," he said, sitting back, shaking his head like he was trying to clear it. "Sorry. I'll stop."

"I don't want you to stop."

Oh, my God.

I didn't sat that.

No way.

His eyes darkened, leaning closer, his mouth by my ear. "Believe me, babe, I don't want to stop either. I want to drag you out of here, throw you into my car, and watch you ride me until you're screaming my name."

Okay.

Wow.

I pressed my thighs together hard, taking a deep breath.

"But I can't do that. Tonight, you aren't mine to have."

Right.

I was a public fucking commodity.

I sat up straight, moving away from him.

And I was never really his. Not the way I wanted to be.

Game face on.

"Okay. So, what now? You're leaving?"

"No. I'll be here. If you need me, come get me. Or call me. I'll keep an eye on you."

So much for my flirt training.

"If someone is really bothering you..."

"I got it, Chase."

"Ava..."

I stood up, grabbing my martini. "I said I got it," I said, walking over to the railing and looking down at the dance floor below, bodies writhing. Women were in small circles, dancing sexually to attract the attention of men, whether they would admit it or not. Then there were men and women, their bodies moving together like an archaic mating ritual. The entire building was oozing sex.

From the corner of my eye, I could see Chase. He had moved to the far end of the bar, swirling his drink, occasionally glancing my way.

It wasn't long until I felt someone move in beside me, blocking out my view of Chase. I looked upward, taking in the fitted blue suit, the white shirt, the dark blue striped tie, then finally his face. He was good looking. Tall. Towering over me even in my heels. His face was broad of jaw with a strong forehead, with short dirty blond hair, and kind brown eyes.

"You with that guy?" he asked, tilting his head in Chase's direction.

Technically, yes.

But, at the same time, completely and utterly... no.

"No," I said, giving him, what I hoped was, a charming smile.

"So I can ask you to dance?"

Oh, God.

Not dancing.

Anything but dancing.

"Sure," I smiled, taking Shay's advice and touching his hand which was next to mine on the railing. I brought my drink up and drained it, hoping some of the liquid bravery would hit me before we got to the dance floor.

"I'm Trip, by the way. I know," he said, smiling easily, "it's a ridiculous name."

"I'm Ava," I supplied, feeling the knot in my belly loosen a little. It wasn't that bad. If that was all there was to flirting, I could totally handle it.

I ducked my head as I turned, not wanting to make eye contact with Chase for numerous reasons as Trip put a hand on my hip, steering me through the lounge and toward the stairs.

We pushed through the edge of the crowd until we were somewhere near the center and, unable to help myself, I lifted my head to look back toward the lounge. Just as another woman, blonde, pretty, breasts all but spilling out of her dress, walked up to Chase, placing a hand on his shoulder and whispering in his ear. Chase turned, tilting his head up toward her, and smiled a megawatt smile I had only gotten to see less than a handful of times.

So that was the way it was.

I felt the quick, nauseating stab of pain accompanied by the twisting sensation of jealousy. My eyes dropped, looking up at Trip.

Well, fuck Chase.

And fuck his rules.

I was three drinks in an hour later, inhibitions low, as I pressed my body into Trip's, his arms going around my back. Way too tight. And if I wasn't dealing with a nice buzz making my skin feel tingly and foreign, I would have pushed him away, freaked out and ran, anything other than sink into it.

"You're so gorgeous," Trip murmured close to my ear.

"Thank you," I said, swaying my hips against him.

"Ava."

Chase.

His voice was the equivalent of having a bucket of ice water dropped on me. Sober. I was suddenly so incredibly sober it was ridiculous.

I felt myself stiffen, moving to put space between me and Trip.

"She said she ain't with you, bud," Trip said over my shoulder, looking like he was ready to defend my honor if he needed to. Which was sweet. I would have realized how sweet it was if Chase wasn't right behind me, no doubt completely disapproving of my behavior and giving me one of those *looks* of his.

"She was mistaken," Chase said, his voice cool. "Ava... it's time to go."

I felt my spine straighten. "No, I think I'm good here, Chase. Thanks for your concern. You may leave without me," I said, not turning around.

"Ava..."

"I said go, Chase."

And then he did.

I entertained the idea of Trip for a while, trying to push past the growing knot of anxiety inside. But soon his arms felt like a prison; his cologne smelled overpowering; the collective energy of the crowd felt stifling. And I couldn't breathe.

"You alright?" Trip asked, watching as my hand went to my throat, as my eyes got wide and panicked.

"I... I have to go..." I said, turning.

His arm closed around my arm, pulling me back, making a rush of panic rise hysterically in my throat. "Wait. How can I get in touch with you?"

I swallowed hard against the knot in my stomach as he pulled out his phone, trying to pull away gently, but his hand was like a vice. I mumbled off the number of Shay's disloyal best friend, which made him smile, wretched my arm away, and ran.

I burst out of the front doors what felt like forever later, having to push through the crushing throngs of people inside to get to the exit.

The air outside hit me, cold and comforting as I stumbled in the opposite direction of the line of people waiting to get inside.

"Ava..."

My head snapped up, looking around and finding Chase leaning against the wall of the club, looking tired. His eyes fell on my face, softening immediately. "Hey... babe..."

Why did he have to be so fucking nice?

I mean, even after being a jerk.

It wasn't right.

It was causing all kinds of conflicting feelings inside.

And I wasn't in any condition to fight them.

So they surfaced. Through the panic. Tears blurred my eyes and I turned away again, walking in the other direction, away from him.

His arm wrapped around my hips before I had even taken two steps, turning me, steering me away from the crowd. "It's alright," he murmured, close to my ear as I blindly followed him as he moved me around the building. "Take a breath, Ava," he instructed and I tried, but it got caught in my throat. "Hey," he said, stopping, grabbing my face and pressing me against the back of the club, "look at me." My eyes slid up slowly. "Breathe." I sucked in a shaky breath, feeling like sulfur, burning my nose and throat. "You're okay," he said, his eyes willing me to believe him. "I'm right here."

The tears slipped over and I leaned forward, resting my head against my spot, taking another breath, breathing him in. His arms went slowly around me, hesitant to trap me. But the effect was like a tranquilizer to my system. Like a warm blanket over my brain.

I blinked the tears furiously away, more angry at myself than I had been in a long time. Giving myself a panic attack because I was trying to be spiteful was so incredibly immature.

And the plan backfired in the worst way possible, not only did I freak out and run away, but I broke down in front of Chase. Again. I clung to Chase. Again. I let Chase fix me. Again.

    I needed to learn to fix myself.

    He wasn't going to be around.

    I couldn't run to him anymore.

    I needed to stop leaning on him.

    I straightened, pulling away, wiping my cheeks before I looked up.

    "You alright, baby?"

    "Yeah, I ... it was too crowded and loud and hot. I... couldn't fight it anymore."

    "You should have left with me."

    I took a breath, dropping my eyes to his collar because I couldn't lie to his face. "I was having a good time."

    I saw the muscle in his jaw start to tick again. "What did you say to your... friend?"

    "I gave him a fake number and just... ran."

    "A fake number, huh?" he asked, sounding almost amused. "I'm assuming that way Shay's idea."

    "Yeah. It's the number of someone she hates."

    Chase snorted, reaching up and slipping out of his jacket, placing it around my shoulders. "She's got a good head on her shoulders."

    "Yeah, except she's sleeping with Jake," I said, shocking myself.

    "They'll probably be good together," he said, putting a hand at my hip and leading me back toward his car.

    "They're not together. They're just sleeping together."

    "Sure about that?" he asked, giving me a knowing smirk. "Those two will be dating in under a week, mark my words."

    "I thought you were a sexologist, not a love expert," I said, cursing myself when his eyes got guarded. I always said the wrong thing.

"True," he said in a clipped tone, opening my door for me then sliding into the driver's seat. Then we drove in silence again until we pulled up next to my car in the garage. "We have our final session on Monday."

"I know," I said, looking at my hands.

"Seven."

"As always," I said, getting out of the car.

As always, but for the last time.

After the Session

I cried. A lot. Then hated myself for it even more. It was a fun weekend.

Tenth Session

    We never discussed what our final session would be. And I had spent my weekend debating my options. I could pick any one of our sessions: kissing and holding each other, chaste naked touching, mutual masturbation, fingering and hand jobs, oral sex, sex, toys, anal sex.

    I considered each and every one of them.

    Because I wanted him to kiss me again. Like we were waiting for the world to end. Like it was the last thing we would ever do. I wanted him to look at my naked body with the wonder of the first time. I wanted him to watch me touch myself, to watch him bring himself to orgasm. I wanted his fingers inside me, and to feel his cock in my hand. I wanted his face between my thighs and I wanted his cock in my mouth, to taste his desire. And, God, I wanted him inside me. I wanted him inside me with a need that was painful, both physically and emotionally.

I wanted him in every position.
I wanted him soft and sweet and loving.
I wanted him fast and rough and wild.
I just... wanted him.
I wanted him so badly.

In the end, sitting at the edge of my bed on Monday after work, I decided to skip them all. I decided to make it a clean break. I needed to move on. It would be easier to do so when things had been strained for the past few sessions. It would make walking away from him hurt a little less. And by "a little less" I meant... not the soul crushing ache inside I had been dealing with non-stop for days.

I showered, towel dried my hair, skipped the makeup, and slipped into a pair of dark skinny jeans and a pale pink sweater. I sprayed on Jake's perfume. And I felt more like myself than I had for a while in all those skimpy dresses and too much makeup.

"You don't have to go," Shay said, sitting on the couch, watching me.

"Yes, I do."

"Do you really think you are going to get closure by doing this?"

I grabbed my keys off the table, shaking my head. "No."

"Then why go?"

I took a breath, looking up at her. "To prove to myself that I can."

I let myself into his office and locked the door, but Chase was nowhere in sight. I took a few steps in, glancing around, checking the time to make sure I wasn't super early. But I was right on time. And he was always waiting. I moved toward his open office door, about to call out his name, when I saw him.

He was sitting in the chair he had sat in during our introductory session, his jacket off, his white shirt looking wrinkled. He had his head resting in his hand, a scotch in his other, resting on his outstretched leg.

And he just looked so... lost.

I had never really stopped to consider the toll his job must have taken on him. Not so much the surrogacy, but the therapy. Having to hear everyone's horror stories, helping when you can, knowing that sometimes you couldn't. It must have always felt like a weight on the shoulders. And that was what he seemed like, his shoulders down- weighted.

"Chase..." I said softly.

He didn't start. He simply turned his head slowly toward me. "Is it seven already?" he asked, his eyes small and tired-looking.

"Yeah," I said, stepping into the room, moving toward him. "Are you okay?"

He gave me a small smile that didn't reach his eyes. "That's my question."

"Well, I'm borrowing it," I said, sitting down across from him.

He chuckled, setting his scotch down. "Do you want a drink?"

"No, thanks. I'm good on the alcohol front for a while."

He ran a hand across his brow, looking at me. "You look

better."

"Better?" I asked, scrunching my brows together.

"Yeah, I don't know... more like yourself." He paused, shrugging. "You're beautiful."

There it was.

I swallowed, looking down at my hands as the blush crept up. "Thank you."

"I figured you wanted a talk therapy session," he said, waving a hand out.

"Yeah, I... yeah," I said dumbly, cursing myself. "How does this go?"

He waved a hand. "We can talk about anything you want. How you think therapy went. Any concerns you have for the future..."

"How do you think therapy went?" I asked, worrying my hands together slightly.

The air in his office felt thick. Depressing. Like he had breathed it out and it stitched itself into every fabric and surface in the room.

He sat up slowly, leaning his elbows on his knees toward me. "Ava, you did so much better than I had anticipated."

"Yeah?"

"Yeah, baby," he said, wincing slightly. "Yes," he said a little more firmly. "I really wasn't sure we would finish the sessions in the allotted amount of time. You were so withdrawn and timid and then you just... is blossomed too cliché a word?"

No. It was just right.

But I only blossomed because of him.

He was the gracious Sun. Me, the ungrateful Earth.

"Chase, I can't thank..."

"Don't," he said, his words heavy. "Don't thank me, Ava."

A silence hung then, long and full of words needing to be said.

"Ava," he said finally, making me jump. "Can you come here for a second?" he asked, holding an arm out.

I wasn't exactly sure what he was asking, but I got to my feet and stepped closer. His hand reached out and touched my arm, pulling slightly. "Closer," he said, sitting back in his chair. With my feet touching the feet of the chair, there was no way to get closer but to move into his lap. When I looked up, questioningly, his other arm reached out for me.

And my first thought was: no.

It was what I had been convincing myself shouldn't happen. It wasn't the clean break I said I needed.

But it was everything I wanted.

So I slid onto his lap and his arms went around me, pulling me close. I rested my head on his chest, his cheek coming down on top of my hair.

And he just... held me.

I closed my eyes, listening to his heartbeat, steady, sure. His arms pulled me tighter and I carefully planted a kiss over his shirt, too soft for him to feel it.

For me, that was therapy.

His touch was a remedy. It was a cure.

A long time later, his hands drifted up and into my hair, stroking through it gently, tirelessly, as the clock ticked the better part of an hour away.

"Chase..."

"Yeah, baby?"

What could I say? What was left?

I sighed, shaking my head slightly. "You made me so much better."

"No, babe. You made yourself better. I just helped you along."

"Geez, learn to take a compliment, would you?" I asked and was rewarded with a small chuckle.

"You're amazing, Ava. Don't ever let anyone try to convince you otherwise. Promise me that."

That was a tall order.

"I'll try."

"Not good enough," he said, kissing my hair. "Try again."

I snorted, smiling a little. Bossy Chase. "Okay. I'll *really* try."

"You're impossible," he said and I could imagine the eye roll I was getting. "In the future, when you are with someone and..."

"The moment," I cut in, surprising myself.

"I'm sorry?" Chase asked, his hands stilling.

I tilted my head up slightly to look at his face. "Someone once told me to be in the moment," I explained. "I think that was pretty good advice," I said, resting my head back against my safe place. I wanted to suck up every last bit of the feeling it gave me, to keep stored away, to bring out when I was lonely and sad and anxious.

I had a feeling there were a lot of those days ahead.

"Okay," he said, and we stayed there, in that silent moment.

Until I drifted off.

Then woke up with a jolt out of a bad dream.

"Hey," Chase's voice said, gruff, like he had been sleeping too. "You alright?"

"Dream," I said, pushing myself up. I checked the clock then quickly got to my feet. I needed to go. The session was over. It was done. It was over. And I needed to leave. Before I kinda... lost it. Which was what I felt on the verge of doing.

"Where are you going?"

"It's almost one," I said, searching for my keys and wallet.

"So what?" he asked, sitting forward.

"I just... it's time to go," I said, turning.

He looked away from me, reaching for his scotch and finishing it in one gulp. "I'll walk you to your car."

"No," I said, too quickly. "No, I'm fine. Stay here. Relax. You look... tired." Which wasn't quite right. It wasn't tired, but I needed to stop looking at him.

"Ava..."

"Thank you, Chase," I said, walking stiffly toward the door and closing it behind me.

I leaned against it for a long moment, looking for the strength to move forward, not go back. I turned, putting my hand against the wood as if I could feel him through it, taking a deep breath... then walking out of his office.

After the Session

<u>Ten Minutes</u>

I managed to keep it together until I got home, opening the door, and falling into Shay's waiting arms. Crying. No... sobbing.

Big, ugly, snot-filled hysterics. And she just stood there and let it run through me. Then walked me to my bed, opening the blankets, and letting me bury inside.

"I'm right here," she said, crawling into the foot of the bed and lying there, "if you need anything, okay?"

<u>Seven Hours</u>

"Seriously, go back to bed," Jake said, looking at my face with a mix of sympathy and disgust. I knew it was bad. I was tear-stained and blotchy. My eyes felt like planets.

"I'm going to work," I said, grabbing an ice pack out of the freezer, wrapping it in a paper towel, and pressing it against my eyes.

"Ava, I'll tell them you're sick," Shay reasoned.

"I've been out twice already. And I need the distraction."

"Still sick with that fake love shit, huh?" Jake asked in typical unfeeling male fashion.

I half-snorted, half-laughed. "I'm not sure it just goes away right away."

"Unless it ain't no transference," Shay supplied.

"What else could it be?" Jake asked.

"She's fucking in love with him, you idiot," Shay said, tapping her heel on the floor.

"It's fak..."

"It ain't fake. The only person who believes that is you."

"And Dr. Bowler," I said, pulling the ice off my eyes.

"Dr. Bowler doesn't know shit then. Because this is love. Straight up, can't eat without them, can't sleep without them love. And it isn't going away. Especially if you keep acting like it ain't what it is."

I shook my head, putting the ice pack away. "We are going to be late," I insisted, making my way to the door.

"You're not even going to think about it?"

"No," I said, finally. She just didn't understand.

It was transference.

And it was going to pass.

Three Days

"Come on, look at all this food," Jake said in the tone like he was trying to trick a dog into eating a piece of lunch meat with a pill wrapped in it.

"I'm not hungry," I grumbled, burying deeper into my robe, turning the volume on the TV up.

"You've said that for like every meal for days."

"And it's been true for every meal for days," I said, the thought of food making my mouth dry up and my stomach turn.

It wasn't getting better.

I was trying to ignore Shay's constant nagging at me to stop being in denial. To admit that I had real, genuine, normal, woman-for-man feelings for Chase.

When that failed, she insisted I set up an appointment for Dr. Bowler because she 'wasn't going to sit around and watch me be a little bitch' about my feelings forever.

So I called.

And I had an appointment for the next afternoon on my lunch break. An appointment I was looking forward to because I needed the reassurance. Especially after three days and absolutely no lessening of the dark pit inside.

<u>Four Days</u>

"Ava, how have..." she trailed off, stepping aside and waiting for me to join her in her office. "What happened?"

My head jerked slightly. "I, um... I ended therapy, remember?"

"When?"

"Monday."

"Why didn't you call me sooner?"

"I was just... dealing with all these... residual feelings and I wasn't really feeling up to talking yet."

"How did your last few sessions go?"

Horribly.

Then great.

Then over.

"Not great. Things were cold. Some... distance I guess. On both our parts. I was trying to, you know, keep myself together. I knew it was ending and I was struggling with that."

"May I ask, and you do not need to answer, what you did on your last visit?"

I nodded, looking down at my hands. "I guess it started with a little talk therapy, but it felt weird. Kind of forced and awkward. And then he..."

"He did what?"

"He asked me to come over and sit on his lap. So I did. And we just... sat there like that for... I don't know... hours."

"Ava," she said, in a tone I knew not to trust. Something was coming. Something I probably didn't want to hear. "I'm not... entirely convinced this is a case of transference."

"What?" I asked, my eyes shooting up to her face.

No.

That wasn't possible.

It had to be.

She held up a hand. "Transference is usually a pretty cut-and-dry thing for doctors to recognize. Because it is so one-sided. One person is bared to the other and one is completely closed off. With sexual surrogacy, that isn't exactly the case. You are both vulnerable. You are both exposed in a very literal, but also figurative, way. Maybe what you feel is genuine, Ava. Maybe you have feelings for Chase Hudson."

I closed my eyes, exhaling hard.

I think a part of me knew.

I think that was why I had been clinging to the idea of transference so hard. As an excuse. As an explanation. So I didn't have to take responsibility.

"Ava..."

"I know," I said, my voice quiet. "I think I've always known."

"What are you thinking?"

I rolled my eyes. "That there is nothing as pathetic as unrequited love," I said, smiling a little.

Of course I would fall in love with my therapist. It was completely inappropriate and needy and co-dependent.

How like me.

"Ava, maybe you should talk to Dr. Hudson about..."

"No," I said, firmly. "No," I added again. "That chapter is over. I'm not dragging him back into my mess. This is my problem. I need to learn to fix it myself. I can't keep leaning on him. It isn't right."

"Did you ever stop to consider..."

"Consider what?"

"That maybe the feelings..."

"No," I said, loudly enough for Dr. Bowler to start. "Sorry," I said, shaking my head. I just... I couldn't let that false hope into my bruised little heart. It wouldn't help. It had been days. Chase could have called. He could have shown up. But he didn't. Because I was just a client. That was all. One of many. Nothing special.

"Okay," she shrugged. "I know right now, this seems impossible and like I am just feeding you platitudes," she said, smiling a little, "but this will fade. I know it doesn't seem like it. And that this is such a unique situation because Chase gave you things that no man has ever been able to before. That feels like a insurmountable thing to get through. But now that you know you are capable of having those kinds of connections with men, you can eventually have that again."

No. Not really.

Nothing would ever be like that.

But something could come in second place.

Something could be almost the same.

And I would just have to learn to feel like that was enough.

"Why don't we consider going back to twice weekly, or at the very least, weekly appointments for a while? Just until you are feeling better?"

"Sure," I said, giving her a very small, very false smile. But it was the best I could muster. "That is probably a good idea."

If nothing else, it would appease Jake and Shay.

Jake and Shay who were, like Chase had predicted, *together* together.

Which made them get together and gang up on me about my wallowing.

Stupid happy couples.

Seven Days

I would like to say something upbeat about moving on. About how it aches and eases as everything heals. How it sounds quietly sad, yet hopeful... like hymns sung by a solemn choir. But it sounds more like worlds falling apart. It feels like walls being built stronger around your heart.

It is all grit and determination. It was the small voice that screams through the urge to curl up in bed all day and cry and tells you to get up, get dressed, eat, go to work, get shit done. To not let it swallow you up. To not let it become all there is to you.

So, after a few days, I listened to it. I went through the motions. I did what needed to get done. I had dinners with Jake or Shay or both of them.

Then I would get into bed, setting the alarm on my phone, and let it all out for twenty minutes. Twenty. Not a second more. Then I got up and wiped all the evidence of it away.

I tried.

And that was all that could be expected of me.

"Hmm," I said, sitting at my computer, looking at my bank account online.

"What?" Shay asked, leaning over her leg to paint her toenails.

"My money is still here."

"What money?"

"My three thousand dollars for... my therapy."

Shay looked up, her brows drawn together. "That's weird. Call the office. See if they messed up or something."

I nodded, taking a deep breath and picking up the phone, hoping I would catch the receptionist before she left for the day. Because if it was Chase...

"Dr. Hudson's office," the voice said, sounding a little frazzled.

"Hi, this is Ava Davis. I have a question regarding a payment I made last week."

"Sure. Davis, you said?"

"Yes."

There was the muffled sound of clicking, then a pause. "Ava?"

"Yes."

"That bill has been canceled."

"Canceled? Why?"

"It doesn't say. Dr. Hudson is in with a patient right now, would you like me to leave a note for him to get back to you?"

"No," I said quickly. "Thank you."

"Have a good night!"

I hung up, staring down at my phone for a second.

"What did they say?"

"That the bill was canceled."

"Canceled?" she asked, putting her polish wand back in the bottle and screwing it.

"Yeah."

"Shiiiit, girl," she said, shaking her head.

"What?"

"Seriously?" she asked, rolling her eyes. "You know what? I ain't even gonna tell you," she said, walking out into the living room. But I knew where she was going. To Jake's room. She hadn't spent a night in our room in days.

I sighed, running a hand through my hair.

He couldn't just... not accept payment.

That was ridiculous.

He offered a service. I used such service. He needed to be paid.

Before I could talk myself out of it, I slipped into my shoes, grabbed my wallet and keys, and left the apartment.

Then went straight to the bank. If I was quick enough, I could get there before the top of the hour. When he would be done with his patient. I got my three thousand dollars, tucked discreetly into a plain white money envelope, and made my way to the garage, parking, and hauling ass to the front door.

My heart was hammering in my chest as I tiptoed across the floor, as if the sound of my flats could rouse the people behind a closed door. I was trying my damndest to not think about where I was. About what had taken place all around me. By the door. In his office. In the bedroom. Every inch of the place felt etched with a memory.

I reached out to put the envelope with his name down, and the door burst open.

"Thank you so much, Dr. Hudson," a woman's voice said and my head snapped over. And there was the blonde from the club. Different outside of the tight dress and makeup, but still pretty. She was looking over at Chase, whose eyes were focused on me.

"Ava?"

The woman's face looked at me, then back at Chase, her eyes brightening as a smile toyed with her lips. "I will see you next week," she said to him, giving me another quick glance as she made her way to the door.

I watched her dumbly for a few seconds, before shaking my head, dropping the envelope, and starting to make my way to the door.

"What is this?" Chase said, too quickly for me to claim I

hadn't heard him, I was barely a few feet away.

I took a breath and turned. "That," I said, my tone a little sharp, "is your payment. Which was apparently and, I assume... *mistakenly*, canceled."

God, why did he look so perfect? Literally. Head to toe male perfection.

Black suit, white shirt, one button.

"You were just going to leave three thousand dollars in cash on the reception desk?"

"You always seem to be... the last one out. I figured you would find it first. But yeah. So, now you have it. And, I'm... I'm gonna go."

"Ava," he said as I turned, making me freeze. My name always sounded way too good on his lips. "It wasn't a mistake."

I turned slowly. "What?"

"It wasn't a mistake. I am not billing you."

That made absolutely no sense.

None.

Unless...

No. Nope. Not going there.

I needed to keep those hopes and pipe dreams squashed.

"Why not?"

Chase sighed, running a hand down his face. "I need a drink," he said, turning and going in through his office.

And, damn it, there was no fighting following him.

I walked into the room, keeping my eyes on the sidebar and no where else. I was absolutely not thinking about all the ways he had touched me on the couch and the bed. Nope.

"Here," he said, handing me a martini I hadn't asked for.

He threw back his scotch and put his glass down.

"Can you come sit down with me for a minute?"

I eyed the couch almost suspiciously, nodding. I chugged my drink and followed him over, sitting down with a cushion between us.

"I'm not billing you," he said, watching me.

"You said that. You haven't said why."

"Fuck," he said, rubbing his brow. He looked up, about to say something, but his eyes squinted, like he was really seeing me for the first time since I walked in. "Have you been crying?"

Not that day. Not yet.

But there was no way to say no to that question.

"Chase, answer my question."

"Answer mine."

I sighed. There was no arguing with him. "Not today," I said.

"Why were you crying at all?"

"You already had your question."

"You're impossible," he said, shaking his head. "Ava... it would be wrong to bill you for those sessions."

"How would it be wrong? You did what you were supposed to do."

"Yes and no."

"How no?"

"Because I pushed the lines of professionalism."

"What because you like... went to my apartment? Or fed me?"

"Yes, those things but..."

"But what?"

He gave me a smile, shaking his head. "Tell me why you were crying first."

No.

God no.

Anything but that.

I hung my head, my hair falling forward like a curtain. "Chase..."

"Baby, tell me..." he said, his hand landing on my thigh.

Maybe it was the 'baby'. Or the hand on my thigh. Or his

refusal to let me pull back into myself... but I didn't want to lie.

"Do you remember when I was drunk and you came over and I started blabbering about Dr. Bowler?"

"Something about something being fake. But maybe not. But maybe yes. You were pretty wasted."

I sucked in a breath, looking at his hand on my knee. "Yeah."

"What was Dr. Bowler right and wrong about?"

Okay. I could do it. Be a big girl and spit it out. I mean... what harm could it do? I was already suffering.

"I went to see her about my sessions with you..."

"That was a good idea."

"Yeah, well. I went to see her because I was... having some issues."

"With our sessions?" he asked, his eyes looking almost sad. "Babe... why didn't you tell me?"

"Because I wasn't sure if what I was experiencing was what I thought it was. Dr. Bowler... well, she confirmed it."

"Confirmed what?" he asked, his hand squeezing my knee harder.

"That I had transference."

There.

It was out.

Sort of.

Half of it was out.

His blue eyes flashed. "Transference. You thought you were having transference?"

"Yeah," I said, swallowing. "But, um, it turns out I wasn't."

"Baby... what are you trying to say here?"

Okay.

Time to spit it out.

"I didn't have transference. I... I was in love with you."

He looked stricken.

His eyes got wide, his mouth opened slightly, his hand

stopped squeezing my knee. He swallowed hard once, looking down for a second, before his eyes found mine again. "Was?"

"Am," I said, shrugging.

"You're in love with me?"

"Yes."

"*Fuck* me," he said, closing his eyes slightly. "*Fuck me*..."

"Chase..."

He needed to say something other than that. I couldn't even tell what that meant. Was it surprise? Anger? What?

His eyes opened slowly. "I couldn't bill you, baby... because this wasn't therapy."

"What?" I asked, my brows drawing together.

"I mean... we followed the schedule, but it wasn't therapy."

"What was it then?"

"It was... *courting*. It was genuine attraction and mutual feelings and..."

"Mutual feelings?" I asked, feeling a tiny light flick on inside of me. On a switch I swear I had disconnected.

"Baby... fuck," he said, taking both of his hands and raking them down his face. "I knew the second I saw you sitting on my couch that first day that this was different. This wasn't a job. I wanted you. I wanted you more than I have ever wanted anyone. And just how you were. Shy and modest and anxiety ridden. I wanted that girl. And then... when you started coming out of your shell around me, letting down your guards, letting me in... I wanted you even more. Every moment with you was like the first time. It was real, Ava. It was real for me. It wasn't work."

"Chase... what are..."

"I love you, Ava," he said, shutting me up. His hands moved out, cradling my face. "I have never loved anyone. No one. I wasn't even sure I knew what it was until I found you."

Oh, my God.

Seriously... *oh my God*.

Then, because it was the only thing to be said, I whispered back, "I love you too, Chase."

His eyes closed on an inhale. "I never thought I was going to get to hear that. I thought..." he shook his head. "There was a time when I had hope that you felt the same way."

"When?"

"Anytime I touched you. When you kissed me. When you dressed up for me. When you said my chest was your spot. When you called it the safest place in the world... but I didn't let myself think... or hope... that it was true."

"It was true," I said, giving him a small smile.

"When did you know?"

"Around the fourth session. I thought... I thought it was a crush. And then I was sure it was transference. So I spent all my time making sure I understood that you..."

"That I what?"

"Saw me as a patient."

"Never," he said passionately, shaking his head. "Not once. Not for a moment."

And then I was reaching for him, pulling him toward me, leaning into his hand as he stroked my cheek, bringing his lips to mine and kissing him with all the feeling I had been trying to repress for so long, with every moment of soaring love, and crashing devastation. With everything inside of me.

His arms went around me, pulling me close, onto his body, then up, pulling me with him toward the bed. He placed me down, pulling his face from mine just long enough to pull my shirt over my head. My hands went between us, tugging at his buttons until they came lose, then running my hands up his strong center, sliding the shirt and jacket off his shoulders.

He broke off the kiss, reaching down to undo his belt, then slip out of his pants and boxer briefs, standing there perfectly naked.

And all I could think was : mine. He was all mine.

I slid back onto the pillows, his body coming over mine, pulling my pants and panties down over my hips, thighs, ankles. His hand ran down the center of my body, watching so intently it was intimidating. "I missed you," he said, looking up into my eyes. "Every day. Every hour. You were all I could think about."

"You too," I admitted. Even when I was trying to not think about him, he was still the dominant thought. No matter what I did.

"So beautiful," he said, leaning down and pressing a kiss between my breasts before shifting and taking my nipple into his mouth, flicking his tongue over it and then taking it and sucking. My hips rose up off the bed, pressing into his cock as he moved across my chest to continue the torment.

He moved back between them, kissing a line downward.

My hands reached out, grabbing his head, and pulling him up. His brows furrowed. "No?"

"No," I said, my voice airy. I noticed his face fall slightly, then the look quickly got pushed away. Patient. But I didn't want patience. I wanted him. "I need you inside me," I said, my legs going up around his hips, pulling him closer. "Now."

"*Fuck* me," he said, bracing his forearms on my sides and resting his forehead to mine for a second.

"Chase, now... please..." I groaned, my desire a hot, twisting need deep in my core.

He shifted his hips and I felt his cock slide between my folds, making me arch up and groan.

"Fuck... so sweet," he groaned, reaching between us and bringing his cock to my slick entrance. "So wet for me."

"Always," I admitted, my eyes heavy as felt him start to press inside me.

"God, I like hearing that," he said leaning down and biting into my lip.

Unable to take the slow torment, my hands moved down his back, grabbing his hips, and pulling him against me, feeling his cock bury deep.

"Fuck," he groaned, closing his eyes. "You feel so good, but baby..."

"It's okay," I said, reaching up to stroke the hair out of his face. We didn't need condoms. We never really did. And I never wanted anything between us ever again.

"You're sure?"

"About ninety-nine point nine percent," I said, wrapping my arms around him. "I want to really feel you," I said, kissing his chin.

His eyes closed as he started rocking his hips into mine. "My baby is so fucking perfect," he murmured, his slow pace sweet and gentle.

But soon, neither of us could take it. Our bodies had been without each other for too long and were too desperate and soon he was thrusting into me: hard, wild, raw. And my hips rose to meet him, drawing him in, driving us both upward.

"Chase..." I gasped, feeling my orgasm crest then crash hard, my muscles pulsating around him.

"Oh, come for me baby," he growled, thrusting hard, then burying deep, his body tense as he came hard. "Fuck..."

"I love you," I said, close to his ear as I felt him come deep inside me.

"Fuck, I love you too," he said, his body jerking.

His weight came down on me for a moment before he grabbed me and rolled us to our sides, our bodies still joined.

His hand went out, stroking the side of my cheek. "I'm done with this," he said softly.

"With what?"

"This," he said, gesturing out to the room. "As of an hour ago. I don't ever want to touch anyone else. I don't think I've ever truly helped anyone until you anyway."

"Chase..."

"I'll keep my practice. But I'm done with surrogacy. It's just you. It's always been you. I just didn't know it until I met you."

Wow.

Just... wow.

My heart felt like it was too big for my chest. Like there was no way it could get any more full. "I think you should keep this room though," I mused, smirking.

"Oh yeah?"

"Yeah... we might need somewhere to sneak off to when I take a lunch break."

"That insatiable, huh?" he asked, smiling.

"Only for you," I smiled back.

"Come here," he said, rolling onto his back and tapping his chest.

I flew at him, my head finding my spot easily, sighing contentedly.

I got to have it.

Forever.

My safest place in the world.

--

Don't Forget

If you enjoyed this book, go ahead and hop onto Goodreads or Amazon and tell me your favorite parts. You can also spread the word by recommending the book to friends or sending digital copies that can be received via kindle or kindle app on any device.

Also by Jessica Gadziala

The Henchmen MC
Reign
Cash
Wolf
Repo
Duke

The Savages
Monster
Killer
Savior

--

DEBT
For A Good Time, Call...

Shane

The Sex Surrogate

Dr. Chase Hudson

Dissent

Into The Green

What The Heart Needs

What The Heart Wants

What The Heart Finds

What The Heart Knows

The Stars Landing Deviant

Dark Mysteries

Stuffed

367 Days

About the Author

Jessica Gadziala is a full-time writer, parrot enthusiast, and coffee drinker from New Jersey. She enjoys short rides to the book store, sad songs, and cold weather.

She is very active on Goodreads, Facebook, as well as her personal groups on those sites. Join in. She's friendly.

Stalk Her

Connect with Jessica:

Facebook: https://www.facebook.com/JessicaGadziala/
Facebook Group: https://www.facebook.com/groups/314540025563403/

Goodreads: https://www.goodreads.com/author/show/13800950.Jessica_Gadziala
Goodreads Group: https://www.goodreads.com/group/show/177944-jessica-gadziala-books-and-bullsh

Twitter: @JessicaGadziala

JessicaGadziala.com

<3/ Jessica

<<<<>>>>

Made in the USA
Coppell, TX
16 November 2020